Heartbeat

Stephanie Bedwell-Grime

LOVE SPECTRUM

Love Spectrum is an imprint of
Genesis Press, Inc.
315 Third Avenue North
Columbus, Mississippi 39701

Heartbeat

ISBN 1-58571-008-3

Set in Schoolbook

Manufactured in the United States of America

FIRST EDITION

Acknowledgments

I would like to express my thanks to Jan, Norah-Jean, and Wendy for their help and advice.

And to the ladies of Toronto Romance Writers who keep me inspired with their support and chocolate.

For my husband, Derek
upon whom all my heroes are based

Heartbeat

Prologue

Maximilian Atonwa Deveraux frowned at the balance sheet on his desk. He'd been over the figures three times and still he couldn't find a way to trim any more fat from Royal Hospital's budget. For two weeks he'd been busily adding, subtracting, reallocating, but if he was to reduce the hospital's deficit, more had to be done. His final report to the hospital's president was due in one week.

Running a hand through his dark curls, he glanced at the clock on his desk. Eight o'clock, and he hadn't eaten since noon. In his rented house, most of his belongings still sat in boxes. He hadn't even had time to unpack the meager possessions he'd brought with him from Ottawa for comfort. He took a sip of coffee gone cold long ago and frowned again at the spreadsheet before him. Something had to go.

Maintenance and housekeeping had been axed completely. From now on the hospital would depend on the services of a much cheaper private firm. Staff in both departments were due to receive their pink slips in the morning. All those people out of work...

The knowledge gnawed at his empty stomach. Max thrust that thought aside. His job was to save hospitals. Like a surgeon removing a cancerous growth, he cut away at bureaucracy, so the institution could thrive and grow healthy again.

Still deeper cuts had to be made. He'd shaved operations, paramedical, even nursing. Development generated its own revenue, medical services could stand a bit more trimming, but that still wouldn't balance the budget. He ran his finger down the column, stopping when he came to Medical Photography. He'd already made some serious cuts in the department's operating budget, but maybe he could trim a bit more. All the other hospitals in the city had closed down their photography departments to save money and were now using the services of the local university. And if the acute care hospitals could make do that way, certainly a small chronic care facility like Royal Hospital could. He drew a red line through the budget allocation and wrote in a number that was less than half. Sighting across to the department head's name, he highlighted "C. Day."

The Medical Photography Department would probably have to be eliminated. He hoped Mr. Day would be able to find another job.

Chapter One

"Fifty percent! Can you believe that idiot just chopped my operating budget in half!"

Carmen's voice echoed through the crowded elevator. Emerald eyes blazing, she brandished the offending piece of paper like a sword.

Her colleague, Barbara Downey, head of Infection Control, held up a hand, warning her to lower her voice until they were in a more confidential setting, a gesture that was as useless as it was futile. When Carmen Day was angry, only a pound of the offender's flesh would suffice as a pacifier. "Did he say why?" she asked lamely.

"Apparently, my department doesn't have a direct impact on patient care. Don't know what management school that hotshot Max Deveraux went to, but they sure didn't teach him anything about health care." Her voice rose. Heads swiveled in their direction. "Medical photography doesn't have an impact on patient care," she repeated in her best executive imitation. "Well, I'll show that pigheaded, narrow-minded number cruncher!"

Barbara blanched a shade paler. All at once, Carmen became aware of her surroundings, the fact that she was announcing her department's difficulties to the captive audience in the elevator. Wait until that hits the rumor mill, she thought, a little abashed. I ought to keep a tighter rein on my temper.

Barbara stared over her shoulder as an extremely attractive man in an expensive suit stepped forward to get off at the next floor. Wonder who he is. Carmen found her eyes wandering over the broad set of his shoulders and settling on his dark, flashing eyes. Jet black hair, high cheekbones and bronzed skin hinted at Native American ancestry. The subject of her examination gave the two women a quick glance. The corner of his mouth turned upward in a smirk.

Carmen noticed the normally reticent Barbara staring up at him in shock. No, it's not possible. After her devastating divorce, Barb had sworn off men forever.

Barbara swallowed hard, then looked up at the handsome man before her. "Good morning, Mr. Deveraux," she croaked out.

Max Deveraux offered Barb little more than a curt nod. His gaze shifted to Carmen pressed against the side wall of the elevator as if the metal might suddenly mercifully open up and swallow her whole. She watched mutely as his eyes flickered to the slow flush staining her cheeks. His smile widened, showing even white teeth. Under other circumstances it might be considered a warm smile. But there was no warmth in the biting expression he offered her. "It's nice to meet you Ms.. Day."

Carmen opened her mouth to reply. But the elevator doors opened and Deveraux stepped off onto his floor. She felt the sharp jab of Barb's elbow connecting with her ribs and thought better of it.

Deveraux was grinning at her as the elevator doors slid closed.

Carmen's cheeks burned with embarrassment as they walked in silence to her office. Barb's look of reproach didn't help.

Once inside, Barb leaned against the door and ran a hand through her graying blonde hair as if the encounter had ruffled it. "Nice one."

"Don't say it." Carmen threw herself into her swivel chair and swung her feet up on her desk.

"You certainly have a knack for making friends and influencing people."

"A talent of mine. My mother was always warning me about it."

Barbara, being a mother herself, took offense. "You should have listened to her."

"My mom used to say I inherited my father's big mouth."

"She had a point."

"Actually it was her forthrightness, but she'd never have seen it that way. My folks had more in common than they liked to admit."

"Nevertheless, you just blew it, sweetheart."

"You can say that again." With one black suede shoe, Carmen pushed the chair away from the desk and stood up. "But like my dad always said, 'There's no defense like a good offense.'"

Barb's eyes widened. "Oh no, where are you going?"

Carmen reached for the door handle, forcing Barb to step out of the way. "To work on that offensive."

Deveraux made drastic cuts in her operating budget, Carmen reasoned as she descended in the elevator. He was the one who should be sorry.

The door to his office swung open more easily than she expected, hitting the wall behind. A flustered secretary looked up from her desk.

"He in?" Carmen demanded before the secretary could offer the expected protests.

"Yes, but he has a meeting"

"Well, he has one with me now." Before the secretary could bar her way to the door, Carmen deftly skirted the desk and yanked open the door to Deveraux's office.

Max Deveraux whirled around in his chair, his phone forgotten in one hand. "I'll call you back," he said quickly to the abandoned caller.

"Nice to meet you, too, Mr. Deveraux." Carmen slammed the paper down on his desk. "Before you obliterated my department it would have been nice if you'd done some research."

Silence stretched between them. Dark eyes snapped from the paper back to her face. With embarrassment, Carmen realized she was panting from exertion. She dragged in a deep breath. Who was this guy who could get her going like no one else? She glared back into his dark eyes and silently asked fate why the most handsome man to walk through the doors of Royal Hospital had to be hell-bent on her destruction. Most handsome, she thought with a bark of mental laughter. Specialized care hospitals were predominantly staffed by women. On her floor she could go weeks without seeing a male.

With his startling good looks, Max Deveraux could have been a male model. Yet, underneath that polished exterior lay a man who was entirely at home in his body. Even sitting behind his desk, he bristled like a lion at rest. A lock of black hair drifted down over his forehead. She suppressed the urge to brush it away. His nose was a touch too long for his face and straight, except for the slight bump from an early break. For all his polish, the expensive suits and the nice office, it appeared Mr. Max Deveraux had a wild youth. Carmen tried to imagine his mother admonishing a young Maxwell and choked on her laugh. Max Deveraux was not a topic for mirth, no matter what his mother called him.

Under her scrutiny, Deveraux's jaw tightened, betraying what she took as a definite stubborn streak. "I'm afraid you're keeping me from an appointment, Ms.. Day. But if you'd like, we can discuss this later, say over lunch?"

"Lunch?" she echoed. Her perusal of his finer points vanished. Who did this jerk think he was? She'd likely lose her temper and stab him with her fork.

"Yes, lunch. My schedule's full until noon. But if you don't mind mixing work with pleasure, we could meet then."

"Fine," she snapped. "I'll meet you in the cafeteria at noon sharp."

"I had in mind a location off-site," Deveraux said with the cool only an executive could muster. She hadn't even ruffled a hair on his head with her outburst, while she stood there before him huffing in indignation. "Unless," he continued, "you'd like the entire hospital eavesdropping on your difficulties."

"No," she reluctantly agreed.

"Wouldn't want to be waylaid by another crusading department manager."

"Of course not," she said tightly.

"Then we'll meet at L'Ambiance at..." The same smirk he'd given her in the elevator. "Noon. Sharp."

Carmen snatched the paper from his desk. After being brandished about, the budget allocation was looking worse for wear, she noticed. She'd have to make a photocopy before their meeting. Didn't want him to see the sweaty fingerprints that came from holding it too tight. "See you at twelve, then."

If Deveraux thought the posh surroundings of a nice restaurant would put her at a disadvantage, would stop her from raising her voice if necessary, he had a big surprise coming.

❏ ❏ ❏

Finally someone interesting in this staid and boring institution. The proverbial breath of fresh air. Max

Deveraux couldn't help smiling as the door to his office slammed shut with a resounding thud. The chief medical photographer had all the subtlety of a flame thrower. And a devastating emerald glare that had essentially the same effect. Eyes that blazed like lasers set in a peaches and cream complexion. Topped off by a thatch of chestnut hair close cropped in a style that was reminiscent of Tinkerbell. The power suit she wore like a coat of armor destroyed any image he might have of her gamine innocence. Oh no, Ms. Day was strictly business. There was no mistaking that. And dangerous as a she-bear when her territory was threatened. A cross between Tinkerbell and Tank Girl.

He'd speculated that "C. Day" might have stood for Charles, or Chuck, maybe even Cedric. "Carmen," he said aloud, rolling her name around on his tongue. Most definitely not Charles.

Max Deveraux laughed out loud, then quickly covered the reflex with a cough as the door to his office opened and Angie poked her head inside.

"Mr. Deveraux, your ten o'clock appointment has arrived."

The president of Royal Hospital was anxiously awaiting his recommendations for the hospital's downsizing plan. Max shoved thoughts of Carmen Day from his mind. Lunchtime would come soon enough. He could wait. He prided himself in being a patient man. Deveraux indulged himself one last smile. Perhaps he wasn't going to die of boredom at Royal Hospital after all.

◻ ◻ ◻

"A man devotes his life to his work, and what thanks does he get?"

Sunlight splashed over the man sitting on a white marble bench in the center of the hospital's landscaped gardens. Around him roses bloomed in a riot of color, scenting the air with their perfume and promise of the coming summer. Sun, unusually strong for late May beat down on the back of his neck, hot enough to burn. But he spared no attention to the beauty around him. His thoughts fastened on the paper in his hands. Words danced across the page in the sun's glare, spelling out his destruction.

High-pitched laughter penetrated his thoughts. A couple of nurses enjoying their coffee break in the warm sun sat on the bench next to him. Laughing, while his whole world crashed down around him, oblivious to his pain.

The president's secretary had been smiling when she handed him the envelope. Shock cooled to calm certain fury. He'd show those fools who thought they could play him like a pawn. Damned if he'd let them take away his life. "Sometimes a man just has to take things into his own hands," he muttered.

The two young nurses looked up at him in surprise, then slid a few feet down the bench away from him.

□ □ □

"I'm sorry the videotape didn't turn out the way you hoped." Carmen tried to insert a calm word into the chief physician's tirade.

And failed miserably.

"This is the third time this month!" he thundered.

"I know." Carmen held up a hand for patience, catching the red faced physician drawing a breath. "The camera desperately needs repairs—if it can be repaired. We needed a new camera years ago, but there isn't even money to repair it. And that downsizing expert the hospital hired just cut my operating budget in half." She searched in vain for an inkling of sympathy on the man's face.

"Your cash flow is your problem, Ms. Day. What do you expect me to show at the conference coming up next week? The great video we would have had if the camera had been working?

"There's really not much I can do"

"And what do you expect me to do? Tell the patient we'll have to perform the procedure again for the camera?"

"Of course not!"

"Then fix the problem, Ms. Day. You leave me no choice but to discuss your incompetence with the president in our meeting this afternoon."

"Surely that's not necessary." Carmen winced at the pleading tone in her voice. But the chief of staff strode off down the hall toward the elevator. She closed the door to her office and leaned against it, still breathing heavily from her encounter with Dr. James Andersen, the physician known among the staff as Andersen the Terrible.

She hadn't expected pity. Not really. The threat of downsizing had staff fleeing, she thought in grim humor, like rats from a sinking ship.

Carmen tossed the videotape into the garbage can beside her desk and came to sit on the stool before her light table. The morning seemed determined to go downhill from her ill-fated meeting with Max Deveraux. After the morning from hell, she had lunch with the downsizing expert to look forward to.

Maybe I could substitute a couple of hours of root canal work instead. Humor deteriorated from dark to dismal. She cast a glance behind her at the slide show the director of nursing needed for his talk on decubitus ulcers at grand rounds. Another look at the bed-sores laid out in brilliant color on the light table made her bury her head in her hands.

If only she could live the morning over.

If only she hadn't ranted on about Deveraux in a public place.

If only she'd seen him first, smiled at him instead. And what woman wouldn't? Deveraux belonged to that rare group of men whose stunning good looks immediately melted the knees, and sent a woman's mind running through scenarios best not spoken aloud in mixed company. The man was gorgeous.

Dark hair a shade longer than was acceptable in business circles swept back off his face. The exquisitely cut gray suit did nothing to hide his broad shoulders, muscular chest and narrow hips. The classical face and windswept hair would seem more at home in jeans and a flannel shirt...or no shirt. In spite of the faultless fit of his clothing, Max Deveraux gave the impression that a magnificent body and an unruly temperament had been imprisoned in a business suit, that at any moment his true nature might burst free.

Why hadn't she offered him a 'good morning' instead. Maybe if he got to know her, liked her, she could convince him of the need to fund a vital service...

Her fantasy evaporated as swiftly as the minutes marched toward noon.

The man the grapevine called Max the Axe hadn't invited her to lunch to romance her. He'd invited her to explain in calculatingly cold-hearted terms exactly why her department was no longer necessary to the smooth running of Royal Hospital. The fifty percent cut was likely only the first step. Fifty percent would soon become seventy-five, then...

She'd better update her resume. Have lunch with her colleagues across town; put the word out that

Carmen Day would soon be seeking employment elsewhere.

Her fist hit the light table. Slides jumped, then
tumbled from their perch like dominoes. Carmen Day
would not be seeking employment elsewhere. Carmen
Day never gave up so easily. On anything. She'd have
lunch with the disagreeable Mr. Deveraux and set him
straight.

"Would Carmen Day please report to the lecture
theater." The sound of her name echoing through the
overhead speakers brought her head up sharply.
Whatever was breaking loose down in the auditorium,
they needed her assistance. No time to plan for her
encounter with Max Deveraux. She'd have to wing it.
Anger would lend her eloquence. Snatching up her tool
kit, Carmen headed for the lecture theater.

Staccato sound burst through the door of the darkened lecture hall. Ghostly images flared drunkenly
across the projection screen. Reams of 16 millimeter
film curled out of the projector into a disorderly pile on
the floor. Curled around the one of the gears, a flap of
film still broadcast its disjointed image onto the
screen. The other end, Carmen noted with a sinking
heart, snapped off in a very long ragged tear.

On top of lunch with Max Deveraux Carmen could
now add a lengthy stint at film splicing to her afternoon. She uttered an inward groan, then rushed to the
projection booth and snapped the film transport control to off, plunging the room into sudden darkness
and silence. Heads turned at the intrusion; watching
the medical photographer struggle with the disagreeable machine suddenly more interesting than what
had been on the screen.

She released the transport gears and fed the
healthy film past the tear, winding the ragged end up
on the take-up reel. The mangled frames she'd have to

salvage later. Fervently she hoped the film wasn't on loan from the university library, which would need to be appeased with a damage fee.

"Don't tell me," snarled a shadow standing between her and the ghostly light from the exciter lamp, "this is another of the pieces of equipment your department doesn't have the funds to repair."

Dr. James Andersen. It figured the interrupted symposium was his. Chalk up another of her incompetencies to the growing list.

"Got that right." Carmen engaged the film projector. The film jumped smoothly ahead. Straightening, she glared at Andersen's shadow. "And if you have a problem with that, why don't you talk to that hot shot downsizing expert, Max the Axe."

That said, she turned into the darkness, leaving Andersen to sputter on to himself. About what, she couldn't decipher over the soundtrack of the film, but she could certainly guess.

Her mood rapidly deteriorating, she returned to her office to assemble the slide show on decubitus ulcers and hoped the slide projector would behave itself at grand rounds.

"So?" Barbara leaned against the side of the light table. Lost in a mental rehearsal for the lunch with Deveraux, Carmen hadn't heard her come in.

"So what?"

"Tell me you didn't storm into Deveraux's office like you were threatening to do this morning."

"Actually, I did."

Barb winced. "I was afraid you'd tell me that." She looked around the office, then back at Carmen. "But obviously you still work here. Security didn't escort you to your office to clean out your desk."

Carmen laughed aloud at her dismal scenario. "No, not yet."

"Tell me what happened already! You're upsetting my ulcer!"

Barbara's theatrics brought another smile to her face. In actuality Barb had one of the strongest stomachs in the institution, built up over fifteen years of eating hospital food. The phantom ulcer was no more than a figment of speech. On more stressful days the ulcer-that-wasn't could mutate to a hernia, or a pending stroke. Barb bantered diseases around the way other people used expletives.

"Relax, we didn't have a chance even to discuss the matter. He had a meeting."

"He didn't throw you out on your ear?"

"He asked me to lunch."

"Say again?"

"We made an appointment to talk about it over lunch."

"What, in the cafeteria with the ears of every staff member in the place tuned in your direction?"

"L'Ambiance, if you must know."

"You're kidding me."

"I'm serious."

"Maybe he's planning to slip you some arsenic over appetizers. That or—"

"Or what? You've been reading too many of those mysteries." Must be a slow morning in infection control, Carmen thought darkly, if Barb had time to spin such ridiculous fantasies.

"He likes you."

"Oh, come on. If he liked me, he'd increase my budget."

"Nobody's getting an increase in budget. Not even the big boss."

"I certainly didn't get the impression that Deveraux guy liked me. He's probably down there in his office red penciling more of my budget allocation as we speak. That's what he's going to dump on me over appetizers, in a public place where he thinks I won't kick up a fuss."

"Carmen baby, the guy's a doll. All the women in the hospital are talking about him."

"Well, he's certainly not making any friends among the department heads."

"Don't tell me you didn't notice the man was good looking."

"Drop dead gorgeous is more like it. But he's also the most cold-hearted administrator to hit the books. It wouldn't matter if he was the last man on earth, Barb, and I was in danger of dying a virgin. He wants to axe my department."

That comment stopped Barbara mid-breath. "He said fifty percent. That's a long way from closing the doors to medical photography."

"I'm sure it's only phase one of his grand plan. And I intend to find that out over lunch." Carmen smiled grimly. "If you hear of a certain downsizing expert being skewered by a baguette, you'll know who did it."

Barbara grasped her by the shoulders. "Now Carmen, don't do anything rash. If the man does like you, a little charm might help smooth over this morning's outburst." She frowned at the grimace on Carmen's face. "You have a devastating smile, you should use it more often."

Barbara's taunts echoed in her mind as Carmen walked up the covered walkway to L'Ambiance. Damned if she'd smile at Max Deveraux like they were buddies when he was trying to obliterate the one thing she believed in above all else. She forced a less confrontational expression and winced when she caught a glimpse of her snarl in the reflection in the glass window. She'd have to do better than that. She'd already

sent a shot across his bow so to speak. It was up to
Deveraux to make the next move.

Deveraux was waiting for her at a table for two set
with a pristine white table cloth. That in itself
annoyed her. First, that he'd beat her there and she
didn't have time to occupy the table and make it her
turf that he was invading. And second, that he'd chosen such an intimate setting, as if they were on a date
instead of the chief medical photographer going head
to head with the Hospital's downsizing expert.

He broke into a smile as she walked toward him.
Carmen tried not to let her annoyance show. What
kind of actor was this Deveraux guy that he could
smile as if he was genuinely happy to see her instead
of plotting her demise. Wonder if he smiles at all of
them before he drops the axe, she thought darkly.

"Thank you for coming," he said, rising to his feet
as she approached.

Carmen was forced to shake his hand. Strong
warm fingers closed around hers, with a brief touch
that promised passion. Carmen jerked her imagination away from that line of thinking. His skin was soft,
unlike her poor abused hands that had been immersed
far too often in developing chemicals. Not like
Deveraux to get his hands dirty, a voice inside
growled, as she forced herself to be civil. No sense getting off on the wrong foot; she'd spent the entire morning with said foot in her mouth.

"Please excuse my outburst this morning." The
words caught in her throat. She forced them past her
tongue.

"Absolutely," Deveraux said, gallantly pulling out
her chair.

So smooth, so practiced. If she hated him it was no
more than a momentary discomfort. By the time she
hit the unemployment line, he'd be long gone, on to his

next assignment. He could afford to be magnanimous. In Deveraux's field there was lots of work.

Deveraux claimed his own seat and stared across the table at her, perfectly composed. All the cards in his hand, she thought, while she sat waiting as if the chair was made of nails. Of course he was composed. He had nothing to lose.

"I recommend the veal," he said opening his menu. "And if you care for an appetizer, the—"

"Mr. Deveraux—"

He held up a hand. "Please, call me Max."

She didn't want to call him Max. Unlike Barb, she wanted to know nothing about him, not even his name. She just wanted Deveraux and the problems he'd brought to her otherwise orderly workplace to go away.

"Max," Carmen spit his name at him. "Let me be straight with you. I don't want appetizers, I don't even want lunch." She paused, wondering what she could say to this piranha who wanted to chew up her department and spit out the bones. "I want you to know that the preservation of medical research, the path of a patient's progress, are things that I am deeply committed to."

"I'm sure you are, Ms. Day." Again that smoothly modulated tone, as if it was the weather they were discussing instead of her life's work.

"Please," she said, copying his tone, his patronizing manner. "Call me Carmen."

"I have no doubt that you're dedicated to your work, Carmen."

"I doubt that you know anything at all about me or my work." The comment came out far more sharply than she intended. And just when she'd sworn to get off to a new start with the oh-so-charming Mr. Deveraux.

He opened his mouth for a swift rebuttal, but Carmen forged resolutely ahead. "Understand, Max, at Royal Hospital, medical photography didn't always command the respect it does now. I educated staff to the usefulness of videotaping procedures, of involving patients in their own progress. I turned this job from a one person operation to a department of three."

"Until the recession hit health care and you were forced to lay off staff."

"Health care was supposed to be a recession-proof industry."

"Weren't they all."

Deveraux missed his calling. He should have been an actor. She would have sworn there was real concern in his voice. "The work didn't go away when the staff were laid off, Max. I am doing the work of three people because there isn't anyone but me to do it. And because I believe in the crucial nature of the service I provide."

A waiter arrived to inquire if they'd like drinks to start. Ignoring the protest of her already upset stomach, Carmen ordered coffee. Deveraux, she noted, ordered bottled water. No tap water for Max the Axe. Cutting costs, it seemed, was a lucrative field.

"As I said, Carmen, your dedication to your work is without question." The mask of pleasantry didn't slip, not even for a second. Only a slight tightening of the corners of his mouth betrayed what was coming. "Bottom line, however, is that in this economic environment we have to consider essential services first."

"You don't consider medical photography an essential service?"

"Not in a specialized care setting."

"I fail to see what difference that makes."

"Royal Hospital isn't a research center, nor a university. There's no emergency, no operating rooms..."

"Nothing interesting. Is that what you're telling me, Mr. Deveraux? If I was in the business of photographing unusual things in people's insides, would there be money then?" Her voice rose with her level of indignation.

"Carmen—"

"Ms. Day to you," she snapped back. "If you don't think the patients in our hospital are worth spending the money for medical photography on, then you come explain that to the man who just woke up out of a coma. And you tell that to the woman who was so paralyzed by a stroke she could only blink her left eye." Her voice cracked. Appalled, she felt the first sting of tears. "She was ready to give up until she saw herself on videotape, until she could see the path of her improvement." Carmen gulped a deep breath of air, steadying herself. She couldn't break down now, not after she'd already humiliated herself once today in front of Deveraux. Too much was at stake. "You stand at her bedside, Mr. Deveraux, and tell her that wasn't money well spent."

Max Deveraux stared back at her, his face impassive. Tears didn't move him any more than her anger had. And she wondered what, if anything, could stir the emotions in him.

They were there, she realized as she caught a flicker in the dark depths of his eyes. Her heart skipped a beat. His silence betrayed the fact that he pondered her words. Or perhaps he had merely a flawless sense of timing. Full lips pursed. Against her will, Carmen found her eyes following the line of them.

Dark eyes caught her gaze, held it, considering. "I have a week to prepare my final recommendations for the president," Max Deveraux said finally. "You have until then to convince me to fund your department, Ms. Day."

"Thank you." Carmen shut her mouth on her surprise and rose to leave.

His gaze followed her lazily. But the compassion she imagined she'd seen in the depths of his eyes had turned to ice. "Be sure of your claims, Carmen. If your department receives its funding, it will be at another's expense."

Chapter Two

"So how was L'Ambiance?" Barb poked her head through the door of medical photography.

Carmen peered at the slide she was examining with a magnifying glass. "About as pleasant as an hour of root canal work."

"Half the city is dying to get into that place and that's all you can say. The food critic for The Lakeview Star just gave it a great review."

"It was the company I objected to, not the food. I didn't stay long enough to order, though Deveraux recommends the veal." With a flick of her wrist she turned the slide upside down and deposited it in its allotted slot in the slide tray. "Maybe you should try smiling at him if you're so anxious for an invitation."

Hurt clouded Barb's face. Carmen turned off the bulb in the slide projector, letting the fan run to cool it down. The low hum was the only sound in the office. "Ignore me." She reached out a hand to squeeze the other woman's shoulder. "I've had a terrible day and it doesn't show any signs of getting better in the near future."

"Tell me you didn't shout at Deveraux at L'Ambiance."

"Okay, I didn't."

"No, really."

"I didn't shout at him, Barb."

"He shouted at you?"

"There wasn't any shouting. He told me my department had no impact on patient care. I explained he was mistaken."

"And?"

"And, that's it. That's all that happened. He didn't admire my smile, okay, Barb? It wasn't a smiling kind of conversation."

"Deveraux sat there and let you tell him he was wrong? Doesn't sound like the Max the Axe I've heard so much about on the rumor mill."

"He gave me a week to prove him wrong."

"Say again?"

"Deveraux's report is due next week. I have until then to change his mind."

"How are you going to do that?"

"I haven't the faintest—"

The crackle of the public address system drowned out the rest of her sentence. "Barbara Downey report to Six West, Barbara Downey..."

Barb turned toward the door. "Gotta go, duty calls."

"If you have any brilliant ideas that don't involve smiling at Deveraux," Carmen said with a wry grin, "give me a call."

Carmen placed the last of the slides in the carousel. Once she handed them in to the director of nursing, hopefully, she'd have a few moments to collect her thoughts and decide the best plan of action for dealing with Max Deveraux.

The phone's shrill ring stopped her halfway to the door. Let the voice mail get it, she thought, her hand on the door knob. But dedication had her reaching for the phone in an instant.

"Carmen?"

Her heart sank as she recognized the voice as belonging to the president's secretary.

"Yes, Judy?"

◻ ◻ ◻

"Mr. Goodman would like to see you in his office."

Wayne Goodman was young for a senior executive. Tall, blond and handsome, he looked more the part of a ski buff instead of the president of the city's leading specialized care facility. In the good old days, before the age of downsizing hit health care, Wayne had been more of a big brother to his staff than a boss. But then came the budget cuts and the president who'd been the life of the company Christmas party now spent long hours hiding a grim face behind the heavy door of his office.

Today, even the perpetually cheerful Judy had a dour expression. Carmen took one look and winced. Whatever lay behind the wooden door to Wayne's inner sanctum, it promised to be bad. Through the closed door, she could hear the muffled bass of male voices. A meeting still in progress.

"Have a seat." Judy waved her to one of the leather chairs beside her desk. "He shouldn't be too much longer."

Carmen leaned across the desk, lowering her voice to a whisper. "What's up, Jude?"

Judy swallowed. Her eyes shifted sideways as if she could see through the door into the intrigue inside. "I'm not at liberty to say."

Carmen sagged back into the chair, letting the chrome arms hold her up. "What did I do this time?"

Judy shot her a tortured look. "I'm sorry, Carmen, I really can't"

"You can't say. I know. Why do I have the impression I'm about to be sacrificed to the god of downsizing and budget restraint."

Judy pursed her lips, biting back a comment she obviously wanted to make. "It's not Deveraux in there."

That didn't make Carmen's stomach rest any easier. If it wasn't Deveraux who'd summoned her down to the boss' office, then it had to be some unknown catastrophe taking place. She glanced at the clock. Four p.m. What else could possibly go wrong before quitting time?

The door to Goodman's office suddenly swung open. A red faced Dr. James Andersen stormed past her. Carmen felt the strength leech out of her spine. She'd given so much attention to her lunch with Deveraux, she'd forgotten Andersen had promised to complain about her at his monthly meeting with the president.

Judy glanced at Andersen and paled visibly. Whatever had gone down in the office before Carmen arrived boded ill for the rest of her afternoon.

A tired-looking Wayne Goodman leaned against the door to his office, arms crossed. With a weary glance in Carmen's direction, he gallantly swept an arm toward the open office for her to enter. "After you, Ms. Day."

She took the offered chair and tried not to wince as the heavy door swung closed, shutting her inside.

"Dr. Andersen didn't look at all happy," Carmen observed dryly.

Goodman rubbed his temples. His normally pristine suit jacket hung on the back of his chair, gathering as many wrinkles as his white shirt. Blond curls lay at odd angles, betraying the fact that he'd spent much of his earlier meeting running his hands through his hair.

"Forgive me for saying it, Wayne, but you look awful." Carmen tried to instill a little of Goodman's self-depreciating humor into the conversation and failed.

"You don't know the half of it," Goodman grunted.

"Did I do it?"

"According to Andersen, you've single-handedly engineered the downfall of this entire institution." The humor was back. A good sign, she decided.

"And what do you think?"

Goodman leaned toward her. "I think, Carmen, that right now we all have to find a way to do more with less."

"Wayne" Humor evaporated. Was it still Wayne, she wondered. Or was it Mr. Goodman?

"We're all in the same boat here. Budgets are being cut. Government funding just isn't there for many of the things we've come to take for granted. Still, we need to be optimistic, creative in our ways of dealing with this new challenge."

"What do you want me to do, Wayne? Tell the video camera I don't like its attitude? That instead of being repaired, I'd like it to be optimistic?"

"That's exactly the attitude you need to avoid."

Wayne was in a Mr. Goodman kind of mood, Carmen decided. The sympathy she'd hoped for, the sympathy she'd always counted on, would not be forthcoming.

"Fine," she said, crossing her arms, mirroring his confrontational pose. "I'll try to be more optimistic about my operating budget being eliminated." Carmen waited for Goodman to signal her release from his office.

"One more thing."

Typical, she thought. Just when she thought she'd heard the worst, there was always one more thing. Her eyes locked with Goodman's as she waited for the other shoe to fall.

"I heard a disquieting rumor this morning."

Carmen froze. "A rumor?" she asked, trying not to sound as uncertain as she felt.

"Apparently a certain medical photographer took it upon herself to go head to head with our restructuring expert in a public elevator. I have to admit this surprised me, Carmen. Discretion is one of the things I've always admired in you."

"If I might say—"

"A word of advice," Goodman said, cutting off her ill-conceived excuse. "Do not make an enemy of Max Deveraux."

"Too late for that," Carmen muttered as she strode past Judy's desk, hoping her cheeks were less crimson than they felt. Judy offered her a sympathetic glance, which Carmen returned with a look of gratitude.

Thoughts of escaping into the sanctuary of the elevator evaporated as soon as the doors opened. Max Deveraux occupied the very center, giving her little choice but to squeeze by him. Hands crossed in front of him, he followed her progress with his eyes only, smiling briefly as she folded herself into a corner and tried her best to ignore him.

"Good afternoon."

"Afternoon," Carmen replied.

"Fancy us meeting again like this."

"Fancy that," she repeated.

The elevator doors whooshed open. A group of visitors prepared to board. But just then the public address system sputtered to life.

"Carmen Day, report to O.T. Carmen Day..."

She seized the opportunity to escape his company. "Got to go. They're paging me."

"Guess you better," Deveraux said. His smile broadened. "It's good to see the service being used to its full potential, Ms. Day."

His sarcastic words followed her down the hall, souring her mood further with each step. By the time she reached the muted green doors to Occupational

Therapy, she felt the gathering clouds of a full blown depression descend upon her.

□ □ □

"Oh, there you are, Carmen." Joan, the O.T. supervisor grasped her arm, leading her toward the corridor away from the patient workrooms. "Tyler's doing really well today. We were wondering if we could do some video taping?"

With a sinking heart, Carmen thought of the slide show she still hadn't finished despite her many attempts. But Tyler was one of her favorite patients. She knew she shouldn't get involved in their affairs, but it was hard not to like the friendly teenager, who only a few months ago had spent most of his days curled up in the fetal position repeating the lyrics to the song "Night Creature" at top volume.

The head injury he'd sustained in a car accident should have killed him. But Tyler was one of the hospital's success stories. His indomitable spirit pulled him through. Carmen glanced over her shoulder into the work room. Having progressed past simple daily activities like tying his shoes, making toast, reading the phone book, today Tyler was learning to use a computer.

"Sure," Carmen heard herself saying. "I'll bring down the monitor as well. When we're finished, Tyler can look at the old tapes and see how far he's progressed."

Clumsy fingers pecked awkwardly at the keys. Gobbledygook filled the screen.

"That's a good try, Tyler," Joan said off-camera.

"My hands don't always do what my brain tells them to," Tyler said. The ends of his words slurred into one another.

"I know, but you have come a very long way. You must be patient with yourself. Let's try it again."

"I want to be like the other kids," he said petulantly.

Joan patted him on the back. "Try it again, she prompted gently.

"Why do I have to type?" Tyler protested, giving up after a few more strikes at the keys still produced nothing recognizable as English. "Don't you have any games? 'Catastrophe'? 'Deep Space Shootout'?"

"No, Tyler, just the typing program."

"How come?"

Joan signaled for Carmen to turn off the camera. No sense wasting time shooting tape that would just have to be edited out anyway. "We don't have the money to buy games," she said tiredly.

Seeing there was nothing more interesting than the alphabet, Tyler settled down to his typing lesson. It was well after five o'clock when they finished.

"Can I see the tapes?" Tyler's face brightened when he saw the monitor sitting on Carmen's equipment cart.

"Sure you can."

Carmen fed the tape into the VCR.

"Show me the ones from the very beginning." Tyler sat back in his chair.

You wouldn't think seeing yourself so injured would cheer someone up, Carmen thought as the first shots of Tyler appeared on the screen. But the proof of Tyler's progress seemed to encourage him. She turned down the volume so the other patients in the work room wouldn't be bothered by his outbursts, and the teenager smiled bashfully.

"I was really bad, wasn't I?"

Joan nodded. "But you're much, much better now."

Next followed Tyler's first fumbling attempts to brush his teeth. He laughed out loud. Images showed a steady progression, culminating with his stint at the computer keyboard.

"Guess typing's not so bad," Tyler said with seriousness after he'd given the matter much thought.

"We all have to do things we don't like," Joan added.

He considered her words solemnly. "Still, I wish you had some computer games."

□ □ □

Scissors sliced through glossy paper. He performed his own brand of surgery on Royal Hospital's annual report. Color photos of the hospital's staff smiled back at him. Physiotherapists in action, medical staff pretending to confer, Wayne Goodman and his secretary engrossed in a mock conversation about something on her computer.

He cropped a neat circle close about her grinning face. The disembodied head clung to the scissors with static, then tumbled to the table. Separating it from the growing pile, he slicked glue on the back and applied it to the circular piece of paper covering his dart board.

Standing back, he admired his handiwork. Who would he put in the bullseye?

□ □ □

Carmen checked her watch. Nearly eight o'clock. Luckily Computer Central was open late. She'd only finished up the Director of Nursing's slide show half an hour ago. Grabbing a salad from the convenience store, she walked the extra two blocks out of her way to the computer store.

This is silly, she told herself. Lakeview wasn't the best neighborhood in the daytime. After dark, drug dealers and junkies claimed the streets. Stately old houses betrayed the evidence it once had been a proud neighborhood. When the hospital had been built in the last century, it had likely been one of the finest neighborhoods in the city.

She had standing plans to move, but her apartment was close to the hospital and on a 24-hour streetcar route. Convenience and a schedule that included evening and weekend overtime kept her there.

"I should be saving my money. If Deveraux has his way, I'll be unemployed," she muttered, stepping into the brightly lit shop. Computer Central had been robbed last month. It was only a matter of time before the proprietor also moved elsewhere. A boy who couldn't have been more than eighteen looked up as she approached the counter.

"Do you have 'Deep Space Shootout'?" Against his fresh-faced youth, her twenty-eight years felt ancient. Most definitely 'uncool' as Tyler would have put it.

"Why, that's my favorite game," said a voice behind her.

No mistaking that voice. Nice to meet you, Ms. Day. Good afternoon, Ms. Day. You have one week to save your department, Ms. Day.

Had he been following her? She'd taken him for the kind of man who'd hightail it out of Lakeview in a moment for the sanctuary of his uptown, upscale neighborhood. No spacious, yet slightly rundown flat for him. No, Deveraux's condo would be one of those concrete and glass monstrosities on Water Street, where all the stock brokers lived.

Carmen turned slowly around, preparing herself for the sight of Mr. Max Deveraux in his expensive suit, his gleaming, black shoes and his leather briefcase. But the Max Deveraux that stood behind her wore faded blue jeans and a pair of beat-up running shoes. His sweat shirt had been washed so many times it was nearly white. He nodded to the package in her hand. "Have you a game sometime?"

"Oh, it's not for me." Carmen's mind raced ahead. If Deveraux wasn't at work, then what was he doing in this neighborhood? "I'm buying it for a young patient who swears he'll spend more time in front of the computer if he has something more interesting to work with than Joan's typing program. We're trying to improve his hand-eye coordination..." The sight of him standing there, hands boyishly stuffed into the pockets of his jeans, stole her thoughts. "Joan doesn't have the budget to buy it for him herself," she finished lamely.

"And you're buying it for him out of your own money?" Deveraux's brows knit together.

"I'm not the only department head subsidizing the hospital," she said crossly. Then, preferring not to continue their earlier argument into the evening, she said, "You must be far from home."

The comment took him by surprise. "Ah no." He nodded toward the nearby block separated by a row of mature trees that arched across the road. "I rent a house a couple of streets away."

"So we're neighbors, then. Visit Computer Central often?"

"This is the first time I've been in. I just moved in last week and the hospital's kept me so busy, I really haven't had a chance to explore."

"I'll bet." The words dripped from her tongue like venom. Deveraux's eyes narrowed slightly, but he ignored her sarcasm. He was an entirely different person outside the hospital walls. She wondered how many masks he wore.

"One of the drawbacks of always being on the move."

Was that regret she heard in his tone? Carmen promptly dismissed the possibility.

"I was just on my way to the store," Max said. There's this old barbecue in my backyard. And the weather's been so warm, I thought I'd fire it up, buy some wine and—"

Carmen stared at him, refusing to believe he could change gears so fast. A moment ago they'd been discussing Joan's budget predicament and now Deveraux was chattering on about the barbecue in his rented backyard.

"Since you refused to let me buy you more than a coffee at lunch, perhaps I could convince you to let me cook you dinner."

She felt her mouth start to drop open. Whatever his other faults were, Deveraux certainly didn't give up. "I don't think that would be very professional."

"Nonsense, we don't even have to mention the hospital. You can fill me in on all the neighborhood gossip instead."

"I'm sorry, but I—"

He stuffed his hands deeper into his pockets, raising his shoulders as if to shrug off her rejection. But then he said instead, "Please come, Carmen. I don't know anyone else here. And I'm tired of eating alone."

The unconcealed loneliness in his voice convinced her when his argument hadn't. "Sure." The word leapt out before she could take it back. "Just let me go home and change. See you in about half an hour?"

He offered her a friendly, open smile, completely unlike the predatorial expression she'd glimpsed during office hours. "Sounds great. See you soon."

Carmen stood in front of her closet and surveyed her meager wardrobe. The suit she'd put on this morning was totally inappropriate for a barbecue. She pulled out a flowered dress, frowned, then rejected that as well. Too early in the season, too frilly. She didn't want to give Max Deveraux the wrong impression. In truth, she owned few feminine pieces of clothing. Photography involved a lot of bending and climbing to capture the right angle, impossible to do in high-heels and a skirt.

She considered a pair of camel, tailored pants before settling on a pair of newly-purchased blue jeans. The denim was still dark, without tears or fading. She completed the outfit with a beige sweatshirt that covered her from neck to wrists.

I can't believe I'm doing this. Carmen turned the corner and headed down Deveraux's street. Toting a bottle of wine, another extravagance she could ill afford, she headed toward the yuppie reno a few houses away. That had to be his house, she assured herself. A guy like Deveraux couldn't be renting the huge old house at the end of the street.

But the reno didn't match the address he'd given her.

Carmen sighted down the street, looking for number twenty. If not the reno, then maybe the bungalow with the neatly manicured lawn. No, that was number twelve. Beside it was a dilapidated, rambling house that had to be rented by students judging by the ban-

ner for a rock group she didn't recognize hanging in
the window. Carmen counted houses, sixteen, eighteen. The house at the end of the block was a stately old
home that had seen more glamorous days. The paint
on the porch needed a new coat of green, but the brickwork was in good shape considering the house had to
be at least a hundred years old. Though it obviously
hadn't been renovated, someone had lived in and loved
the place for most of a century.

And it didn't look like the kind of house Max
Deveraux might inhabit, even temporarily. Carmen
glanced down at the address on the crumpled piece of
paper in her hand. Twenty Lake Road. Brass numbers
on the door confirmed the address. Unhooking the
latch on the low red fence, she strode up the narrow
walkway.

The door opened before she could lift the brass
knocker. The small entrance way was suddenly filled
by Max Deveraux. Up close, in such an intimate setting, she found herself gone suddenly shy. He was
wearing the same over-washed jeans and frayed sweat
shirt and looking not at all like the kind of man who
spent his days counting money and rolling heads. The
scent of charcoal smoke drifted through the open doorway from the garden beyond.

"You came," he said, as if he hadn't expected her to.
And she wondered for a second if this was all just a
ploy, either to ferret information out of her that she
wouldn't normally give him in the hospital's professional environment, or to throw her off kilter. The
crease between his eyebrows deepened, and it was
Deveraux who seemed off balance, as though now that
he had her company he wasn't quite sure what to do
with her. Then his smile broadened. Obsidian eyes
sparkled in the last light of the setting sun. He

stepped back from the door and waved her inside. "Come on in, then."

She followed him through a series of narrow hallways and small, darkened rooms. Ancient wallpaper decorated the walls in stripes of gold, faded and stained here and there, but none peeling. A glance inside the sitting room showed threadbare furniture that looked to have been expensive fifty years ago. Comfortable, Carmen thought, memories of her grandmother's house springing to mind. A house well-loved, well-lived in. The kind of home in which you wouldn't mind throwing your feet up on the coffee table while you read the newspaper.

"The place came furnished, I take it," Carmen said, for lack of a better opener. The narrow hallway was cramped with the two of them in it. Built in an earlier time when people were smaller, Deveraux's shoulders practically touched the walls as he passed through.

"An estate sale. With the market so soft, the family couldn't sell the place. I agreed to rent it."

"Who lived here?" It became important to know. It was her downfall, the desire to know the details of people's lives. Though she strove for impartiality in her work, she never quite achieved it.

"A ninety-five year old woman," Deveraux said, leading her through a closet-sized kitchen that still had the original tub sink. An ancient refrigerator hummed noisily in one corner and a stove that had to be the first electric oven ever built took up the other. "She lived here for seventy-five years."

"Seventy-five years," Carmen repeated. She couldn't imagine being that old, never mind living in one place that long.

"Apparently, she was widowed quite young. Lived here alone for over forty years."

"In this big house?"

"Said she'd rather die in her own bed than in a place like—"

"Like Royal Hospital. That is what you were going to say, wasn't it, Mr. Deveraux?" The battle lines were drawn once again. It hadn't even taken five minutes.

"Carmen—"

"Was it?" Damned if she'd let him get away with that horrid stereotype. People heard the term specialized care, chronic care and they thought of nursing homes, of old age, of all the things they preferred not to think about, to lock away and forget about instead. Their work didn't seem as important as heart transplants and incubators. People wanted to forget and so they did.

"I'm only repeating what her son told me," Deveraux said earnestly. He led the way past the rickety porch. The backyard desperately needed a gardener's attention, but the view stole the sharp comeback from Carmen's lips. Lake Road ended with Max's backyard. His rented property jutted out, hiding the highway that ran beneath the property and revealing a startling panorama of the lake beyond.

White-capped waves crashed on the shore, their moisture adding a sparkle to the setting sun. The rush of the waves hid the dull roar of the nearby highway. Water stretched in every direction, merging with the horizon. Standing on that outcrop of land, she could almost forget the city existed.

Max waved at the quiet neighborhood, the glory of the sunset. "Look, it's a nice evening, we've both had a trying day. I'm willing to give you a second chance. Say you give me one too?"

Carmen nodded hesitantly, the gesture warning him he'd better not blow it.

"How about we make a pact. I won't talk about work if you don't."

That seemed like a wise idea. The subject of Royal Hospital practically brought them to blows.

She smiled. "Deal."

"Good." Max turned his attention to the barbecue sitting in the middle of the overgrown lawn. "Hungry?"

Carmen assumed Max's choice of a grilling appliance would run more along the line of a fancy gas model instead of the rusted-out hulk filled with charcoal. But the aroma of steaks grilling made her stomach rumble. "Starving."

Max Deveraux turned out to be a passable chef. His steaks, a baguette from the local bakery and the salad Carmen had meant to eat alone on the sofa watching late night television formed a satisfying meal. The unseasonable heat lingered long into the evening as they sat on the old wooden chairs and watched the coals fade from red to white and then cool completely.

Deveraux (she wasn't quite able to make the jump to "Max" in a social situation just yet; that would require a great deal more trust), glanced at her over his coffee mug. "Did you study medical photography in university?"

Carmen froze, the coffee mug halfway to her mouth. "I thought we agreed not to talk about work."

His eyes glinted in the light of the dying fire. "The question was a personal one, Carmen."

And a loaded one, she thought. But Deveraux couldn't know that, unless he was a better detective than she thought. "I didn't go to university," she said finally. "My mother became ill, and I was needed at home. I had to help support the family."

In the gathering darkness, she saw the outline of his dark brows knit together. "I'm sorry."

Easily enough said. He couldn't possibly know the sacrifices she'd made. "Look, it's getting late said, we've both had a hard day, and I'm expecting another one tomorrow. I should really get to bed."

"I'll walk you home."

"Oh no, I'll be fine, really."

"I insist. They tell me this isn't the best of neighborhoods."

Now he was patronizing her. "And who will walk me home tomorrow night, or the night after that?" she asked crossly. There'd never been a man to protect her. Deveraux was a man she needed protection from, she reminded herself.

"I'd be happy to be your escort," he said, a little hurt. That wounded expression tore at her heart. And that made her even angrier. "Then stand on your doorstep. I only live in the next block. I promise I'll holler if I run into trouble on the way home." Carmen softened her tone in spite of her rising annoyance.

"You're sure?" he asked.

"Positive." She started down the walkway. "Thanks for dinner," she called back, remembering her manners.

"You're welcome," he said right behind her, making her jump. "Perhaps we could do it again some time."

"Sure," she said, heading for the sidewalk. But he followed her.

"I'll come with you to the top of the street." Fatigue stole away the energy to argue with him. Getting mugged, losing your job, dangers, it seemed, were all ldn't he see that?

in silence between yellow pools of

that house." Carmen pointed out a at sat like a dark mountain against

ind him close beside her. Heat radi- the cooling night air. Caught in the dark pools of his eyes, she could only stare up at him. His head dipped toward hers. Her eyes dropped to his full lips. For a moment she was sure he would kiss her. Instead, he smiled and said, "Go on, then. Get inside before we get mugged out here on the street."

"Good night." Carmen took that as her chance to escape.

He just couldn't do it, Max Deveraux thought as he watched her lithe form disappear inside the rambling old house. He'd broken his own cardinal rule and looked beyond the black numbers on the page at the person behind them. Now that he knew the enigmatic C. Day, he just couldn't axe her department and leave her without a job.

He leaned against a streetlight, watching the front door swing closed, following her invisible footsteps through the house until a light came on upstairs.

And then again, perhaps there was a way to balance the budget and have the lovely C. Day as well.

Chapter Three

*C*armen dumped cream into the vat-sized cup of coffee sitting in the middle of her desk. Sandy's Cafe made the strongest coffee in the city. Half a vat down and she still couldn't keep her eyes open. Though she'd left Max Deveraux's house before midnight, it had been well after three a.m. before she fell asleep. Outside the hospital walls he was completely different. Kind, funny, gentleman enough to want to walk her home, to care for her safety. And it had been so long since someone had cared...

She yanked her mind from such blearyeyed thoughts. Lack of sleep made her foolish. Deveraux was lonely. So was she. It seemed only natural they might share fixings for dinner. Deveraux's position at Royal Hospital, like his residence in Lakeview, was temporary at best. He'd do his job, then move on to the next.

And take away her life in the process. Damned if she'd make a gift of her heart as well.

Suddenly she remembered why she so rarely went out on work nights. Sleep deprivation clouded her judgment. Carmen took another gulp of coffee strong enough to stand a spoon in and winced.

"Up late last night?" the voice said.

Carmen jumped, frayed nerves kicking in all at once. It was Barb. "I do wish you'd knock sometimes."

"Didn't want to wake you up." Barbara leaned against the corner of her desk. "Not losing sleep over that bean counter downstairs, I hope?"

"The same." Carmen rubbed her eyes. "Actually, I had dinner at a neighbor's."

Instantly, she regretted saying it. Barb had sensitive antennae when it came to gossip. Nothing got by her. "Now this is news. I don't recall you mentioning this particular neighbor before. Not the counselor from the group home?"

Carmen took another sip of coffee and shook her head. She'd come to know the counselor of the group home very well after several of his charges had set her garbage on fire. He'd been asking her out since Christmas, but persistence was the only quality of his she admired. "Someone on the next street."

"Ohhh..."

Carmen could almost hear the gears turning in Barb's devious brain. It would only be a matter of time before Barbara extracted the truth from her. Though Barbara ran her department like the tightest of ships, she'd find any excuse to wander by Carmen's office on the way to her own in the neighboring hall. In brief visits in the hallway, on the elevator, Barb would wear her down over time.

"Does this neighbor have a name?" Barb asked, the first of a multitude of questions to come.

"He does." Carmen took another sip and grinned at Barbara over the rim of her coffee cup. "Max Deveraux."

To find Barbara Downey struck suddenly speechless was a truly spectacular sight.

"You had dinner with Max The Axe?"

"Barbecue, actually."

"What did he say? Did you convince him to give you funding?"

"We agreed not to talk about work."

Barbara thrust her hands against her hips. "Now that, darling, was a missed opportunity."

"It was dinner, Barb. That's all."

"On second thought..." Trust Barb to find the most profitable angle in any venture. "Maybe that's the way to tackle this problem."

"Oh no you don't." Carmen rose from her chair to escort Barbara from her office.

But the irrepressible Barb would not be silenced so easily. "Charm him. If he likes you, he'll be less likely to chop your budget."

"Barb—"

Barbara glanced up at the clock over Carmen's desk. "I'd better go. I have an eight o'clock meeting. We'll talk later."

"I can hardly wait," Carmen muttered.

Seven fifty-five. She was booked to videotape in Speech Pathology at eight sharp. Giving the camera a warning glare, she stocked the cart with lights, tripod and sandbags and headed for the elevator.

□ □ □

Magda Barrons was a grandmother in her seventies whose retirement had been cut short when she'd been struck on the side of the head with a hockey puck while watching her grandson play. A puck-shaped scar still showed where one side of her head had been shaved. Her punk hair cut, Magda called it, and threatened to dye her hair purple.

Today, she wore a navy dress that didn't resemble punk attire of any sort. Complete with navy pumps and button earrings, she looked as though she belonged at a ladies' luncheon rather than a special-ized care hospital, until she turned her head. Then evidence of her injury was painfully clear.

Magda had returned to her volunteer work at Royal Hospital and, bravely, to watching her grandson play hockey once again. Looking at her, Carmen thought she still belonged back in the rehab ward, but Magda was determined to reclaim her life.

"How's your volunteer work going?" Carmen snapped the locks on the tripod in place.

"C—coming along," Magda stuttered in reply. "But I—I'm glad to be back. It's nice to feel n—normal again." She glanced in the mirror on the desk and offered Carmen a rueful grin. "Well, almost."

"Hope they're not being too hard on you."

"Everyone's been n—nice."

They had been through this routine several times in the past couple of months as Carmen documented Magda's recovery. An edited version of the tapes would be shown at an upcoming symposium, assuming the unpredictable camera deigned to cooperate long enough to tape the final chapter.

Carmen adjusted the last of the lights and checked the camera. So far, so good. "Okay, I'm ready," she told Rani Sandhu, the speech pathologist. "Hold as you are for five seconds to make my editing easier, then go ahead.

Careful that the camera was recording audio as well as video, Rani gave a silent nod. Carmen held up a hand and counted down five seconds on her fingers.

Rani led Magda through a series of mouth and tongue exercises designed to strengthen abused muscles and train the mouth and brain to work in sequence once again. It sounded like nonsense, like children daring each other to complete tongue twisters. But it was entirely serious. The difference between Magda having her life and her career back instead of being disabled.

An hour passed, timed only by the tape coming to an end. Carmen longed for another cup of coffee. Rani went on to her next patient, and Magda hurried to make her nine-thirty volunteer shift in the gift shop.

◻ ◻ ◻

Carmen maneuvered the video cart off the crowded elevator and wheeled it into her office. Closing the door, she leaned against it and wondered if she could sneak down to the cafeteria for another coffee.

Someone knocked on the door behind her. She felt the vibrations through her back before her mind registered the intrusion. Please, she prayed silently, don't let it be Deveraux or Andersen.

She opened the frosted glass door and peered out into the hall. Looking at the sign on her door in confusion was an elderly man.

"Can I help you?"

"I'm looking for the medical photographer."

Carmen forced a smile. "Well, you found her." She watched his confusion escalate. They all came expecting a man, she wasn't sure why, except that Raymond Carter, her predecessor, had been male. "Can I help you?"

He pulled a wrinkled photograph from the pocket of a rumpled pair of wool pants. His shirt was just as wrinkled, Carmen noticed, with a pang of pity. She recognized the signs. A widower, having trouble coping with all the housekeeping details his late wife had always taken care of. "I was wondering if you might have the negative for this picture on file?" he asked.

Carmen glanced at the worn photo in his hand. An elderly lady surrounded by balloons grinned for the camera. Happy eightieth birthday was written on the cake placed on the table in front of her wheelchair. She was surrounded by a ring of smiling staff mem-

bers: nurses, ward aids and John Forbes from maintenance, who'd been working on the unit that day.

The patient was the late Mrs. Harding. Carmen
matched the face to the name. She had taken the picture herself just over a year ago. "You must be Mr.
Harding."

"Why yes." His face brightened. "Did you know my
wife?"

"She was a sweet woman." Carmen glanced down
at the picture in his hand. "This is from her birthday
party."

Mr. Harding's expression clouded with grief. "She
took a terrible turn for the worst shortly after. This
was the last time I saw her smiling..."

"I'm sorry. We miss her here at Royal Hospital."

"I'd like an enlargement to hang in the living room.
You know, to remember her, like she was."

"Well, I can certainly dig out the negatives for you,"
Carmen said, trying to inject some cheerfulness back
into the conversation. "I do my own printing here at
the hospital, so we can give you a good rate. Shouldn't
cost you more than ten dollars for an eight by ten."
She mapped out the dimensions with her hands.

"Ten dollars..."

Carmen could tell the meager sum was well beyond
his budget.

"Perhaps you could just make me a new copy of the
small one."

"Sure." Carmen pulled a requisition from her drawer. "That would only be about two dollars."

Mr. Harding rummaged in his pockets.

"That's okay," Carmen said quickly. "You can pay
me later. I should have it finished within a week. If
you leave your number, I'll give you a call."

Her pen hovered above the box to specify the size of
the photograph. Carmen looked up at poor dejected

Mr. Harding standing by the elevator. With a deep
sigh, she ticked off eight by ten inches. She'd make up
the difference in price herself. It was only a few dollars, she thought. After all, what price could she put
on the enjoyment he'd get from looking at his late
wife's smiling photograph every day? Normally, she'd
just run it through on her supplies budget, but with
Max Deveraux running a fine-toothed comb through
every expenditure, she didn't dare. Max the Axe would
never consider brightening an old man's day a bottom
line expense.

□ □ □

He surveyed the faces in their colored ovals decorating
his dart board. A fitting revenge.

For the past twenty years his life had revolved
around Royal Hospital. All that hard work down the
drain, he thought dismally. Anger, keen and pure,
welled up inside him. Damned if he'd let them destroy
his contribution, his sacrifice.

"Man devotes his life..." he snarled.

He backed up, aimed the dart, and threw.

Stepping up close to the dart board, he yanked the
dart from the hole dead center in the circular photograph. Oblivious, the picture grinned back at him still.

As good a place as any to start, he thought with a
shrug.

And left to make his preparations.

□ □ □

"Oh wow!" Tyler exclaimed in delight. "Deep Space
Shootout! Where did you get it?"

Carmen ruffled Tyler's hair. "It was recommended to me by a young man who promised me he'd spend more time at the computer if he had something more interesting to work with."

"You bet," Tyler said with a quick glance in her direction. Already he was engrossed in destroying an enemy ship. Joan and Carmen might as well have been part of the furnishings.

"I think we've lost him," Carmen whispered to Joan as they left the treatment room.

"As long as he works on his hand-eye coordination, I have no complaints." Joan squeezed Carmen's shoulder. "That was sweet of you, thank you."

"Don't mention it," Carmen started to say, but her words were drowned out by a male voice.

"Ah, Ms. Day, crusader for the underfunded. Might I have a word with you?"

Carmen forced herself to turn slowly in his direction. Didn't want Max Deveraux to know he'd startled her, or how much his glib words offended her. If you'd loosen up the purse strings, she wanted to tell him, I wouldn't have to be a crusader. But Joan was casting nervous glances in Max's direction. "Be right with you, Mr. Deveraux," Carmen said aloud.

He motioned to the elevator. Mercifully there was no one else inside.

"That was insensitive," Carmen said fiercely as soon as the doors closed.

"The kid seems to be enjoying the game."

"It's not just a game," she hissed as the elevator plummeted. "It's a tool to help improve his hand-eye coordination."

"That shoot 'em up game?" he asked incredulously.

"Of course." She glared hotly at him. "I wish you'd do your research before you criticize. Joan's been trying to get that kid, as you called him, to spend more time on the computer for six months."

Deveraux looked chastened. Then the corner of his mouth twisted into a half-smile. "As you recommend, Ms. Day, I will allocate more time to my research."

His admission to his ignorance took Carmen by surprise. "What did you want to talk to me about?" she asked, having nothing left to lecture him about.

"I wanted to say that I very much enjoyed your company last night."

"That's all?" Just when she thought she had Max Deveraux figured out, he changed tactics completely.

"Not quite." He stepped up close to her. Carmen found herself trapped against the side of the elevator. "And I'd like to do it again, some time very soon."

"Well, I"

Warm lips smothered the rest of her sentence. Strong arms enveloped her, pulling her close. Carmen caught the scent of sandalwood soap, felt the hard imprint of a male body against hers. Feather-soft lips traced the firm line of her mouth, softening it, teasing her into parting her lips. Carmen sighed. Almost against her will, her arms closed around his neck, pulling him closer still, demanding more of that enticing, intimate caress.

Her fingers curled, bunching the smooth wool of his suit jacket. The resolve with which they'd armored themselves last night evaporated. Max wove his fingers through her short hair, sampling all the different textures of her. Demanding more. Carmen's hands slid down his back, over taut muscles sheathed in layers of linen and wool.

Suddenly there was only air beneath her questing fingers. The elevator doors whooshed open. She blinked in the unexpected light, finding them both silhouetted in the doorway of the elevator which opened on the ground floor. A sea of faces looked back at them. Deveraux motioned for her to precede him.

"After you, Ms. Day."

Carmen sincerely hoped her face wasn't as red as it felt. "Why you—"

But she was deprived of the stinging comeback she wished to fling at him. Wayne Goodman strode down the corridor toward them.

"Max," he said with a brief nod in Carmen's direction. "Could I have a word?"

"Certainly." Max Deveraux was suddenly all business, as if the moment in the elevator had never happened. He turned to follow Goodman to his office, then abruptly turned back toward Carmen. "I take it we have a meeting." A slow smile crept across his face. "Same place, same time?"

"Oh, you bet." They'd have a meeting all right. But it wouldn't be the kind Max Deveraux was expecting.

Carmen glanced at the arrows pointing to the lobby, realizing she'd followed Max Deveraux all the way to the ground floor instead of heading back to her office as she'd intended. Venting her frustration, she stabbed at the elevator button. But even the elevator refused to cooperate, stopping at every floor and taking another five minutes to reach her office.

Red-faced, she rushed by Mandy, the department secretary, who waved a pink message slip at her. "I'll get it later," Carmen called over her shoulder as her office door closed behind her.

Collapsing into her swivel chair, she rested her elbows on her desk and her head in her hands. The only sound in the office came from the persistent ticking of the clock above her desk.

Damn, she thought fiercely. Damn Max Deveraux who'd not only shaken up Royal Hospital, but her entire life as well.

Someone knocked loudly on the door to her office.
Carmen glanced at the shadow silhouetted against the
frosted glass and ignored it. She couldn't talk to anyone until she collected herself.

"Carmen!"

Carmen recognized Barb's voice even muffled by
the heavy fire door and winced. Barb could sense a
problem from a mile away.

"I know you're in there, Carmen," Barbara said. "I
saw you go in."

Resigned to the inevitable, Carmen opened the
door. "I was trying to get some work done," she said as
lightly as she could.

Barb strode into her office. "Well, forget it for a second."

"Okay..." Carmen frowned at her friend.
"Something wrong?"

Leaning against the desk, Barbara folded her
arms. She took a deep breath, as if searching for the
right words. "Forget everything I said," she blurted.

"Forget what?"

"Everything I said about Max Deveraux."

Carmen nearly laughed with relief. "Don't worry,
I'd be only too happy to forget Max Deveraux completely."

"I'm serious."

"I'm glad you've given up on that ridiculous plan of
yours that I should romance him." The irony was
almost too painful to bear.

"Yes!" Barb said emphatically. "Because according
to the grapevine, Max Deveraux has romanced nearly
every female department head he's fired."

Chapter Four

 arb's words struck Carmen like a blow to the chest. In the cool air of her office, she could still feel the warm pressure of his lips on hers. It took the sum of her will to keep from blushing as she remembered in vivid detail the imprint of his hot body against hers, the way they had practically clawed at each other trying to get closer.

And then the elevator doors opened and the impervious mask Max Deveraux usually wore slid back into place. She indulged herself in a completely inappropriate manner. Wrapping herself around the downsizing expert in a public place was hardly the way to maintain a professional image. And image counted more than ever these days. As unprofessional as it sounded, funding decisions were based on such things. No doubt about it, she'd made a complete fool of herself. Well, it wouldn't happen again.

Problem was, she wanted it to. Despite her indignation over his ill-timed kiss, she had to admit watching the sun set over the lake with him last night had been...well, pleasant.

She could count the number of kisses she'd received on one hand, and none had fired her passion the way the simple brush of Max's lips had. Embarrassment stained her cheeks crimson. Carmen came to a swift decision.

Devastating dark eyes and knee-weakening kisses aside, Max Deveraux would have to go.

"Relax, Barb," Carmen said, feigning nonchalance in spite of her sinking heart. "According to the grapevine, Deveraux eats babies for breakfast. Trust me, the real Max Deveraux is not nearly so larger-than-life." It took the last of her resolve to sound so glib.

"This is serious, Carmen. I can give you names and dates. Our Mr. Deveraux has quite the scarlet past. I don't like any of what I've heard."

"You can hardly expect a man that good-looking to live like a monk."

"There's a difference between a monk and a philanderer."

"I'm really not interested either way."

But Barb Downey, on the scent of a good story, would not be distracted from her tale. "Tamara Brown over at the General said—"

"Tamara's the biggest gossip in the city. I'm surprised they haven't given her a column in the association newspaper."

"Say what you will, the woman knows everything."

Carmen smothered a laugh. "I can tell the story is practically burning your tongue. Okay, what did old Tamara say?"

"Apparently our buddy Max had quite the torrid affair with the assistant administrator at the General in Kanata."

"And?" Now that Barb had dropped her bomb, she was going to let Carmen squirm in anticipation.

"And then he dumped her cold."

"That's it?" With that kind of build up she'd been expecting some hot revelation. That Deveraux was married, that the administrator was married. "He didn't run off and leave her pregnant with triplets?"

"He dumped her, and then he fired her. Isn't that bad enough?"

Probably had her over for a barbecue, too. The scenario was starting to sound sickeningly familiar. Was the kindred spirit she'd sensed in Max Deveraux just a clever modus operandi? Too late to take back last night, Carmen decided with a stab of embarrassment. Not even Barbara could know how far and how fast she'd fallen for Max Deveraux.

"You're losing your touch, Barb," Carmen said. "What will the grapevine do without you?"

Instead of taking the comment with the humor it was intended, Barbara reached out and grasped Carmen by the shoulders. "Listen to me. The assistant administrator was merely his latest conquest. The most recent on a very long list. Max the Axe is a very busy man."

"Spare me the details."

"Tamara knows the Administrator. They went to university together."

"So she'd take her friend's side. I'd expect you to."

"I don't want to be taking your side, Carmen. I don't want to be commiserating your devastating break-up with Max Deveraux."

"We had dinner. That's all there is to it."

"And lunch."

"It was coffee, Barbara."

"Stay out of his way."

"You were the one that told me to charm him."

"And now I'm telling you to run for your life."

"I can't do that, either. I have one week to convince Don Juan Deveraux to keep my department."

"So write up a report, make a speech to senior management, but don't spend time alone with Max Deveraux."

Before Carmen could open her mouth to protest, Barb swept out of her office with a last parting comment. "Rumors are already flying about you two."

"What rumors?" Carmen demanded as the heavy door swung shut behind Barb. "You're just saying that," she muttered to the quiet office.

A glance at the clock told her she'd wasted far too much time on Max Deveraux. She was booked to videotape the walking program in physiotherapy in ten minutes. By the time she finished, it would be early afternoon. Hopefully she could steal some time after lunch to work on her strategy for convincing Deveraux to keep medical photography.

Was that how Max worked? Did he keep the women he was planning to fire so preoccupied, they didn't have time to prepare a decent defense? Well, if that's what he was planning, she had a surprise for Mr. Deveraux.

□ □ □

Margo Haynes shuffled awkwardly down the long hallway, stopping now and then to clutch at the wooden railing for support. Diane Green, her physiotherapist, walked closely beside her, reaching out to steady her like a nervous parent catching a toddler. Her progress would be agonizing to watch if Carmen didn't remember that only a couple of months ago, Margo could barely pull herself along the parallel bars.

A sudden stroke had stolen the past few months of her life. Margo hated Royal Hospital, hated being unable to care for herself. But at fifty-two, she was determined to reclaim her life and return to her floral design business. Walking was the first step. Gaining the use of her right hand would be a greater challenge.

Carmen checked the viewfinder, making sure Margo was still well centered in the shot, then straightened. Muscles in her neck and lower back protested vehemently. She rolled her head from side to side, trying to shake the tension that seemed to radiate out from the base of her neck.

"Watch that posture," said a male voice behind her. "The last thing this hospital needs is another back injury. Compensation costs are already through the roof." Spoken in an engaging manner, the words held a grain of truth. Compensation costs were through the roof.

Carmen froze, muscles seizing despite her efforts to unkink them. Max Deveraux. Damn him. Though she'd tried desperately to concentrate on the videotape she was producing, her thoughts kept straying to the topic of what to do about Max Deveraux. The walking program was routine work and her mind refused to stay glued to it. No one, she decided, deserved that much of her time, mental or otherwise. Especially someone determined to see to her extinction.

"Shh!" she said loudly, indicating the on-camera microphone. It didn't really matter, an audio track with commentary would be added later when the program was complete. Assuming there still was a medical photography department to complete it. His intrusion into her thoughts had annoyed her, but his callous disregard for suffering sharpened her feelings to anger. Trust a bean counter not to see the human misery behind injury, to count only the cost of compensation fees. She whirled, eager to do battle regardless of the microphone.

To her surprise, Deveraux looked properly chastened. Backing away from the camera, he mouthed, "See you later," and tiptoed off down the hall.

Disloyal thoughts slid back to the topic she was trying to avoid. What was she going to do about Max Deveraux, especially since she'd somehow led him to believe she was interested in a relationship with him?

She'd just have to convince him otherwise, Carmen decided. Starting immediately, she would make it

clear she was concerned only with the future of her
department.

Mercifully, she finished videotaping without further interruption. Patients left to eat lunch in the dining room and Carmen returned to her office to stow
her equipment on the allotted shelves.

Her stomach growled as she unpacked her video
camera. What would they do with all this old equipment if the hospital closed down the department?
Audio-visual equipment was expensive to buy, but had
little value on the resale market. Its true value lay in
the vision of the person using it, the research it uncov-
ered, the motivation it provided.

She glanced at the clock. Almost two o'clock. If she
didn't hurry the cafeteria would close and she'd have
to settle for a greasy burger from Sandy's.

The cafeteria was practically deserted by the time
Carmen arrived. She claimed one of the last scoops of
macaroni and a wilted salad. The macaroni looked
appetizing enough with its Parmesan topping, but
Carmen knew from past experience it was hopelessly
bland inside and would lay like cement in her stomach
all afternoon. Still, she fell for it every time. It reminded her of her mother's. Mom had been a superior chef,
she decided, sprinkling on a liberal dose of hot sauce.

Barb had grabbed lunch hours before, so Carmen
ate alone with only the whir of the ventilation system
and the fragmented snatches of conversation from a
table in the far corner to keep her company. With little else to occupy her thoughts, her mind returned to
Max Deveraux.

As much as she wished it, she couldn't relive yesterday. She couldn't undo dinner last night, nor the
aborted lunch at L'Ambiance. The problem with trying
to decipher what was going on in someone else's mind,
was that you never really knew, Carmen thought

morosely. Max Deveraux could just be lonely. And
then again, he could be making a case against her, for-
tified by innocent snippets of conversation over dinner. The rumor mill certainly wasn't kind to him. And
if any of what Barb said was true, she'd just made a
giant fool of herself.

Confronting him would only make the situation
worse, especially if she was wrong about his motives.
As Wayne Goodman had advised, she didn't want Max
Deveraux for an enemy.

No, the only way out of this dilemma was an hon-
orable one. She'd just be too busy. Certainly a worka-
holic like Deveraux would appreciate her dedication to
the job, and if she was run off her feet, she wouldn't
have time to spend in his company. Finding work to do
posed no problem. Requests overflowed her in basket.
She'd put in so much overtime in the next week that
even Deveraux would be impressed.

Starting with overtime tonight.

"Mind if I join you?" a voice said.

Startled, Carmen jumped. Her fork clattered to the
floor, impossibly loud in the quiet cafeteria. She'd been
so deeply submerged in thoughts of Deveraux, she
hadn't sensed his approach. At the table in the far corner, heads swiveled in their direction, taking in Max's
presence and exactly who he was talking to.

Rumors are already flying. Barb's words echoed
through her mind. She reached under the table, using
the excuse of retrieving her fork to cover her embarrassment.

"It's okay, I'll get you a new one," Max said, starting for the cutlery stand.

"Please, don't bother." She had to stop him, could-
n't allow him to offer any more of those chivalrous ges-
tures like walking her home, getting her a new fork.
She straightened, too quickly. Her head connected

with the underside of the table with a loud bump. Rubbing her head, she looked up, catching Max's eyes sliding upward over the tailored wool pants stretched tight as she bent for the fork.

"You okay? That sounded like it hurt."

The staff at the next table had their eyes riveted in their direction. Carmen cursed the flush working its way across her cheeks. "I'm fine, really."

"Let's see."

Before she could object, he bent over her head. Tingles traced the path of his fingers as he parted the layers of her hair. She realized suddenly she was staring straight at the silver buckle of the belt that circled his slim hips. She could only imagine what that looked like from across the room.

Carmen shut her eyes, refusing to indulge herself in a quick glimpse of the exquisite fit of those tailored pants. With her eyes closed, the effect of his touch intensified. Abashed, she bit back the moan ready to spill from her lips.

His hands slid down the back of her head, sending shivers down her spine as they mapped the contours of her jaw. He tipped her head back and looked down into her eyes.

If she stared into those eyes another moment, she'd be lost. Covering his hands with hers, she gently pushed them away. It took every once of her will to break away from his touch. The touch she'd like to feel...

"I'm all right, Max." She winced at the tremor in her voice.

"You sure?"

"Relax, I promise I won't file a compensation claim." Her attempt at a joke came out with an edge far more cruel than she intended.

"I wasn't worried about a claim," he said, looking truly wounded. "It sounded like you really hurt yourself."

"No harm done."

"Sure I can't get you another fork?"

"Actually, I was on my way back up to my office. I'm on a deadline this afternoon." The excuse sounded as lame as it felt.

"You've barely touched your lunch."

"I'll take it with me." Carmen snatched up her plate and beat a hasty retreat.

"Eating on the job isn't good for you, Ms. Day," he called after her. "But I do admire your dedication."

"Don't worry, indigestion isn't covered by compensation," Carmen said, and backed through the swinging doors. She caught a last glimpse of him sitting down in the chair she'd vacated and deftly reaching under the table for her forgotten fork.

Max laid Carmen's fork on the table and stared down at his plate of macaroni. With Carmen gone the pasta seemed even less appealing. It would take at least a vigorous game of squash to undo the damage that meal would cause. He pushed his plate away. The sight of those pants stretched tight across her shapely hips had been feast enough.

And yet he sensed she had no idea of her effect on him. A layer of innocence wrapped around a core of tempered steel. Carmen Day was unlike any other woman he'd met. She seemed entirely devoid of feminine wiles. Until he held her in his arms.

His head warned him that as an employee of Royal Hospital, she should be off limits. His heart? His heart demanded he do just the opposite. Intellect won the battle, reminding him with a cold stab of humiliation just what had happened the last time he'd followed his heart.

Max tossed her discarded fork onto the plate of macaroni. Life was no more than a series of risks, he told himself. Question was, how much of a risk was Carmen Day?

□ □ □

Seven o'clock. Carmen rubbed her eyes. It seemed like an hour since she'd last blinked, she'd been staring at the computer screen so long. Dry, tired eyes protested the abuse. Enough, she thought. Almost twelve hours had passed since she had walked through the doors of Royal Hospital that morning. Time to call it quits. She could finish up Andersen's stupid slide show in the morning.

All the office doors were shut as she made her way down the hallway toward the back elevators. The last thing she needed was to run into Deveraux. Even Max the Axe ought to have called it a day by now. Carmen let go a breath of relief. If she couldn't control her response to him, at least she could avoid him. But the sensation of his lips on hers, his hands laced through her hair stuck to her thoughts like glue.

With a quick glance around the quiet first floor, she made it out the back doors without incident. Even the security guard was missing from his post by the switchboard, presumably off on his rounds. It was still light as she walked the two short blocks home. A quick stop at the dry cleaners and a few items from the corner grocer and she'd be safely locked in her flat for the night.

So far so good, she thought, draping the plastic wrapped gray suit over one arm. She glanced out the door checking right, then left, and spied Max Deveraux rounding the corner at the top of the street.

Carmen ducked behind a row of pressed suits in plastic bags, hoping Max would simply pass by on his way to the grocery store. But no, he was heading right for the dry cleaners. Her heart sank.

Her situation deteriorated from annoying to intolerable. Working in the same building and living a block away from each other made it nearly impossible to escape Max Deveraux. He turned up everywhere, in hospital corridors, on the street, in the variety store. Not tonight, Carmen thought, and vowed to spend the evening without Max Deveraux's company.

A line had formed at the counter, and hoping Max was busy paying for his clothes, which would afford her a chance to escape, Carmen darted out from behind the suits, and—

"Oomph!" She barreled straight into something hard and muscular. Breath squashed from her lungs. She put out her hands to steady herself and found her fingers digging into thin t-shirt material that did nothing to disguise the muscle beneath. Her entire body pressed along the length of his, matching every contour of the tight denim jeans, the strong legs against hers.

Warm hands fastened on her upper arms as if deciding whether to pull her closer or push her away.

"I'm terribly sorry," she got out at last.

"Carmen?"

She knew instinctively just whose body she was pressed against even before he spoke. Knew him by the scent of his sandalwood soap, the gentle pressure of his hands that promised so much more. Not wanting to look, her eyes were nevertheless dragged upwards.

He gazed down at her in a combination of surprise and humor, and she caught a distinct mental image of what they must look like squashed against each other in the doorway.

"Excuse me," said another patron squeezing by.

They needed to step out of the way before Mr. Lo started shouting at them for blocking the doorway to his store. But Max didn't relax his grip and though her mind screamed at her to pull away, Carmen couldn't bring herself to move.

Because it felt so right, the symmetry of their bodies together. Even though Max was a good head taller than she, her head fit perfectly against the contours of his chest, his arms falling in exactly the right place around her shoulders. And as he bent his head lazily toward hers, she knew their lips would fit together just as perfectly.

Why was everything you wanted desperately bad for you? Carmen wondered as his warm lips brushed hers.

"I was just on my way home," she blurted against the soft barrier of his mouth.

His lips fastened once more upon hers. "Good, I'll walk with you."

From some hidden well of resolve inside, Carmen found the will to push away from him. "No, Max, I can't. Not tonight. I have work to do." It wasn't a lie exactly. She did have a ton of work to do.

"I thought that's what you were slaving away at all evening."

"I didn't get it finished."

She finally levered her arms between them, straightened her elbows. With a deep sigh, Max let her go.

"If you're trying to impress me with your dedication, Carmen, you can relax. You already have."

"Is that what you think?" she demanded hotly. "That I'm putting in all this extra work to earn brownie points with the boss?"

"Are you?" he asked coolly.

Deep in the pit of her stomach, Carmen felt a cyclone of rage stirring. "Is that all it is to you? A balance sheet? You earn brownie points, you win. You fail to impress, you lose? Did you ever think for a moment, Mr. Deveraux, that there are real people behind all those numbers on your damned spreadsheets—people trying to reclaim their lives? Have you ever walked through any of our patient units, talked to the people there, seen their suffering?" She snatched up the gray suit that had fallen to the pavement and offered him one last glare. "Perhaps it wouldn't matter to you anyway."

He had her all stirred up again, Carmen realized, as she charged down the street toward the grocery store.

"Wait a minute!" She heard the soft slap of his running shoes against the pavement behind her. "I resent that."

"Fine," she snapped back and let the door to the grocery store swing shut in his face.

He was through the door in a second, grasping her arm, whirling her around to face him. "Did it ever occur to you that what I'm trying to do is to save hospitals from being shut down, to find a way to keep the doors open even in the face of cut-backs, so there will be places for people who need help to go? Did you think of that, Carmen?"

She swallowed, realizing they were blocking another proprietor's doorway.

"And as to your other comment—yes, I have walked through the patient wards—"

"Units," she corrected. "People live there, Max."

"Units, then. If you must know, today I visited that kid you bought the game for."

"Tyler."

He sighed impatiently. "His occupational therapist says they can't keep him off the computer."

Carmen dragged in a shuddering breath. She didn't want others to see her panting with anger at Max Deveraux in public. He'd done enough to tarnish her public image as it was. "Really?"

"Apparently, he's even willing to do a half hour of the typing program to play the game for fifteen minutes."

"He is?" The thought of Tyler meticulously hunting and pecking on the keyboard brought a smile to her face in spite of her anger.

Taking that as acquiescence, he said, "And now, I'd appreciate it if you'd stop seeing me as such an ogre. I'm only doing my job, Carmen. Just like you are."

At the moment she saw him as anything but an ogre. With his hair tousled and his dark eyes blazing, that wild side of him was clearly visible. She wondered what happened when Max Deveraux burst out of his uniform and really let himself go.

But you're not going to find out. You're going to do as Barb says and go home. Alone.

"I'm sorry."

He accepted her apology with a curt nod.

"All this talk of money, this cost/benefit analysis stuff makes me crazy. How can you put a price on people's lives?"

"It happens every day." There was a strange sadness in his smile.

"That doesn't make it right."

"I do believe you're an idealist, Ms. Day."

"Perhaps," Carmen said, stepping away from him. Her anger had run its course, leaving her feeling completely drained. What was it about Max Deveraux that he could shake up her emotions and leave the pieces to lie as they fell? "And now I'm going to take my stupid convictions and go."

He moved out of her path, motioning for her to precede him with a grand sweep of his arm. "I didn't say they were stupid," he said as she passed, "just naive."

Just had to get that last dig in, didn't you, Max. That clinched it. If she didn't get away from Deveraux, she'd spend the night arguing ideologies. More importantly, if she didn't get away from Max Deveraux, she'd forget what her convictions were.

"Night, Max," she said, letting the ball drop in his court. Damned if she'd stay for another public display of temper. Never in her life had anyone had the power to move her like that, to passion, to anger, to jerk her emotions about as though she were a giant puppet.

Well, Max Deveraux might control the purse strings to Royal Hospital, she decided bitterly, but he could keep his hands off the strings to her heart.

□ □ □

Carmen stuck a low-fat frozen dinner into the microwave and poured herself a glass of diet cola while it heated. It was a far cry from the barbecued steaks she'd had last night, but safer. A night in Max's company was like walking an emotional and political minefield.

The microwave beeped. Balancing the hot cardboard gingerly, she took it into her cramped living room to eat while she watched the news.

The doorbell chimed. She ignored it. It chimed again, followed by a loud knock. Whoever was on the doorstep two flights below was adamant she answer.

□ □ □

Max knew she was in there. He could tell by the flick-ering silver light that danced across the ceiling. He rang the doorbell again and then knocked loudly.

He looked down at the picnic basket he carried and felt like a fool. He'd found the old basket, complete with its own cutlery and linens in the dining room cup-board. That evening, instead of takeout, he'd opted for traditional corn soup. He rarely cooked, even in his own kitchen. But marooned in Lakeview in the middle of a difficult contract, he found himself longing for the comforts of home.

The aroma of soup reminded him of his mother's house. His mother favored soups and stews, anything that could be put into the slow cooker during the long hours she spent at work and school. Hard work was no excuse to ignore tradition, she'd often reminded him. She'd adapted Mohawk recipes handed down from her elders and found time to take him to powwows and potlatches. She wove a richly-textured life for them that he had not fully appreciated during his rebellious teen years.

Max then found his thoughts turning to another woman as hard-working as his mom. Carmen certain-ly shared his mother's determination. Though they came from different cultures, they were both militant defenders of what they believed in.

By the time he'd finished grilling the vegetables, he knew he had to see Carmen. Even if she slammed the door in his face and left him standing on her porch like an idiot.

He wrapped the vegetables in foil and added a loaf of crusty bread as well. Wicker picnic basket, a small crock of corn soup, two crystal bowls, two antique glasses and a bottle of wine made a romantic gesture. Now it seemed like a bad idea growing worse with every passing second.

Watching the setting sun over coffee last night, he'd been sure she was starting to open up to him. And this morning in the elevator...well, there was no mistaking her intentions then. He'd had to walk into a meeting with the president with the imprint of her hands permanently creased into his lapels.

Suddenly this evening she wanted nothing to do with him. He was experienced enough with women to know when a deliberate cold front was blowing in his direction. Something he said while they argued ideologies in the grocery store? Or did she regret showing him that tiny piece of herself last night?

Whatever troubled her, Max was certain of one thing. He wanted to make it go away.

Dinner was ruined. His gesture wasted if she wouldn't even open the door. He glanced up at the top floor flat again and wondered, not for the first time, why he was hanging out on her doorstep like some love-sick teenager. He should leave now with his dignity intact.

The door flew open. Light spilled out over the threshold. He caught a sudden glimpse of her in a white t-shirt and leggings silhouetted in the doorway. Light ringed her hair like a halo, and for a second she looked like angel dressed in white and splashed with gold.

"Max?"

He squinted back at her, his eyes protesting the unexpected brightness, and found himself struck suddenly dumb. "I brought you some dinner."

"Dinner?"

"I didn't want you to starve," he offered for lack of a better excuse. "Being so busy and all."

Damn, he sounded like a love-sick teenager. She stared at him, green eyes round like an owl's.

"You were worried about me?" Her tone made it more an accusation than a question.

"I was thinking of you."

"Why?"

"Wish I knew." Max leaned against the doorway, bravado having fled him the moment she opened the door. "But I can't seem to stop thinking about you."

Her eyes darted to the wicker basket. The pink tip of her tongue flickered between her lips, then she caught herself and the frown settled firmly back in place.

"Hungry?"

"Starving. I was just going to eat one of those cardboard frozen dinners." She stopped, having revealed more than she intended.

"Traditional Mohawk corn soup and grilled vegetables." Max pulled up the corner of the cloth, letting the aroma escape.

Guilt nagged at his conscience. He'd never earn her trust if he pushed the issue. No, the elusive Carmen Day required a light hand. He pushed the basket toward her. His own share was in the package. Lord knew what he'd do if she took it and didn't invite him in. Probably go home and heat up one of those cardboard dinners. But his bet was placed. "Listen, I'm not asking to come in or anything. I just wanted to make sure you had a decent meal."

"Thanks." Carmen took it hesitantly. "You do this for all your staff?"

The bet laid and the money lost, Max thought with a sigh. And a TV dinner as reward for his stupidity.

"No." He stepped back down off the porch. *"Bon appetit,* Carmen."

Pride kept him walking without a backward glance until he'd turned the corner.

□ □ □

Carmen set the picnic basket down on the coffee table and eyed it cautiously. The enticing aroma alone was enough to make her push the microwave dinner out of the way with a grimace.

Gingerly, she pulled back the dark green cloth that covered the top. Her heart sank. Inside were cloth napkins that matched the table cloth on top. Antique silver cutlery and crystal goblets complemented the china plates. Excavating further, she found the promised corn soup in its earthenware crock and the grilled vegetables wrapped in foil. Another napkin insulated a bottle of Chardonnay to keep it chilled.

A gesture as thoughtful as it was romantic, and she'd sent him away.

And he'd gone, without a word, too much of a gentleman to let her know she'd thrown his offering in his face. Too proud to admit he was about to go hungry.

To call him back would only embarrass them both further. He'd meant to share dinner with her. Another whiff of chowder and grilled vegetables and hunger would have overruled her good sense. Once upstairs, her most private of secrets would be his for the asking. The old photos of family and friends, her choice of furnishings, all spoke volumes about a person. Not to mention the report on the medical photography department lying open on the couch.

All that information for the taking and still he'd gone home hungry.

Carmen surveyed the picnic laid out on her coffee
table with a frown. The basket and its antique acces-
sories obviously belonged to the house Max was renting. She'd have to return it. What would she say?

Her stomach growled insistently. She couldn't
waste the meal he'd gone to so much trouble to prepare. Carmen sampled a morsel of corn soup and
hastily scooped up another. After a moment's deliber-
ation, she opened the wine and poured a mouthful into
one of the goblets. Raising it in a silent toast, a
thought brightened her dark mood.

She'd never met a man more interested in seducing
her stomach before.

☐ ☐ ☐

The seven o'clock alarm cut through her head like a
knife. Carmen dragged herself from the depths of
sleep. Thoughts of Max Deveraux had claimed another night's rest. The last time she'd glanced at the clock
it read 5:29 a.m.

An ice-cold shower and a giant cup of Sandy's coffee later, she headed for her office. A niggly feeling
she'd forgotten something developed into a disaster in
the making as soon as she glanced at her calendar.

Written in red ink was an eight o'clock video shoot
with Dr. James Andersen. Carmen glanced at the
clock. Five minutes late already.

A knock at the door only intensified her panic. She
stared at the shadow through the frosted glass. Please
don't let it be Andersen.

Delaying the inevitable would only send Andersen
back down to Wayne Goodman's office with another
complaint. She wondered if the president ever felt his

job amounted to nothing more than refereeing the squabbles of his staff.

A reprimand was coming her way regardless, Carmen decided. And opened the door.

Barbara Downey marched into her office without so much as a good morning.

"I can't talk, Barb, I'm late." Carmen reached for the camcorder on the shelf above her desk. Silence answered her. "Barb?"

The sound of her voice seemed to shake Barbara from her stupor. "You've heard of course?" she asked.

Carmen set the camera down on the desk. "Heard what?"

"Judy Connors was attacked in the parking lot last night."

"Attacked?" It didn't seem possible. Carmen conjured up images of tiny Judy sitting behind her desk. Despite her lack of stature, the president's petite secretary had always been a solid shoulder to lean on during all Andersen's tirades against her.

"On her w-way out the back door to the parking lot." Barb's voice shook as she tried to describe what had happened to her friend.

Carmen put her arm around Barbara's shoulders. "Is Judy all right?"

"Pretty shaken up." She shot Carmen a look of uncharacteristic uncertainty.

"Shh," Carmen said gently. "It's going to be okay. They'll catch the guy. When Judy feels better, she can give the police more information."

Barb shook her head. "Judy said he was wearing a ski mask. All she saw was that he had a scar on his hand. That's not much to go on. And here's the weird thing, she said he seemed more interested in her than her money."

"What do you mean?"

"Well, according to Judy, she was just walking out the door about seven-thirty, and this guy grabs her from behind. He didn't ask for her wallet or anything, just roughed her up a little, you know, shook her, threatened her."

Seven-thirty. Carmen had left herself, only moments before. She took a deep breath to loosen the knot of fear clenching her stomach. "Threatened her?"

"He said she didn't deserve to have a job, that she had a husband to take care of her, that people like that..."

"Like what, Barb?" Carmen probed gently, "Tell me what he said."

"People like that didn't know what they had," she paused, dragged in a shuddering breath, "until it's gone. It really spooked me, Carmen."

"Spooks me, too," Carmen admitted. "Do you think it's someone Judy knew? I mean he knew she was married."

"That's the creepy part of it."

"Well, she does wear a wedding ring." Already Carmen's mind was busy whittling away at the problem. "A nice one, too. Maybe this guy knew her husband is a doctor. Maybe he was jealous for some reason. Maybe it had more to do with Judy's husband than Judy. Someone he angered somehow."

"It's not just what happened with Judy." Barb broke out of her embrace and stood staring out the window. "Royal Hospital used to be a pleasant place to work. I used to really believe in what I did. I thought that even if we weren't curing people here, at least we were making their lives better. Now we've got budget cuts, that bean counter downstairs deciding who's going to stay and who's going to get fired. The staff are fighting among themselves. And some maniac's hanging out in the parking lot preying on women! What's happening to this place, Carmen?"

Carmen reached for her hands, turning Barbara to face her. "Those things are all separate events. None of them are related."

"What makes you so sure?"

"This is Lakeview, Barb. It's hardly the best of neighborhoods. And since the budget cuts to the mental health center, there are lots of people on the street who really need help. Who knows, this guy could have been a patient of Judy's husband who thinks Judy stole his soul. I've heard stranger things."

The phone rang, making them both jump. Carmen reached for the receiver.

"This is Wayne Goodman," the president said without even a good morning. "I need to see you in my office, immediately." He hung up.

The dial tone sounded unusually loud in the quiet office.

"Goodman," Carmen said in response to Barb's puzzled look. "He didn't even say hello."

Barb shot her a sympathetic grimace. "When it rains, it pours."

"Why do I have the feeling there's a tornado watch in effect."

"Good luck," Barb said, and fled to look after her own problems.

Chapter Five

Wayne Goodman acutely missed Judy's presence, as evidenced by the ringing phones, the paperwork piled up on the president's desk. Without Judy, the office had a cavernous feel to it. Carmen had never appreciated how fully the five-foot secretary could fill the room with her calming manner. She wished Judy were there to give her the "inside" on what had Wayne summoning her for an early morning meeting.

The door to Wayne's inner office flew open as she crossed the carpeted floor. The president looked as if he'd been up all night. Perhaps he had. Even though the shirt he wore was freshly pressed, Carmen knew he had an assortment of them hanging in his closet, along with a couple of extra suits.

"I gather you've heard," he said without preamble.

"About Judy? Yes, I'm terribly sorry. Is there anything I can do?"

Carmen looked up, catching Wayne in the act of ruffling more of his blond hair. It stood out at all angles like a misused broom. She had to bite the inside of her mouth to keep from laughing.

"As a matter of fact, there is. I need your help in catching this creep."

Creep really wasn't a Wayne Goodman kind of word. Nor was the venom with which he said it characteristic of the mild-mannered president. Carmen's eyes widened. "My help?"

"We managed to catch a blurry image of the guy on the outside surveillance camera. It's not much of a photo, but I thought perhaps you might have some equipment upstairs to enhance it with."

If any of it's still working, Carmen thought, then decided to keep that comment to herself. She ran through the possible ways to do what Wayne wanted of her, matching them against working equipment, discarding unviable options as she went. "If I could get a reasonably clean dub off the VCR in security, perhaps I could run the videotape through the computer, see if I can't clean it up a bit."

Wayne Goodman looked immensely relieved. "I knew I could count on you, Carmen."

She smiled, seeing for a moment a tiny piece of the old Wayne. "Don't hold a parade for me yet. Let's wait until I get a look at that tape."

The president unlocked his top desk drawer. Almost reluctantly, he handed her a video tape. The timed surveillance tape. It wasn't compatible with her machine, but hopefully she could make a clean copy. "Be careful with this, Carmen. It's our only evidence. I'll have John Forbes bring the recorder from security up to your office."

□ □ □

Could the morning get worse? Carmen wondered as she opened the door to her office. The sight of the abandoned camcorder on her desk told her it was about to.

Andersen! She glanced at her watch. Nine o'clock already. She was supposed to be taping with Andersen at eight sharp.

Someone banged on her office door. Oh no! Her stomach did a sickening somersault. Hopefully, it was Forbes with the tape deck from security. She threw open the door and came face to face with Dr. James Andersen.

"Clinical hours start at eight a.m.," he bellowed, striding into her office without invitation.

"Yes, I know, I—"

"You what, Ms. Day? Did you have a late night meeting with our downsizing expert?"

So Barb wasn't exaggerating about the rumors, Carmen thought. That sickening knot of fear snarled her stomach again. "I have no idea what you're—"

"Oh, don't play innocent with me, Ms. Day. It's all over the hospital."

"As a matter of fact, I had a meeting with—"

"I really don't care," Andersen said, looking down at her from his superior height. Not for the first time, Carmen cursed her lack of stature. She'd like to pop Andersen one. Right on the nose it would be an effort to reach. "I just wanted to remind you that we did have an appointment this morning. To tape the procedure that I was forced to use as a back-up for the symposium. As you recall, your last attempt to record my research also failed."

Carmen ran a hand through her short hair, and wondered idly if she looked as disheveled as Wayne Goodman. "Look, neither of these things is really my fault"

"Of course not, Ms. Day. Nothing is ever your fault. Blame it on the downsizing expert occupying the extra office downstairs. Actually, in this, it probably is his fault." He crossed the office with a couple of strides and hauled open the door. "Just be advised, I will be documenting all of this in my report to Wayne Goodman."

The door swung shut with a resounding boom as he left her office.

With her foot, Carmen pulled out her chair and sank down into it. The day was only an hour old. How could things have gone so wrong so quickly?

Another knock on the door roused her from self-pity. She approached it cautiously, but the shadow visible through the frosted glass was a good deal shorter than Dr. Andersen. John Forbes. She opened the door.

"Mr. Goodman asked me to bring up the VCR," Forbes said.

"Just put it in the back room."

Carmen suppressed a stab of guilt as the maintenance supervisor walked past her. A blue workman's uniform one size too small didn't complement Forbes' heavy-set frame. The uniform was in need of laundering. She'd heard that the services of housekeeping and maintenance would soon be contracted out. Maybe a man destined for the unemployment ranks didn't think it necessary to waste money on new uniforms or dry cleaning. Poor guy, she thought. Where is a man a couple years shy of retirement going to find another job?

"Terrible thing," Forbes said as she wired up a cable from the back of her VCR to the one from security and started to make a copy. Usually, she hated when people watched her work, but John Forbes seemed to have an interest in the project. Probably wanted to feel like he was helping. "Pretty young woman like that." Forbes shook his head. "Hope they find the bastard and lock him up good and throw—" He looked up at her in shock, realizing the language he'd used. Embarrassed, he stuffed his hands into his pockets.

"Me, too. But—"

The phone rang, cutting short the rest of her sentence. Carmen left the tape to run by itself. But the interruption only brought her more bad news. In the lecture theater, the slide projector was in the progress of mulching her carefully prepared presentation for the director of nursing.

"Gotta run," she said, reaching for her tool kit. Forbes stared at the tape. The expression on his face was difficult to read. The horror of what happened to Judy affected them all, Carmen thought. "Thanks for bringing up the machine," she said pointedly.

Forbes took the hint. He shrugged, thrust his hands deeper into his pockets and wandered to the door. Locking it behind him, Carmen fled for the elevator.

Maniac film projectors, crazy chiefs of staff, slide projectors that picked the worst moment to eat slides, Carmen wondered if the lecture theater might be haunted. Enough weird things certainly happened down there.

The normally docile slide projector had crunched one of the slides on decubitus ulcers she'd prepared for the director of nursing. Rather than turning smoothly through the carousel, the slide had become lodged beneath, providing a slippery slope for a number of others to join it. The only way to get it loose was to take apart the top of the projector. Charles had called a break in his in-service, but even the normally mild mannered D.O.N. seemed annoyed at her this morning.

She managed to salvage two of the slides by bending the cardboard mounts back into shape. The other needed to be re-shot. Redoing her work because of equipment failure put a definite cramp into her schedule. Carmen thought of Andersen's next report to Wayne Goodman and winced. Perhaps if she made some headway with the security videotape, Wayne would overlook the equipment problems.

"Not much I can do with this one." Carmen held up the shredded slide. Bedsores looked all the more lurid crumpled in her hand. "We'll reshoot it next time—"

"The next time what?" the D.O.N. demanded. "The next time someone's in pain?"

"I'm sorry about the projector," Carmen said, refusing to get into yet another whining argument about budget cuts. She hit the forward button. Mercifully, the slide projector advanced smoothly.

Appeased, the D.O.N. turned back to the seminar participants coming back into the lecture theater. Carmen gratefully escaped into the hall.

No end to it, she thought, letting herself into her office. Budget cuts bred desperation. Normally kind people got edgy. They did as much damage to each other as the bean counters and senior executives trying to put a lid on runaway health care costs.

All the time, the work load got heavier. Carmen glanced down at her calendar in panic. She had the luxury of fifteen minutes before her own in-service this morning. Budget cuts and the loss of her staff made teaching others to do her job the only alternative. A dangerous one. The more people who knew how to do her job, the less need there was for her. Her conscience wouldn't let patients suffer or research go without documentation. So each week, she taught another group of staff how to use her equipment.

Maybe she should teach Dr. Andersen, she thought with a bitter smile. Then if the tapes didn't turn out, he would have only himself to blame. But Andersen would never lower himself to what he disdainfully called "a technical job."

While she appreciated the enthusiasm of the group of physiotherapy students from the nearby university, they were more interested in photographing each other than in learning the rudiments of video production. Carmen packed up the camera, which miraculously had decided to behave itself for once, and closed the door to her office.

She couldn't be more than five years older than
most of them, but their youthful rowdiness got on her
nerves. Carmen sat down at her desk and wondered
when the last time she'd felt carefree had been.

At least a millennium, she thought. First her
mom's death, then the harsh reality of trying to support herself, and now the challenge of saving a department doomed to extinction. Did the worries never
cease?

Someone knocked loudly at her door. Apparently
not. She should keep it open, she mused, then she'd be
able to spot them coming.

This dark, fatalistic mood wasn't going to go away.
She might as well face up to whatever awaited her.
Max Deveraux, however, was the last person she
expected.

In his flawless dark suit, he looked strikingly different from the man in jeans and sweats standing
uncertainly on her doorstep last night. Self-assured,
armored by the office uniform, rested, Max hadn't
been up late thinking of her. Well, at least one of us
got a good night's sleep. Carmen resolved to get herself one, starting as soon as she could escape from the
walls of Royal Hospital.

"Did I catch you in the middle of something?" Dark
eyes swept over her. Deep inside, she thought she
caught a glimmer of interest, but Max the Axe never
revealed the path of his thoughts. The awkwardness of
his departure last night stretched between them.
Fervently, she hoped that wasn't what he'd come to
discuss. Because when it came to her feelings for Max
Deveraux, she had no answers.

Carmen became aware she was staring. "Ah, no. I
just finished the physiotherapy in-service." Best to
keep the topic of conversation safely—however cow-
ardly—upon work.

"Good." Max strode past her. "Then you can spare me a minute."

Carmen caught the phrasing of that non-question. Rather than resenting Max Deveraux, she should take lessons from him. No "Can I come in?" Just the assurance that of course he could.

"Come on in," Carmen said dryly. Max didn't seem to notice.

She sat in her chair, leaving Max to lean against the desk. A tactical error, she realized as he looked down at her. But Max didn't seem bent on intimidating her.

He pulled a ream of paper from an inter-office envelope. "Carmen, I'm taking a great risk sharing this with you, but I thought you should know. I'd like your word that nothing will be said beyond this office."

Resisting the urge to fidget, Carmen nodded. Max handed her the paper.

It took a moment to understand the ramifications of the name and dates of the meticulously laid-out graph. The following pages proposed a financial forecast on how the budget of medical photography could be better used in medical services. Each of her mishaps, the broken video camera, the disagreeable film projector, the forgotten videotaping session, were given a dollar value. Careful manipulation of the figures made it look like medical photography was costing the hospital more than it produced. A complete work of fiction. The report was signed "Dr. James H. Andersen"—the "H" stood for Hellion according to malicious rumor. Addressed to Max Deveraux and copied to Wayne Goodman, President, Carmen noted.

"I suppose you agree with this?" she asked. Max was watching her carefully, dark eyes alight with interest.

"I thought knowing the contents of this report might help you plan a reasonable rebuttal," Max said, completely side-stepping the topic of what his feelings might be on the matter.

Silence stretched between them, neither mentioning the aborted dinner last night, nor the ramifications of Andersen's report. One of those male maneuvers, coached in sports terminology that Carmen never understood. Drop the ball in your court as it were. Somehow she still had to find a dignified way of returning his picnic basket. Drop the ball in her court, indeed.

"I can't allow you to keep the report, of course." Max indicated the report with raised eyebrows. "But like I said, I thought you should know. So take a good look, because I'm going to have to take it with me."

Take a good look. The contents of the report were already burned into her mind. She handed the report back to him. Andersen would have a fit if he knew she'd seen it. As he pointed out, Max was taking a risk showing it to her. The question that burned through her mind was, "Why?"

Why was he taking risks on her behalf when he'd seemed intent on her destruction? Why was he worrying about whether she made it home safely? Why did whether she ate properly concern him? Could it all be just a game of good cop, bad cop, to use another male metaphor, designed to win her trust, while doing her out of the one thing she trusted most, her job?

"Thanks, Max. I do appreciate it." Carmen rose to her feet, signaling the end of their meeting. She could play these male games just as well. She shut her mouth firmly, resisting the feminine urge to sputter some more.

It was harder to resist the urge to invite him to dinner. It was nearly impossible not to follow the line of his sensuous lips, to imagine how they'd felt covering hers yesterday. But if she was going to play games, Carmen Day intended to win.

The look he gave her was truly tortured, as if he too, had a lot more to say. Thanks for dinner. The words burned the tip of her tongue, but Carmen watched mutely as he stuffed the report back in its envelope and let himself out of her office.

Her stomach uttered a ferocious rumble. She had to eat something today or she'd never make it through the afternoon. Carmen headed for the cafeteria for a muffin and coffee, the only things her churning stomach could handle.

□ □ □

Dr. James Andersen was waiting to see Max when he arrived back in his office. "Did you have a chance to review my report?" the chief of staff asked as soon as he stepped through the door.

"I received your report," Max said noncommittally. "But I have to tell you right now, I'm saving all the material until the end of the week. That way, I can review it all together."

"You could at least let me know what you thought." Andersen moved into the room, occupying it, staring down at Max from his superior height. Did he think that maneuver would intimidate him? Max wondered. Max the Axe, he thought wryly, using the name the grapevine had given him, had been intimidated by the best.

"I'm afraid I can't do that. My recommendations will be published within the week. Until then, I'm considering all reports equally. There are enough rumors about my intentions," he finished pointedly.

"You mean you can't even give me your impressions, off the record?" Andersen stated the comment as a question, but it came out more of a threat.

"That's what I mean," Max said firmly. And yet, he'd shared his impressions with Carmen Day, off the record, his guilty conscience pointed out as Andersen left fuming. Why on earth had he done such a thing?

First the fiasco with the picnic basket, now this. Max waited until Andersen had closed the door behind him and rested his head in his hands.

□ □ □

The door to the office was locked, but that was hardly an obstacle for the intruder. He cast a glance over his shoulder to make sure the hallway was quiet, then pulled on the thick black gloves he'd brought with him. No sense leaving fingerprints. He'd made that mistake last night in the heat of the moment. But he prided himself in being a man who learned from his mistakes.

The key slid smoothly into the lock and the heavy door opened with a loud click. He looked furtively behind him, but the traffic in the corridor was sparse in the late afternoon. Letting the door close behind him, he moved to the back room where he knew the videotape machine would be waiting with enough evidence to incriminate him. He thought she'd never leave her office. First she'd had all those physiotherapy students crammed in there, then that rat of a downsizing expert. Didn't the woman ever eat? Use the ladies room?

Didn't matter, he thought, ejecting the tape from the VCR. He slid the tape into one of his large pockets.

The sound of the door opening stopped him in his tracks.

Silent curses echoed through the intruder's mind. Another minute—that's all it would have taken to accomplish his task. But the conscientious Carmen Day couldn't even grant him that. She was going to be a problem, he could tell that right now. In his haste last night, he'd made a number of mistakes. Fate intended to make it up to him, though. Wayne Goodman had been kind enough to spill the secret of the security tape, the only evidence of his crime. It wouldn't be a problem if he could make it vanish.

He pressed himself harder into the space between the editing console and the cupboard beside it and hoped she couldn't see him from her desk. Seconds stretched into minutes. The intruder watched helplessly as Carmen settled in at her desk with no intention of leaving. He tightened his grip on the rope in his pocket and prayed he wouldn't have to use it.

□ □ □

Carmen set the muffin down on her desk and proceeded to break it into bite-sized pieces. Halfway through the first mouthful, she remembered the security tape in her back room. She rose, reaching for her coffee as she turned to check the back room.

The phone ringing drew her back to her desk. She washed the muffin down with a mouthful of scalding coffee and caught the phone on the fourth ring.

"You still alive in there, Carmen?" Mandy, the floor secretary asked.

"Just barely."

"Well, revive yourself and pick up your messages. I'm starting to get complaints."

"Be right there." Carmen realized with a pang of guilt she hadn't even thought of her messages since yesterday. Poor Mandy. As floor secretary she was the front line for everyone's complaints.

Carmen crammed another piece of muffin into her mouth and topped it off with another gulp of coffee. Letting her door swing shut, she rounded the corner to the floor reception area. "Sorry," she said, wincing at the stack of pink message slips.

"I don't mind taking the messages," Mandy said, "but the people who think I can conjure you out of thin air get on my nerves."

"Tell them I died and there's to be an open auction for my department budget." Her gallows humor got only a glimmer of a smile from Mandy.

Some people just can't take a joke. Carmen glanced down at the stack of messages and all attempts at levity fled. Andersen, Andersen, Andersen. Goodman. Andersen. She groaned.

The gaping door to her office stopped her cold. Carmen eyed the open door from several feet away. Had she left it open? She distinctly remembered locking it, yet she also remembered that she had no appointments that morning.

Carmen bolted through the open door, racing around her desk toward the back room. She hit the eject button on the security VCR.

Nothing.

Her heart pounded hard in her ears. A thin sheen of sweat broke out on her lip. She slid her hand into the thin slot in a vain hope the tape was merely jammed.

The tape deck was empty. Carmen checked the console, the floor, even the top drawer of her desk. But the evidence hollered what she already knew.

Someone had stolen the videotape containing the only evidence of Judy's attack.

Chapter Six

"*You* left the door open," Wayne Goodman snapped. "That's the only logical explanation."

"I never leave the door open," Carmen insisted for at least the tenth time, "not even to visit the ladies' room."

"That's right," Barb said hopefully, "I've teased Carmen about being paranoid several times." Wayne shot her a withering look. Barb who'd dropped by to offer Carmen moral support quickly found a reason to return to her own office.

Wayne ran his hands through his blond curls. "All right," he said to the detective in charge, "could you have another look at the lock?"

Uniformed officers swarmed through her small office. Two detectives in trench coats questioned the president. They really do wear those beige trench coats, Carmen thought. Just like in the movies. At another time Carmen might have found that observation funny. But the forensics expert dusting her doorknob was a grim reminder that her office was now a crime scene. He finished with the door and moved on to the videotape recorder still sitting on her back counter.

It didn't look as though the verdict would fall in her favor. No signs of tampering marked her door. The lock hadn't been broken or forced open. Even the president was convinced she'd left the door unlocked when she went around the corner to retrieve her messages from Mandy. That's what she'd think, Carmen had to admit.

A vivid memory of locking the door on her way out of the office burned in her mind. She had locked the door. Carmen knew that much for certain. Someone had breezed through the secured door as easily as if it had been standing open. She'd only been gone a couple of minutes.

"Gloves," the fingerprint expert announced, pointing to a finger-sized smear on the eject button. "Same as on the door."

Carmen breathed a breath of partial relief. That proved someone had gone to the trouble of putting on gloves. Someone meant to steal the videotape and took steps to conceal their identity. But that still didn't solve the mystery of how the thief got through a supposedly locked door.

"This tape should have been turned over to the police yesterday," the detective in charge said accusingly to Wayne.

Goodman caught the accusation in his tone and set his jaw. He shot a withering glance at Carmen. "We thought we could enhance it." The excuse sounded lame even to Carmen's ears.

"In future, leave that to the experts."

Goodman looked as stung by the remark as Carmen did. Forensics wasn't her specialty, Carmen thought. Why hadn't she told the president that this morning?

Because she wanted to be a hero? Isn't that why she stayed in this job, even though the health care system was falling down around her? She wanted to save someone because she couldn't save her—

Carmen wrenched her thoughts out of that futile line of thinking. It did nothing to help her current predicament.

Wayne Goodman had entrusted her with a valuable piece of evidence. While she'd been out of the office, someone had barged through a locked door and stolen the one clue to the attacker's identity. A chilling thought occurred to her.

The intruder had a key.

That would explain why the lock hadn't been tampered with. And if the intruder had a key, it meant he (or she?) had to be an employee of Royal Hospital, someone who could walk the halls and no one would take any notice.

The chill snaked further down her spine. Carmen shuddered. It could even be someone she liked. Someone she said hello to in passing every day, sat next to in the cafeteria, danced with at the Christmas party.

Someone who could enter her office any time they pleased.

"It had to be someone who had a key," she said firmly. "I know for sure I locked the door."

By his ominous frown, she could tell Wayne Goodman didn't care for that idea. That there was a maniac loose on the grounds of Royal Hospital was one thing. That the maniac was also a member of the hospital staff didn't sit well at all.

"That would explain how he got past the lock," the forensics expert said. "Who in the hospital has keys to this office?"

"I do," Goodman said, daring the detective to add an accusation to that statement. "As well as all the senior staff, security, maintenance, housekeeping, the head of volunteers so they can get equipment on the weekend, and Carmen herself."

"What you're saying is that it could have been just about anyone," the detective finished.

"Any one of about twenty people," Wayne said. Obviously, he'd been hoping to pin the mishap on Carmen's carelessness. This new development added a sinister dimension to what originally seemed like a fluke occurrence.

"Would have helped to have that security tape. Make it easier to weed the guy out."

Wayne ignored the sarcasm. "Come down to my office. I'll have my secretary prepare a list of..." He paused, realizing what he'd just said—the Judy he'd come to depend on was still off on leave, recovering from the attack. "I'll get you that list," he finished lamely.

The knot of investigators began to dissolve, some dispatched to other assignments, a couple to Wayne's office. Carmen let the heavy door swing shut, grateful for the solitude. In the sweeping arc of the closing door, she noticed Dr. Andersen standing at the elevator with Wayne Goodman. Snatches of their conversation reached her. "Videotape...stolen." Wayne's voice, followed by "incompetent," kindly added by James Andersen. One of the police officers muttered something in reply, but the door whooshed shut, muffling the rest of the conversation.

"Thanks a bunch," Carmen said. Then it occurred to her that Dr. James Andersen, as a member of the senior staff, was one of the people who had a key to her office.

No! She dismissed the thought as soon as it formed in her mind. Determined to survive the downsizing process with his department intact, Andersen challenged anyone he considered a threat. But Dr. Andersen had always been ruthless when it came to his priorities. Certainly he wasn't desperate enough to improve the odds by attacking the competition or stealing. Was he?

Once the police had left, she had the acute feeling of being watched. Carmen found herself glancing over her shoulder into the equipment room. She stood up, forcing herself to walk to the spot where the intruder would have been standing. Not so bad, she told herself. Her breath caught in her throat. She hadn't looked in the back office when she returned from the cafeteria. What if the intruder had been lurking in her office while she sat at her desk blithely eating a muffin?

Don't think about it! her subconscious pleaded. That someone might have been hiding in her back room made her stomach clench. At the very least he'd been watching the office, had used the few minutes she spent with Mandy to make his move. In her attempt to help Judy, Carmen had become a target.

She looked nervously around the familiar walls of her office. For the past five years it had been her sanctuary, the place where she did her most creative, most important work. At Royal Hospital she knew she was needed. Until Max Deveraux and his downsizing plan. Until some maniac stalked the hospital grounds. Now even her office wasn't safe.

She should have told Wayne enhancing the tape was beyond her capabilities. But she desperately wanted to help Judy. She wanted to be a hero. And instead she'd made everything a lot worse.

Wait until Max Deveraux hears about this one. I'll be standing in the unemployment line for sure.

Carmen reached behind the security videotape machine and unhooked the connecting cables. Might as well return it to the security office. She disconnected the cables from her editing equipment and turned the power off.

The machine spat out a videotape.

And then she remembered. She had started making a copy before she'd been called away. Whoever had stolen the tape didn't understand video equipment, didn't understand the significance of the cables hooked up to transfer the picture from one machine to another. Or had he merely run out of time?

Her heartbeat pounded in her ears. Carmen turned on the power and shoved the tape back in the machine. She peered into the outer office, but despite an overactive imagination that conjured images of masked intruders wearing black leather gloves, the office was empty.

She ran the tape back. It showed a black and white scene of the hospital corridors, empty due to the late hour. The security cameras were timed to rotate through all the corridors, inside first, then out. Carmen rushed through the inconsequential footage, then slowed the tape as the scene switched to the exit to the parking lot.

Judy walked into the scene, digging in her huge leather purse for her car keys. Carmen bit her lip, choking back the urge to scream at Judy to watch out. But she was watching the events of last night as the time code in the lower corner reminded her. Carmen clapped a hand over her mouth, resigned to the fact that she was going to have to watch her friend get attacked.

Finding her keys, Judy straightened and stepped off the concrete step onto the asphalt. Here it comes. Carmen winced.

But the picture broke up at that point, slanting across the screen in black and white bars. Then the signal turned to snow.

The thief hadn't needed to worry about the copy in progress. He took the original out of the machine before the crucial scene could be copied.

Her shoulders slumped. Circumstances offered no way to redeem herself. Carmen ran the tape one more time to be sure.

Judy searching in a purse almost bigger than her for her keys. Judy walking ahead towards her car. A shadow in the frame, then the breakup of the signal.

A shadow.

Carmen rewound the tape and peered at the monitor. Sure enough, just before the tape broke up, a shadow appeared in the side of the frame. She paused the tape. Definitely a shadow.

She ran it forward frame by frame. The shadow crossing into the frame from the left side. The slanting bars as the tape broke up. Still, she was certain she'd seen something else besides the shadow just before the tape broke up. Holding her breath, her nose nearly touching the screen in concentration, Carmen backed the tape up again.

Just as the signal disintegrated, she caught a glimpse of a hand reaching into the frame.

Gotcha! Carmen reached for the discarded cables and hooked the videotape machine up to her computer. She glanced back nervously, certain the phantom had disappeared like the videotape, but there on the monitor, frozen in place was a man's shadow, and a hand reaching into the frame.

Not much of a victory. Identifying the man was a priority, but Carmen was somewhat relieved the tape ended before Judy's attack. She didn't think she could sit and watch her friend get hurt. But it also meant she had no way of knowing if this was the attacker or just another staff member walking towards his car.

It was all she had to go on. Carmen sent the signal to the computer. The frame of video appeared on the screen, a blurry smudge from the long range security camera. She drew a box around the hand and enlarged it, blurring it further. Entering a computer command, the picture dissolved into squares of light and dark. Carmen worked meticulously, making the light squares lighter and darkening the dark ones until she'd made a high contrast image of the attacker's hand and his shadow.

The long shadow cast by the setting sun offered no clues. Distorted by the sun's angle, it was impossible to determine the height of the shadow's owner. Definitely male, though, but then Judy told them that already. Carmen went back to work on the hand.

Neck muscles protested violently. She straightened, realizing she'd been sitting with her back at an impossible angle, her nose practically touching the screen. All hospital employees were given lessons in back care. The penalty for injuring herself was sitting through ten weeks of Barb's back care classes. Carmen sat back and surveyed her handiwork.

Up close the image was still a mass of black and gray squares, but from a distance of a couple of feet, she could see the shadow of a deep scar cutting across the attacker's hand.

So the attacker had a scar on his hand. Carmen rubbed her neck. It wasn't much to go on, but it would help narrow down the list of possible suspects by matching those who had keys to her office to anyone bearing a scar on their hand. Assuming of course that it was the attacker's hand she'd captured on video.

Her excitement evaporated. The police, even Wayne Goodman already thought her a klutz. How could she convince them this was a clue worth following up? And if the police wouldn't believe her, what then? She could hardly skulk the halls demanding to look at people's hands.

A knock on the door made her jump. She hadn't realized she was so nervous. But then she hadn't realized there were people who wanted to break into her office, either.

"It's me, Barb," came a muffled voice through the glass. "Are they gone?" Barb asked as soon as Carmen opened the door. But Barb's eyes were busy scanning the office behind Carmen. She suppressed a grin. Barb already knew the answer. Barb knew everything that went on at Royal Hospital.

Carmen slumped against the door, realizing for the first time just how drained she felt. "C'mon in."

"You okay?"

Carmen opened her mouth to reply politely in the affirmative. A glance at Barb's face made her give up all pretense at bravery. "No, Barb," she said in a tiny, broken voice. "I'm not okay. In half a week I've managed to make enemies of our new downsizing expert, the chief of staff, and the president himself. Not only has one of my friends been attacked, but I've lost the only piece of evidence we had."

"You left out becoming romantically involved with said downsizing expert." Barb's attempt at levity failed miserably. "Ignore me."

"We aren't romantically involved," Carmen insisted. "We had dinner. And last night—"

"Last night! Carmen, you promised me you were going to disentangle yourself from Max the Axe."

"I tried. I ditched him at the dry cleaners, the grocery store. But then he showed up on my doorstep with a home-cooked meal."

"And you let him in?"

Barbara looked so entirely scandalized, Carmen couldn't help laughing.

"He didn't ask to come in. He said he was worried about me and left me this great dinner all wrapped up in a picnic basket, with wine and everything. Honestly, I can't figure the man out."

"Obviously he was looking for more than dinner."

"But if that's true, why didn't he ask to come in. I think it was his dinner as well in the basket. But he went home without a word."

Barb considered this new development, head cocked to one side. "Don't give him too much credit. You still have to return his basket. It's an old trick, Carmen. You leave something at the potential love interest's house that they have to return."

"Barbara Downey, you have a suspicious mind." The protest sounded hollow even to her own ears. "But the thought had occurred to me," Carmen admitted aloud.

"So are you?"

"Am I what?"

"Going to take his basket back?"

"It would only be polite. But tonight I think I'm going to go home, order pizza and crawl into bed where no one can find me."

"The way things have been going it sounds like a good strategy. I'll give you a lift."

Carmen started to say thank you, then changed her mind. "Don't wait around for me, Barb. I only live on the next street."

"There's a maniac loose, Carmen. Have you forgotten?"

"I refuse to be held hostage at work, in my office or on my street. This has always been a bad neighborhood, Barb. That doesn't mean I have to cower inside."

"I wish you'd be reasonable." Barb crossed her arms. "About your safety and getting entangled with Max the Axe."

"Max is the least of my worries," Carmen said. She reached out, steering Barbara by the arm into her back office. "Tell me what you make of this."

Barbara glanced blankly at the screen. "What is it?"

"I think," Carmen drawled the word in emphasis, "it's a blurry shot of Judy's attacker."

"But it doesn't look like anything more than a shadow."

Carmen pointed to the hand in the enlarged box. "It is only his shadow, but this looks like his hand. Can you think of anyone who might have a scar on his hand. Someone who might also have keys to my office?"

"No, but I'll have a quiet look around."

The prospect of Barb's help made Carmen feel slightly relieved. Suddenly, she wasn't alone in this mess. She had an ally. "Can you do something else for me?"

"Sure."

Carmen put a disk into the computer and saved the file. Ejecting the disk, she handed it to Barb. Keep this safe for me, will you? I don't know what I've really got here, or whether it's important, but I can't run the risk of having anything else stolen from my office."

Barb stuck the disk in the pocket of her lab coat. "I'll keep it safe, don't worry." She looked sternly at Carmen. The "mother look," as Carmen called it, when Barb insisted on mothering her the way she mothered her teenage daughter. "And you take care of yourself, too. I don't like what's happening around her. It scares me."

"Okay, Mom." Carmen used the nickname to let Barbara know when she was nagging. "I'll be careful."

"I've got to run." Barb turned back, her hand on the doorknob. "Let me know if you change your mind about that ride home."

"It's only two blocks." Carmen opened the door.

And nearly screamed to find John Forbes standing there.

Barb clutched her chest. "You scared us half to death."

John Forbes grasped the door frame, as if they'd scared him as well. He looked from one to the other and stuffed his hands deep into his pockets. "Ah, Mr. Goodman sent me to pick up the video machine."

Carmen willed her heartbeat to return to normal. "It's in the back room."

Barb returned to her own office to settle last minute problems for the day. Carmen watched as John Forbes bundled the VCR under his arm. She saved the image to her hard drive, and decided to call it a day herself. Enough had gone wrong. Best to start over fresh tomorrow.

She looked up to find John Forbes staring in puzzlement at the fading monitor. It really didn't look like anything, Carmen thought, viewing the image with skepticism. Just a blurry shadow and that's probably all it was.

John Forbes trudged out of her office on his way down to security. Carmen turned off the lights and locked the office, checking at least five times to be sure the door was indeed locked.

Hopefully, it would still be locked when she arrived at work tomorrow morning.

Once out on the street, however, familiar surroundings took on a sinister cast. The setting sun filled the tree-lined road with foreboding shadows. Carmen caught herself walking faster than usual, counting the blocks home. Three more to go.

Behind her came the echo of footsteps. She forced her legs to move faster. Two blocks. Footsteps hurried to catch up with her.

She was just about to give up on dignity and start running full out for home, when a breathless voice called, "Carmen!"

Carmen nearly tripped over her own feet as she
slowed down. Turning to peer down the dark sidewalk
behind her, she saw Max Deveraux hurrying toward
her. His suit jacket was unbuttoned at the front and
flapped out behind him like dark wings. Wind caught
his hair, ruffling it in all directions. He would have
looked every bit as wild and untamed as she suspected, were it not for the slim, expensive-looking briefcase in his hand.

"You raced out of the hospital like the devil was on
your heels," he said, breathing heavily himself to catch
up with her. "What's the hurry?"

"The devil is on my heels," she said, then just as
quickly wished she hadn't. Oh, brilliant, Carmen. Why
did I tell him that. "Bad day," she finished lamely.

"So I heard."

Of that she had no doubt. News traveled fast at
Royal Hospital, especially when the news was bad.

"I'm sorry, Carmen."

His heartfelt sympathy only made her angry. "Are
you, Max? I'd have thought it would make your job
easier."

His dark brows drew together. For an instant she
saw pain flash within his dark eyes. Then he composed himself. "Why would you think that?"

Guilt stole her glib reply. "If the manager could be
proven incompetent, it would make it easier to close
down the department."

"You're jumping to a lot of conclusions, Carmen.
One thing has nothing to do with the other."

"Oh right," she snapped and started walking again.
"Do you expect me to believe that?"

"If the manager is incompetent, but the department is still needed, then the question is really
whether to hire another manager."

"Especially if you could get one cheaper."

Max dashed after her, grasping her arm and pulling her gently around to face him. "I never said you were incompetent. In fact, I've given you an opportunity I rarely give to anyone to put together a report. A chance to make a better impression, Carmen, and you took it as an outright attack."

"You mean when you asked me to write that report, you were trying to help me?"

They walked together now, his hand still on her arm, like lovers. Except that they were still at war.

"I gave you an opportunity."

"Did you give James Andersen the same opportunity to prepare a report against me?"

His eyebrows lowered threateningly again. "Andersen did that of his own initiative."

"And were you impressed by his 'initiative,' as you put it?"

Max seemed to struggle with the answer. "No," he said at last. "While I have to admire his industriousness, I would have been more impressed with a report on why we should maintain his funding as opposed to why we should cut someone else's."

"I see."

He pulled them to a stop again, in the pool of light cast by one of the streetlights that suddenly winked on. "I don't think you do. I'm trying to help you, Carmen, in the only way I can. I can't fund your department simply because I like you, because I admire your spirit. As much as I'd like to, I can't. But I've done what I could, and you've done nothing but throw my kindness back in my face."

She'd hurt him. She could see the pain, unmasked now in his dark eyes.

"Forgive me," Carmen whispered. "I've been too wrapped up in my own problems to notice you were trying to be kind." It sounded lame, it sounded insincere. "But I did notice dinner last night. It was wonderful. And I wish—"

He drew closer, so close she could feel the warmth of his breath on her cheek.

"What do you wish, Carmen?"

Should she tell him? "I—I wish I'd invited you in." There, she said it. And if he made her feel foolish, she'd never forgive him.

"So do I."

"You could have said something."

Max offered her a wan smile. "I'm not in the habit of barging into women's apartments. Especially when I'm not invited."

"I wouldn't think you'd find invitations that hard to come by."

Wrong thing to say! She could tell by the way his smile faded back into that pained expression. She'd managed to wound him twice in the space of five minutes. "Forget I said that," she said. "It would appear I'm doomed to spend the entire evening with my foot in my mouth."

"Perhaps we should start over. You had a disastrous day, mine was no pleasure, either. So let's not continue it into tonight. Why don't I go to the video store, rent something funny, we could order pizza—" He stopped. "Except that I just remembered my VCR is sitting in my apartment in Ottawa."

"I have one." Oh no, am I really inviting Max the Axe to my apartment? But she couldn't stop her lips from moving. "I owe you at least two dinners, and I have to give you your picnic basket back. Why don't you come over to my place?"

It would seem inviting Max Deveraux home to her apartment was just what she'd done.

Chapter Seven

*U*nlike a business meeting, there were no rules when it came to the courting of a human female, Max told himself as he climbed the steps to Carmen's apartment. In the last century it had been easier. His male Mohawk elders had gone to live with their wives' families. His European ancestors asked a father's permission to court his daughter. And if the answer was no, well, you took it like a man. But Carmen never mentioned her father, whatever that meant, except that he was most definitely in uncharted territory.

Women baffled him. They seemed to like his looks well enough. Obviously the outward package pleased them, but when it came to matters of the heart, Max had to admit he was sorely lacking a procedures manual. It wasn't like a spreadsheet, you couldn't explain it in a cost/benefit analysis.

Well, he'd just have to write the manual as he went. Max was a man accustomed to getting what he wanted in life. And what he wanted was Carmen Day.

She answered the door wearing jeans and a crisp white t-shirt. He wondered how she managed to keep it that white.

He still hadn't mastered the knack of dividing up his wash so that the dark colors didn't ruin the light. Eventually, he'd just given up. When it came to the cost/benefit analysis, he decided it would be prudent to hire a professional and called a laundry service.

Carmen looked relaxed. He took that for a good sign. Though she'd had a long day, her eyes brightened when she saw him and she smiled warmly. In the light from the hallway behind, he could see the spattering of freckles across her nose and longed to get

close enough to count them. He submerged those
thoughts under a layer of polite interest as she ush-
ered him up the steep narrow staircase to her apartment.

Well, he was in, Max thought to himself. So far, so
good.

□ □ □

Carmen leaned back on the couch, more relaxed than
she'd been for a long time, and a little amazed at
Max's revelation that he was a race car driver.

The rented videotape still sat in its black plastic
box, unwatched and forgotten. Pizza had been delivered an hour ago and devoured with the appetite of
people who hadn't eaten since breakfast. They'd polished off the rest of the wine in the crystal glasses Max
had borrowed from the collection in his rented house.
No romantic music played on her CD player. Max's
company was entertainment enough. He practically
filled her tiny living room.

Being short in stature, Carmen rarely thought
from the perspective of anyone larger than herself.
But in the cluttered living room with the remnants of
her mother's life in the two china cabinets, Max was
like the proverbial bull in a china shop. The narrow
spaces between furniture were easy to traverse with
her slight figure, but Max moved gingerly as though
he was afraid to stretch out so much as a leg for fear
of toppling some curio cabinet or unseating an antique
lamp. The wildness in him chafed to get out, and in
that moment she could see him quite clearly racing
down the track at Indy, black hair escaping from his
helmet and blowing in the breeze.

"I'd never have taken you for a race car driver!" she said.

"Would-be racer," Max corrected. "I never got to drive myself, though I watched my dad from the time I was a little kid. When I think of him I can still smell rubber and gasoline." He laughed. "But he must have had great plans for me, after all he named me Maximilian."

Carmen swallowed hard on the laughter burbling up inside her, and covered the reflex with a sip of wine. The wine went down the wrong way, and she coughed. "Your name is Maximilian?" she croaked.

Dark eyebrows drew together, revealing his displeasure at being teased. "What did you think it was?"

She swallowed past her raw throat, remembering how she'd imagined his mother calling him Maxwell, and tried not to blush. "Maxwell?"

"Maxwell is a nerd's name."

He sounded hurt that she had assumed he had so unappealing a name, but she couldn't help asking, "What's your middle name?"

"Atonwa. It's Mohawk or Kanyen'kehaka for Thomas."

"Maximilian Atonwa Deveraux. That's an auspicious name."

Max laughed. "A Mohawk activist and a French-Canadian race car driver made pretty auspicious parents."

"Sounds like an interesting relationship."

"Tumultuous is probably a better word. Suffice it to say they had radically different approaches to life. I don't think they agreed on anything, except their love for each other."

Maximilian Atonwa Deveraux, descendent of Mohawk warriors, and would-be race car driver, seemed out of place sitting in her Victorian parlor.

From her new vantage point, Carmen couldn't remember why she'd kept it that way. The intricately decorated china wasn't her taste. She abhorred clutter. Still, part of her couldn't let go of the remnants of the life she'd had, her mother's life. Her history. "Why didn't you become a race car driver?" she asked, distracting herself from that unsettling train of thought.

It never occurred to her there might be a painful answer behind her innocent question, but Max's face clouded. For an instant, she caught a glimpse of the pain behind his brusque exterior. His eyes flickered to hers, capturing her glance and holding it, as if he debated whether to tell her the truth. "Well, I probably would have," he said finally. "If my dad hadn't died in a car crash."

Carmen's hand flew to her mouth. "Oh God, I'm so sorry, I didn't mean to pry, I—"

"It's okay." Max waved her protests from the air. "It was a long time ago. Dad died doing what he loved best."

"What about your mom, what did she do then?"

"Mom decided the best way to change things for The People was through shaping the minds of the future. So she went back to school and got a law degree."

His face clouded. Carmen read loneliness into that expression. In a way he must have felt as if he'd lost both parents with his mother so busy.

"She became a professor at the university and moved the two of us to Ottawa."

"Your mom sounds like an admirable lady."

"She certainly taught me a great deal about surviving in an unpredictable world. Max paused. "My Dad taught me a valuable lesson too."

"A lesson?" She couldn't image finding wisdom in such a tragic event. But infinitely practical, Max Deveraux would.

"That some risks just aren't worth taking."

So that's what was behind the impenetrable wall he built around himself. The triumph of good sense over his unruly nature. If in fact it did triumph. Wildness bulged out at all the seams, there for anyone vigilant enough to see. Max took his risks with other people's futures.

"Why do I have the feeling it isn't race car driving you're talking about."

She expected him to be insulted, to accuse her of prying. But instead he threw back his head and laughed heartily. "And now I'm on dangerous ground, aren't I, Ms. Day?"

"I don't know what you're talking about."

"Sure you do." Max poured the last dribble of wine into their glasses. "You intend to find out all about me, and leave me wondering about you."

"I had no such thing in mind."

Onyx eyes stripped her defenses. "So as long as we're spilling our guts here, tell me, what is a woman who insists she didn't have the time or the money for university doing in an institution where everyone has a Ph.D. or M.D., or at the very least a master's in something?"

Carmen felt her face reddening with fury. His question touched a nerve she didn't like to admit existed. And he was right. At Royal Hospital, everyone was more educated than she—and she fought every day to show them with the hard evidence of her skill that she was neither stupid, nor uneducated. "I believe in my work," she ground out between clenched teeth.

"And fight like a banshee to protect your turf," Max supplied, laughing, but there was good-natured

respect in his amusement. "Now you look like you did
when I first met you, ready to bang down my door and
give me what for."

"I did bang down your door and give you what you
deserved."

"So you did." Sometime in their conversation they'd
moved closer. Had he moved or was it she? Carmen
couldn't be sure. Now only inches separated them. She
was hyper-aware of how small her couch seemed with
a larger male body occupying a good portion of it.

"Tell me, Carmen, why does Royal Hospital inspire
such loyalty?"

"My mother died there." The words slipped out
before she'd even made the decision to tell him.

"I'm sorry." He reached for her, grasped her hand.
Lost in his bigger hands, hers felt tiny, but his warmth
was comforting.

"Like you said, it was a long time ago." Might as
well tell him all of it, she thought. "I hung around the
place so much, Raymond Carter, the medical photographer at the time, took me under his wing. He
trained me, gave me some work after school, developing film and stuff. It helped me to pay for some of
Mom's expenses. Help out, you know."

The unasked question hung between them, but she
purposely avoided mentioning her father. Excavating
old wounds had its uses, Carmen decided, but some
wounds ought to stay buried.

"A lot of responsibility for a kid," Max said.

She smiled sadly. "Not like I had a choice."

"Sure you did. Lots of people are devastated by the
events of their lives. Not too many people could make
it into a career."

"Thanks, I think."

Max moved closer still. So it was him. She gazed into the dark depths of his eyes. "I could see it in you the first time we met, that fire."

It was Carmen's turn to laugh. "I don't remember you being too impressed."

"Oh, I was," Max said with mock seriousness. "But I was too busy trying not to get burned."

"And now?" This time it was Carmen who inched closer. So it was me!

"Now," Max said, his face inches from hers, "I'm willing to risk getting a little singed."

Warm lips covered hers. His hands let go of hers to move upward and clasp her closer. As in the elevator, she felt the soft movements of his mouth on hers, the delightful spirals of pleasure that emanated out from the point of their contact.

His comforting warmth was all it took to burst the dam within her. As he parted her lips, seeking more of her, he drew out all the day's disappointments. The theft of the tape, her failure to keep it safe, the upcoming report on which her job depended, all disappeared in a wave of sensation. His arms clenched around her, crushing her closer still. Her hands traveled upward over the strong muscles in his back that were evident even through the fleece of his sweatshirt.

And then abruptly he released her, holding her back, gazing down at her with dark eyes that smoked with desire. "If you're going to tell me to leave, Carmen, now's the time," he said hoarsely.

Gallant of him to give her an out, a chance to blame it on the wine, to bring up those protestations of mixing work with pleasure. But the damn once burst could not be rebuilt. She had needed too long to turn back now.

Carmen buried her face against his shoulder. "Don't go."

"Oh God," Max groaned. "I was hoping you'd say that."

This time he was more thorough in his exploration. Starting with the top of her head, he buried his face in her cap of auburn curls, mapping her with scent, touch and taste. His lips ironed out the worried crease between her eyebrows, lingered to smooth both of them before offering a wisp of a kiss to each closed eyelid. Her eyes flickered open, drinking deep of the desire mirrored in his gaze. She laced her fingers through his silky dark hair, pulling him nearer, wanting more of what was certain to come.

His lips dipped lower, planting a brief kiss on the tip of her upturned nose. "I've wanted to touch you like this since I first met you," Max whispered.

The brush of his lips against hers made her shiver. "You have?"

"And you teased me mercilessly."

"I did not!" Carmen pulled away from him, only to be caught within his embrace again and lured back.

"Oh, I'm sure you didn't know what you were doing." He punctuated the remark with a probing kiss that said he knew exactly what he was doing. "The worst kind of a tease is a woman who's completely unaware of the effect she's having."

Max created his own effect on her. Linking her hands behind his neck, Carmen anchored him in place, demanding more of those silken kisses that melted her to the core. "I thought I was just making you furious."

Max chuckled, his breath warm against her cheek, and moved to nibble her left earlobe. "Oh, you did that, too. But I like a woman who can move me to strong emotions."

"Is that so?" Carmen answered his offensive with a line of her own kisses along his jaw.

"Mmm hmm." He groaned as her lips drifted lower, down the now stubbled column of his neck to bestow one last kiss in the hollow of his throat. The ribbed collar of his sweatshirt brought her exploration to a halt. "I thought you would drive me to distraction standing there in my office in your self-righteous anger, those beautiful green eyes blazing at me. I've barely had a moment's peace since."

"Serves you right," she answered boldly, and he laughed again.

"Carmen, I think you might just be the death of me."

The collar of her t-shirt offered no barrier to his perusal. He teased the crook between her neck and shoulder with tiny nibbles that sent shudders of pleasure down her spine. With teeth and lips, he tugged at the collar, pulling it open so he could place a gentle kiss on the swell of her breast.

Still not ready to divest her of that covering, he lowered his mouth to the taut peak shrouded in gauzy layers of t-shirt and bra and sucked tenderly. Carmen arched against him.

"Max"

"What?" he asked, lifting his head to tease the other.

"I—"

"We're moving too fast for you." A softly worded statement, not a question.

"Well, no, it's just that—"

"You've changed your mind." The expression on his face said he'd die if she had.

"No."

"You need more convincing." He lowered his head again and applied himself to the task.

They were moving again, Carmen shifting down oɪ the couch, Max lowering himself gently atop her. ᵀ gathered her close to him. "Trust me, Carmen. Just this once."

She shouldn't trust him. Barb's warnings rang in her mind. It was a bad idea in the extreme to get involved with someone from work, yet every feather-soft caress promised that he did care. Oh, sweet damnation, Carmen thought. And surrendered entirely.

Her hands traveled upward under his sweatshirt, mapping the broad contours of his back, the muscles bunched now to grasp her even closer. Max was in great physical shape. His was a body born to movement, and she suspected he never did quite keep the wildness at bay.

Wild even now, his hands moved over her body in broad strokes as if he sought to memorize her shape. His fingers fumbled with the button front of her jeans, and he cursed every button, until the front parted and he could touch the silky curve of her hips.

Beneath her hands his skin warmed until she felt a fine sheen of sweat break out. Impeded by the material of his sweatshirt and growing impatient, she pulled it over his head. Max tugged it off his arms, signaling he was as impatient as she. The cloth tousled his hair, making him look even wilder.

He tore the hem of her t-shirt free of her jeans, bunching it up as his hands moved over her torso. He sucked in a breath at the sight of her small breasts trapped by the gauzy material of her bra. Nuzzling his face between the lacy peaks, he pushed her t-shirt further still.

"Max, I'm going to suffocate."

" He raised his head, dark hair tousled even she fancied she could see the red embers of ning in his eyes. Urgently he pulled the t-her head and just as urgently went to work on the hook of her bra. But the tiny closure offered a challenge to bigger male fingers. "They make these things for women's hands," he complained.

"Women fasten and undo them more than men."

"Not if I had my way," he said through clenched teeth. He uttered a triumphant sigh as the clasp sprang free.

Carmen felt his warm weight settle atop her once again. The downy hair on his chest rubbed erotically against her bare nipples. For a moment they lay quietly, getting used to the feel of each other's bodies bared to the waist. Max looked down at her, searched her face thoroughly, reading the reluctance still there.

"God, Carmen, if you're not ready for this, you better stop me, now, because in a minute, I don't know if I'll..."

But she couldn't stop, even if she wanted to. Carmen realized with a certainty that shocked her that she didn't. Her body, primed and ready, was already committed, drunk on the feel, taste and smell of him.

In answer she reached up, pressing her lips against his heart already pounding rapidly beneath her touch. "Don't stop."

Her hands followed the broad expanse of his chest to where it narrowed over his slim hips. His fly zipped up, she noted with a smile, popping the top button. Neatly, she undid the zipper so his hardened length sprang free, hampered only by the mesh of his underwear. Taking up the momentum of her actions, he slid her jeans down over her hips, lifting himself as she kicked them free. He slithered down, trailing a line of blazing kisses from her breasts, circling around her belly button and settling on the equally blazing mound between her thighs.

He went to work with teeth and lips, easing the elastic of her panties further down to expose the hot flesh beneath. Carmen moaned at the first contact of his mouth, shocking herself with the huskiness of that sound. The walls in the old house kept no secrets. Mrs. Landreth downstairs would be scandalized. Carmen decided she didn't care. Max Deveraux's wildness was catching.

Max raised his head. Following the path of her thoughts across her face, he asked teasingly, "Should we adjourn to my place?"

"No—" she wailed, then added more strongly, "No! I can't wait."

His wicked laughter was muffled against her thigh. He tracing the contours of her inner thighs with hot kisses before circling back to his goal.

Carmen arched against him as he probed gently deeper, parting the soft folds of her flesh. His tongue found its target, and she moaned again, not caring if Mrs. Landreth had her ear pressed to her door, not caring if the windows were open, or if the entire staff of Royal Hospital stood out on the street listening. Her hands groped for his pants, pushing them lower. "Take these off, I want to feel you."

He raised his head again, provoking a moan of protest. "Not yet, little vixen, I want to make sure you have no regrets whatsoever."

His tongue roved in scandalous circles, slowly at first, then faster, then teasingly slow again. She ground herself against him, threading her hands through his hair, making no secret of her intentions. Her body turned to liquid fire, the flame burning at the core of her anchored by his mouth. She felt the fire rush toward him, drawn in, until she was soaring, bursting in a blaze of light. Distantly, she heard her own hoarse cry, and fervently hoped Mrs. Landreth had her television on downstairs.

Carmen came to her senses cradled beneath Max's comforting warmth. Her limbs seemed turned to lead. Sweat beaded on her forehead and between her breasts. She dragged in a long sigh of contentment.

"Regrets?"

She shook her head. "My God! And you thought it was me tormenting you."

His laughter was warm against her ear. "I don't see why we can't both be tormented. It's only fair."

Passion churned deep within his gaze, but he was gentle with her as he stripped off his jeans and underwear and settled himself between her thighs. She felt the hard weight of him against her moist opening, and angled her hips toward him, taking him deep inside. His eyelids drifted shut, sweeping her cheeks. He held her there for a drawn-out moment suspended in time, savoring the feel of her. Then he began to move.

Carmen sucked in her breath at his slow seductive movements, each gentle probing thrust aimed to discover the very depths of her. There was nothing rushed or urgent, though she could tell by the tension in his shoulders that he held himself in check. Wildness restrained.

Each tender push filled her with the promise of ecstasy to come. Each pull filled her with dismay at the loss of him. His hands slid beneath her buttocks, controlling their movement. She gave herself over to his rhythm, angling her hips to take even more of him.

Moments ago she wouldn't have believed she was capable of more lovemaking, yet with each thrust the fire within her grew until she found herself moaning for more, demanding it.

The sounds ripped from her own throat ceased to shock her. It was as if he'd reached inside her, found

the wildness aching for release and ripped it free. Her
hands cupped the round hardness of his bottom, pressing him closer. She arched against him, flung her head
back, lost in another wave of that sweet torture.

"Vixen," Max said hoarsely, followed by an oath
smothered against her breast.

"Seducer," she countered. The rest of the sentence
deteriorated into another incoherent cry.

His rhythm became more purposeful. She flung
herself against him again, heedless of the creaking
springs of her mother's old couch, forgetting Mrs.
Landreth downstairs, lost to everything except the
building passion that emanated out from the center of
their contact.

Within her the coil of desire wound tighter. She
heard her breathless cry, followed by his deeper one as
the entire world shattered into splinters of white-hot
ecstasy.

Carmen felt the tension go out of him all at once
and realized she could barely move. Every ounce of
energy in her body seemed drained. Muscles in her
thighs protested their abuse. One of the old couch
springs poked at the small of her back. She could
scarcely believe what she'd done here, in the living
room for God's sake, on her mother's couch.

Max sighed, levering himself up on one arm that
sunk up to the elbows in the cushions. "Carmen, you
practically killed me."

She heard her own dusky laughter. "I think we
broke at least two couch springs."

He kissed her tenderly now, all the fire gone out of
him. "I guess I should say I'm sorry, but I'm not."

"Sure, ruin my furniture."

Max kissed her again. "You can ruin my furniture
any time."

The couch creaked ominously as he stood up and pulled her up into his arms. Hooking his arm beneath her legs, he scooped her up and headed down the narrow hall.

"Where are you taking me."

"To bed," he said, burying his nose in her short hair. "Unless you'd prefer to spend the night on that noisy couch."

But the bed in her closet-sized bedroom was the same one she'd been sleeping in since childhood. She'd never had a reason to replace it. Until now.

Max pulled off the lacy coverlet and lowered them beneath the sheets. He looked out of place in the child's bed and lacy comforter, like a bad little boy caught where he didn't belong. She'd never given much thought to the decor of her apartment, yet since Max's arrival earlier that evening, Carmen suddenly found herself wanting to make her own mark upon it.

The china could be boxed and put in the hall closet. Perhaps she could find storage for the curio chests. If she took her mother's double dresser out of the bedroom, there would be room for a bigger bed. Maybe she should consider one of those butter-soft leather couches for the living room.

If she still had a job to finance it all with.

The thought stopped her cold. What was it about Max Deveraux that after a short time in his company, she acted in ways that would have made her blush even to imagine before? Max had been in her apartment only a few hours and she was ready to throw out lifetime possessions.

"Such serious thoughts."

Carmen looked up to find Max leaning over her, searching her face.

"Don't know where you get the strength," he added. "I'm exhausted myself."

"I was thinking of work," she lied.

"Don't," he said. "Don't think of work. Don't think, Carmen. Just be here with me."

He rolled to his side, pulling her with him, offering her more space in the bed he practically filled. Carmen buried her face in the downy hairs of his chest, slicked flat now with sweat. His arms came up around her, drawing her protectively closer, as if he feared she might run away.

"So," she said into his chest, "Will I see you this weekend?"

He stiffened, pulled away from her slightly. In the fading light, she saw caution in his eyes. "Not this weekend, I can't."

A knot of dread settled in her stomach. Tendrils of ice crept down her spine. So this was it, then. A one-night stand. She'd always wondered what it would be like to have one, had never dared. And now she knew. It was hell. Carmen managed to say, "Oh," and steeled herself for his excuses, the I'll call you's.

Max read the fear in her eyes, misinterpreted it. "Don't look so mortified, Carmen. I don't have a hot date or anything. I promised Jim Andersen I'd go fishing with him up at his cottage."

"You're spending the weekend with Andersen the Terrible?"

"Sure. Why not?"

Because he wants to see me fired, because he's the enemy. She couldn't say either of those things, so she said instead, "Isn't that kind of unprofessional."

"Ouch!" Max clutched his heart. "What's got into you?"

She couldn't tell him. No matter what she said, it would sound whiny, petty. "He's buttering you up, Max. Can't you see that? So you'll decided in his favor."

"Asking me up to his chalet isn't going to influence my decisions about his budget." Hurt flashed in his dark eyes, unconcealed this time.

Obviously, neither would sleeping with the medical photographer. She understood the way of it now. He'd romance her, bed her and coldheartedly destroy her life, just as Barb said.

Dread became horrible certainty. Max was spending the weekend with the one administrator who desperately wanted to see her canned.

Dr. James Andersen, who also had one of the only keys to her office.

Chapter Eight

There was a coldness coming from the other side of the narrow bed, the intensity of which he hadn't experienced in a long time. Max shifted his weight gingerly against Carmen's silent form. She lay with her back stiff against him. He could tell by her breathing she wasn't asleep, yet he could think of nothing to say that would ease the tension between them.

He should leave, but that in itself had its implications. Above all he didn't want her to think he'd used her. He wanted to spend the night with her, the two of them curled up in each other's arms (as if there were any other way two people could sleep in such a narrow bed).

Red lighted numerals on her clock showed 3:00 a.m. Obviously neither of them would get any rest tonight. She was furious with him, and for the life of him, he couldn't figure out why.

It had something to do with his fishing trip with Andersen. Why she would care was beyond him. Andersen was senior staff, it only made sense to do some additional consulting, get another's viewpoint. In the end his own best judgment would prevail, but why waste a fishing trip? Especially when he hadn't had a break all year. He needed time to reflect on this difficult contract. He was dying to get away from the city, its noise and pollution and the constricting boxes people lived in and worked in. He needed to get closer to the land, to feel the pulse of the earth, to remember his connection to it. The hubbub of the city made him feel tense, as well as caged and confined. More than anything else, he wanted some quiet time to sift through his conflicting feelings about Carmen Day.

The situation had a distinct ring of familiarity to it, one that set all his mental alarm bells ringing. He'd thought he was certain of her intentions. Their frenzied lovemaking left little doubt of her feelings for him. Or did it?

Doubt solidified into a dull ache in his stomach. He'd been through this once before. And it had proved disastrous to both his personal and his professional life. Carmen was different, he insisted. Never had he met anyone like her.

Or had he misjudged the entire situation? Was she pretending to be interested in him in a desperate ploy to keep her job?

Say something, he urged her silent form. Say you care. Say tonight was wonderful. Say anything! But Carmen kept her thoughts to herself.

Max dozed, waking with a start. The clock on the beside table read 6:00 a.m. He had a breakfast meeting with Wayne Goodman. If he hurried, he'd just have time for a quick shower.

Carmen had fallen into an uneasy sleep. He could tell by the way she muttered and tossed about. She burrowed gratefully into the warm spot he left. This wasn't the way he'd hoped to end it, but she left him no choice. What point was there in waking her, robbing her of what little sleep she was going to get, only to have his doubts confirmed? Quietly, he gathered his clothes from the living room floor and made his way to the door.

He'd almost made his escape to the front porch, when the inner door to the first floor apartment flew open. For a moment he thought it might be Carmen, but turning, he looked into the wizened face of an elderly woman. The disapproving glare she shot at him told him she knew exactly what he'd been up to last night. Damned if he'd blush like a sixteen-year-old.

The way things were going it was unlikely he'd be back.

"Good morning," he said politely. Seeing a rolled up newspaper on the porch, he picked it up, bowing gallantly as he handed it to her. As the elderly woman's mouth dropped open in surprise, he made his escape.

□ □ □

Carmen glanced at the pile of requests in her in-basket and buried her face in her hands. A bowl-sized cup of coffee sat in the middle of her desk. Her belly sloshed with the warm liquid and she still didn't feel remotely awake. Days had passed since she'd had a decent night's sleep. Not since she'd met Max Deveraux, she reflected darkly. After what happened between them last night, she doubted she'd sleep well for some time to come.

He waited until she'd fallen asleep to sneak from her bed, like the coward he was. Not a word of regret at how he'd betrayed her. Not even a "Thanks for last night, you were wonderful."

Carmen took a sip of scalding coffee. That's what hurt the most. It had been wonderful.

She had work to do. Might as well do it now, while she still had a job. Carmen sifted through the requests in her in-basket. Requests for photography from physiotherapy, social work wanted to make a new slide show for new patients and their families. Three requests for videotaping from Joan in O.T. This week's events had even robbed her of time for her favorite patient, Tyler.

Another request fell from the pile, drifting like a snowflake to fall on the carpet under her desk. Carmen reached for it, smacking her head against the underside of her desk. Fate simply had it in for her lately. She glanced at the requisition and groaned. She'd promised Mr. Harding she'd have the photograph of his late wife developed within the week.

An hour or so in the dark room might just be the remedy for her black mood. She wouldn't have to answer the door or talk on the phone. The prospect was tempting. But hiding in the darkness wouldn't make the pile of requests on her desk vanish. Work was the only remedy for that. Carmen scooped up her video camera and headed for occupational therapy.

□ □ □

HU, MY NANE IS TYUILER.

Carmen took a close-up shot of the garbled words on the computer screen. Better than last time, Tyler's typing skill showed a definite improvement—but deep down Carmen had hoped for a miracle.

"Can I play 'Deep Space Shoot Out' now?" Tyler asked brightly. "You said if I typed for half an hour I could," he added, his voice full of accusation.

Laughing, Joan unlocked the overhead cupboard and produced the promised game. "Okay sport, load it up."

Carmen couldn't help taping a couple more minutes of Tyler's enthusiastic playing. But even as she packed up her camera, she couldn't seem to shake the feeling of disappointment. Problem is you want to save the world, she told herself sternly.

"You're looking down these days," Joan remarked. "That downsizing guy still giving you a hard time?"

Does the entire world know about Max and me? Carmen used the truth to steer the conversation away from Max and the budget. "Life's giving me a hard time."

"I heard about the tape being stolen from your office."

"I'm sure you did. It's hard to keep a secret with police officers crawling all over your office."

"That must have given you the creeps, knowing someone had been in there."

"It did. But that's not what's bothering me at the moment." Carmen glanced over her shoulder at Tyler still merrily murdering aliens in the tiny back room. "I hoped the game might help a bit more."

"But you did help, Carmen. Look how happy he is. Remember how we practically had to drag him kicking and screaming to typing practice."

"He didn't even want to see the videos this time."

"That's because now he can see concrete evidence in his recovery. He wants to get better so he can go home and play with his own computer. He's even been talking about what he wants to do when he finishes high school."

Sounds of explosions echoed from the back room. "Point is," Joan added, "at least he is thinking about high school."

"Do you think he'll make it?"

"I don't know." Joan's voice turned serious. "Tyler was terribly injured. He's lucky to be alive. We have to be patient in our expectations. But the kid's going to try to get well enough to go back to school. Who knows, he just might do it."

"Thanks, Joanie." Carmen put the camera case back on the cart and started to wheel it out into the hall, but Joan reached out to stop her.

"You can tell me it's none of my business, Carmen." Joan lowered her voice to a whisper. "But I've heard some rumors."

She knew the answer, but Carmen asked anyway, "What kind of rumors?"

"About Max Deveraux." Joan looked over her shoulder, as if the topic of conversation might be wandering the halls even as they spoke.

Carmen felt her stomach knot into what was becoming a habitual dull ache, a torment that started the day Deveraux arrived and persisted no matter what she did to extract him from her life. "Max Deveraux has an entire mythology built up around him," she said noncommittally.

"This particular rumor was about you and Max Deveraux."

What does it take to keep a secret around here? Carmen thought, resisting the urge to spill her guts by telling Joan the truth. She longed to have someone to talk to. Anyone who'd tell her not to worry, that it would all work out all right. That one-night stands happened all the time and they were rarely the downfall of anyone's career. But she couldn't run the risk of more rumors hitting the grapevine. "They're simply rumors," she said. "I intend to have nothing to do with Max Deveraux other than turning in my report on why the hospital should keep my department." That, at least, was the truth.

"That's good," Joan said, plainly relieved. "Because what I heard wasn't pretty. Apparently, he's quite the womanizer. The list of his conquests was impressive. He didn't seem like your type." She eyed Carmen shrewdly. "But you never know."

"You were right, he's not my type." Carmen wheeled the cart out into the hall. "I'd better go. I've got a stack of requisitions a mile high waiting in my office."

"He's not my type!" she insisted, alone in the elevator. By the time she reached her office on the eleventh
floor, she had almost convinced herself.

"There you are!" Carmen heard Barb's voice before
she rounded the corner.

"Oh no, what is it?" There was no mistaking the
look of concern on Barb's face. "Not another attack?"
Carmen tried the door to her office and found it locked
the way she'd left it.

"Relax." Barb held the door while she wheeled the
cart into her office. "No one's been attacked. And your
office hasn't been robbed today. But I found out a few
things I thought you should hear."

"Not about Max Deveraux." Carmen closed the
door behind them and made sure it was locked.
"Because I'm sick of hearing about him, Barb. And I
just heard far more than I wanted to know from Joan
in O.T."

"Remember I was telling you about Tamara Brown
and her friend the assistant administrator at the
General in Kanata?"

Carmen nodded, resigned to listening to what Barb
had to say, whether she wanted to or not. Barb keeping a secret was like a helium balloon waiting to burst.
The secret would explode with a big bang, but usually
what it amounted to was little more than hot air.

"Well, that's only half the story. An old friend of the
administrator's was director of nursing at Children's
Hospital in Ottawa."

"So this gossip comes from a friend of a friend who
lived next door to Max's mother, right?"

"Listen to me, Carmen. I know you're finished with
the brute, but apparently he not only dated the D.O.N.
while he was working on the restructuring project, he
even asked her to marry him. Then he dumped her—"

"So he's fickle. What's that got to do with me?" It was desperately hard to remain nonchalant faced with a list of Max's bedroom conquests.

"Not only did he dump her, he fired her. But wait, there's more."

"There always is," Carmen said morosely.

"The administrator from Kanata hadn't seen her friend the D.O.N. for a couple of years. They meet at this party last Christmas in Ottawa, and start commiserating about the disaster of their careers and their love lives. Well, they find out they have much more in common than they thought."

"Oh no, not—"

"They'd both been loved, then left in the unemployment line by Max Deveraux!"

"I don't want to hear any more."

"You should hear this," Barb insisted, "just so you'll know you made the right decision."

"But, I don't—"

There was no stopping the barrage of words. They tumbled over her protests, until Carmen fell silent, resigned to hearing Barb out, whether she wanted to or not.

"So after they found out how much they had in common, they started to do a little digging, networking if you will, at the association conference. And guess what they found out?"

"I shudder to think."

"And so you should. Apparently, Max the Axe has a habit of romancing all the female department heads over lunch."

"I can't see what good that would possibly do him."

"No? Think, Carmen. He gets them out in a nice, romantic setting. He's a handsome man. They're taken in by the ambiance, the attention of a good looking guy. He earns their trust. They have a couple of drinks. And then they start telling him things that they'd never tell him around the boardroom table. Good old Max the Axe collects all these intimate facts, then uses them against them when it counts most, when they're making decisions on whose heads are going to roll."

Carmen felt the telltale flush spread across her cheeks. Barb's assessment of the situation was damningly accurate.

Barb read the meaning behind those pink cheeks and nodded, taking it as a tacit agreement to hear more. "They start asking around at this conference and they find out that Max didn't just confine his conquests to his home turf. They found former colleagues and lovers of his in Kingston, Sudbury, London and Hamilton!" Barb's eyes widened theatrically. "Enough to fill a bus."

"Perhaps they should form a support group," Carmen remarked darkly.

Barb held up a hand for silence. "And more than a few here in Lakeview."

"Not what's her name from the General again."

"Tamara? No. But she's tight with several clinical supervisors from the psych hospital and the West End Health Center."

"I'm sure she is."

"Point being, he made some friends there as well."

"Okay, who?" Enough of this conjecture. Carmen wanted hard facts, name and dates.

"I didn't recognize the names. They weren't women I knew, but there are a couple of clinical specialists looking for work in Alberta."

"There are a lot of people looking for work in other provinces. The job market's a disaster right now."

"Tamara said she'd talk to you if you wanted, tell you what she knows."

Carmen's cheek darkened to crimson. She gave in to the rush of anger. "You told her! Barb, how could you!"

"I didn't tell her everything," Barb said defensively. "I just wanted to put your mind at ease that you made the right decision about dumping the jerk."

"The right decision—" The words sputtered from her lips. "I didn't dump him, Barb."

"What?" For the second time in less than a week, Barbara Downey was struck speechless. At any other time, Carmen might have enjoyed the spectacle. Barbara paled, her hands flew to her mouth. "Oh, Carmen! Oh no!"

Taking a perverse enjoyment in her friend's discomfort, Carmen continued mercilessly. To her shock, she found she reveled in the idea of destroying the myth of the perfect Carmen Day who always did the right thing. "I didn't dump him, Barb. I slept with him. And if you tell that to Tamara Brown, I swear I'll never forgive you!"

"How could you sleep with that brute?"

"I could because I wanted to. For once, I wanted to do something daring instead of the right thing, the comfortable thing, the safe thing."

Barbara, who devoted her life to the prevention of disease, was thoroughly scandalized. "Was it worth the risk, Carmen? To your health? To your job?"

Carmen leaned against the wall, her false bravado forgotten. "I don't know. I'm still trying to figure that out."

"It's just so unlike you," Barb blurted.

"Exactly."

"I mean, I can't imagine you making such a rash decision about something so important."

"I didn't, really. I was all set to dump him, but then I met him on the way home. I'd had such a horrible day, and he was so sweet, so kind..."

Barb looked genuinely hurt. "You could have called me if you were feeling bad."

"Well, I might have. But I wasn't alone. I invited him in."

"And he was only too happy to oblige, I'll bet."

In for a penny..., Carmen thought. "It was wonderful, until he told me he was spending the weekend with Andersen."

"Andersen?" Barb's eyes took on a malicious gleam. "I wouldn't have thought a womanizer like Max the Axe would fancy guys, but—"

"That's not funny," Carmen snapped. "We had a big fight, and we haven't spoken since. So now it's over, my heart is broken, and I'm probably going to lose my job as well." Her voice cracked, threatening the tears to come. "If you say 'I told you so,' I promise I'll bawl like a little kid."

Motherly instincts got the better of Barb. She wrapped her arms around her. Carmen leaned against her, the sleepless nights stealing what little strength she had left.

"I'm sorry, Carmen. I didn't know."

"It gets worse," Carmen said, her voice muffled against her friend's shoulder. "Not only is he spending the weekend at Andersen's fabled chalet, probably discussing how best to reallocate my budget, but Andersen's one of the only people who has keys to my office."

Barb stiffened. Holding Carmen away from her, she said, "He wouldn't!"

"Wouldn't he? Why not?"

"I don't know. I mean, he's probably the biggest pain in the butt in this entire hospital, but he's not a criminal."

"You don't know that. What if there was something on that tape he really didn't want me to see?"

"Like what?"

"Like proof that he attacked Judy."

Barbara pulled out Carmen's desk chair and sat down. "He couldn't be the attacker."

"Why can't he, Barb? Because he's a respected physician?"

"He took an oath, Carmen. Besides, Judy would have recognized Andersen's voice. She talks to him more than to any other administrator in this hospital."

"Not if he took pains to disguise his voice."

Barb considered this new thought. "Okay, I'm with you so far. But does he have a scar on his hand?"

"It would be easy enough to find out. I'm sure he'll find a reason to yell at me again today."

"I have a reason," Barb said. "There have been several cases of flu on his unit. I've got to see him about it anyway."

Carmen walked into her equipment room and flicked on the computer. "I'm going to have another go at that frame, see if I can enhance it further. I want to make it up to Wayne somehow, for losing the tape."

"It was stolen, Carmen. That's not your fault. Be careful, will you? I don't like all the things you've gotten yourself into lately."

"I'll be careful, Mom." She looked back at Barb. "Do you still have the disk I gave you?"

Barb patted the pocket of her lab coat. "Right here."

"Hang on to it for me. I'll probably have a new disk to give you for safe keeping."

Looking more troubled than Carmen could remember her being, Barb let herself out of the office. As the door swung shut, Carmen heard her greet John Forbes in the hallway. A chime signaled the elevator doors opening. The doors closed, cutting off their conversation.

Chapter Nine

*C*armen looked at the image on her computer screen. She had spent two hours systematically enlarging parts of the image, then painstakingly enhancing the light and dark boxes of individual pixels, until they formed a pattern. Up close, it looked like nothing more than a checkerboard of black and white boxes. Carmen rose, rubbing the kinks out of the back of her neck.

From a few feet away the image was definitely recognizable as a hand. The palm faced the camera, grasping as if reaching for someone, jutting barely into the frame. Carmen dearly wished she'd seen the entire tape before it was stolen, so she'd know if this was in fact the attacker's hand, not just another staff member on the way through the parking lot. She tilted her head to one side, examining it from another vantage point.

Enlarged as much as the software would let her, the image was still blurry. But the afternoon's work revealed a long scar running diagonally across the palm. Must have been a nasty cut. Carmen winced. An accident with a knife or a saw blade, perhaps. She'd pushed the software to the limits of its ability, but she needed more. Carmen sat back down in her chair. She'd have to go on her own instincts now, use her basic abilities to put in what the computer image didn't show.

Reconstructing a scar she could barely see was tricky work. It was difficult to tell if what she added to the image was actually there, or merely her wishful thinking to find some identifying mark that would identify the attacker, make up for the theft to Wayne and help Judy seek justice.

After another hour's work, her shoulders ached. Shadows of black and white boxes lingered in her vision even when she looked away from the computer screen. Friday evening had arrived and she had no weekend to look forward to. Somehow this weekend, she needed to draft a report that would convince the senior administration of Royal Hospital and Max Deveraux to fund her department.

Her abused neck muscles clenched in anger. Max Deveraux wasn't spending the weekend working. Max the Axe had two days of sun, fishing and country air to look forward to. A glance out the window reminded her it was already going dark. She couldn't remember the last time she'd eaten. The caffeine she'd consumed during the day was wearing off. What she needed was a nap, a shower and then some time to do some serious thinking. She'd start in on the report bright and early, visit the reference library, see if she could dig up some statistics on the rehabilitative uses of computer and audio-visual technology in health care.

Carmen stretched the kinks from her back and shoulders. She saved the image to her hard drive, then to another disk for insurance. She'd have to give Barb the disk on Monday, Carmen thought, certain she'd left hours ago, anxious to start her weekend. She toyed with the idea of locking it in her desk drawer over the weekend, then stuck it in her jacket pocket instead.

That nap felt infinitely appealing as she left by the back door, conscious of the security camera pointed in her direction.

She shouldn't be walking home this late, but she was too tired to call a cab. Should save the money anyway. Just in case I end up unemployed next week.

"Carmen!" The sound of her name yanked her from her dark musings. She turned to see Max Deveraux coming down the back hall after her.

He'd changed from his expensive, tailor-made suit into a pair of jeans and a thick flannel shirt. He looked rugged, every bit the fisherman. Carmen tore her eyes from the fit of those well-worn jeans, the muscular shoulders the flannel did little to hide, and wondered just how many masks Max the Axe wore. Max the administrator, Max the lover, Max the fisherman. He seemed to be able to change shape as easily and as thoughtlessly as a chameleon. He stopped just a few feet before her, in the center of the security camera's focus. She imagined the security guard sitting in the front office watching. No wonder rumors flew like wild fire through Royal Hospital.

"I only have a minute," Max said.

"Must be nice to be so popular," Carmen countered, refusing to wince at the bitterness in her voice.

"I wish I knew why you're angry with me," he said, taking in her blazing green eyes, the set of her jaw. "I really don't understand why me going fishing with Jim has got you so bent out of shape."

"'Jim,' is it?" Her voice inched up an octave. Carmen wrapped her will around her temper. It wouldn't do to have a screaming fight with Max right under the security camera. That would entertain the staff all weekend. "I don't suppose it occurred to you that 'Jim' would like nothing better than to see me gone from this place."

"It's just a fishing trip, Carmen."

"Sure, Max. Well, you have a great fishing trip with 'Jim'. I'd bet my pay check he spends the weekend finding new ways to allocate my budget into his department."

"It wouldn't make any difference if he did. That's what I want you to understand. I don't want it to end this way between us, not after last night."

She wanted to yell. She wanted to cry. She longed to have him wrap his arms around her, tell her it was all right, just a mistake, that he'd come up with ways to reallocate Andersen's budget into her department. But that was an unfair thing to expect from any relationship. Carmen could see that now.

"I understand far too much, Max." She walked away from him before the tears betrayed her in front of Max the Axe, in front of the security camera. "Have a good weekend. Say hi to Jim for me."

Carmen fled around the side of the building. But then strength deserted her and she leaned against the brick, even the thought of a nap and a hot bath having lost their appeal. Footsteps started after her, then stopped. She heard Max's smothered curse, the sound of a stone ricocheting off the pavement.

Andersen's voice echoed in the vestibule as he greeted Max. "I just have something I need to see to before we leave. Pick you up at your place..." Their voices grew distant as they started back down the hall.

The sweep of a Jeep's headlights turning out of the parking lot brought her back to her senses. Better watch where I'm going. Don't want Andersen to inherit my budget by attrition!

Determination dealt her a mental jab to the ribs. Damned if she'd give up. Andersen might have Max's ear for the weekend, but as the saying went, "The pen is mightier than the sword." And "a picture is worth a thousand words." She'd pen a killer report with statistics and graphics. And she'd highlight it with the faces of Royal Hospital.

If that didn't work, she'd go willingly. And leave Royal Hospital to the likes of Max the Axe and Jim the Fisherman.

Carmen levered herself away from the wall. Walking down the path, it was hard not to keep her shoulders from slumping. *Should have called that cab, whether I have the money or not.*

A hoarse scream shattered the silence.

Shoes slapped against the pavement. People rushed toward the emergency. Carmen dashed back down the path.

A black shape hurled toward her out of the darkness. They collided, superior weight throwing her heavily back against the brickwork, crushing the breath from her lungs. She gasped for a burning mouthful of air. The shadow disentangled itself. Carmen caught a glimpse of dark eyes, all that was visible in the black ski mask he wore.

He shoved her backward. Her head hit the brick. As sparks cleared from her vision, she caught a glimpse of him disappearing into the shadows of the nearby parkette.

Carmen dashed after him. Emerging from the bushes that marked the edge of hospital property, she scanned the parkette.

And found it empty. The four-foot fence the attacker leapt with ease provided more of a challenge to someone little more than five feet tall. Cursing the waste of time, Carmen skirted the fence and dashed into the center of the tiny park.

The park benches were empty. Inky shadows bled between ancient trees. Bushes rustled. Carmen jumped back with a cry.

A disgruntled raccoon bolted from beneath a bush, skittering across the parkette until the sight of an overflowing garbage can eased its fear to a self-confident swagger. Carmen sucked in a deep breath.

Shudders racked her body. Her lungs ached from the sudden activity. A dull ache radiated out from back of her head where her skull had hit the brick. Realization dawned that she was a woman alone in a deserted park. And someone had just been attacked at Royal Hospital.

What on earth am I doing?

With the last of her strength, she bolted back toward hospital property.

A crowd had gathered in the vestibule around the back door. The fence of bodies, all taller than she was, made it impossible to see. As she drew nearer, Carmen recognized Stan from security in his black and white uniform, looking concerned and more than a little guilty.

Sirens shrieked down the street, coming to an abrupt stop as two police cruisers and an ambulance barreled through the gates and into the parking lot. As a specialized care facility, Royal Hospital didn't have an emergency room. In cases of emergency, patients had to be sent by ambulance to other facilities.

Uniformed officers hurried toward the knot of people. Rotating red, white and blue lights cast eerie shadows off the white brick building.

Paramedics unloaded a stretcher with a garish orange blanket on it. Following close on the heels of the police officers, they raced the stretcher across the tarmac.

Headlights swept the parking lot. Carmen recognized Wayne Goodman's car. Someone must have reached him on his cellular phone on his way home.

The crowd parted to let them through.

In the center of the commotion, still lying against the sidewalk where she'd been thrown, Carmen caught sight of a familiar figure in a white lab coat. She leapt forward.

"Barbara. Oh my God, no!" Carmen elbowed her way through the crowd, reaching Barbara just as the police and the paramedics burst through with the stretcher. Stan from Security helped her to her feet and she stood unsteadily, supported by Stan and one of the paramedics.

Carmen took one look at Barb and gasped. Her pantyhose hung in shreds from the knees down, evidence of where she'd been dragged along the rough pavement in the struggle. Streaks of dirt marred her normally immaculate lab coat. The white coat hung from one arm, as if it had been pulled off while Barb tried to make her escape. Her graying blonde hair hung in a disorderly mass so different from the usual sprayed bob, Carmen wouldn't have recognized her. Beneath pale gray eyes wide with panic, Carmen saw the red marks left by a man's hand that likely would become an ugly purple bruise. At the sight of the stretcher, Barb grew even more agitated.

"Oh no, I don't want to go to the hospital."

"We'd just like to take you in for a quick check, ma'am," a tall blond paramedic said. He was young enough to be Barb's son, Carmen noted.

"I work in a hospital. I was on my way home. I just want to go home."

"We just want to make sure you're okay, ma'am," the paramedic repeated. "Royal doesn't have an emergency, so we'll have to take you to the General."

"I don't want to go to the General. I just want to go home. My daughter will be wondering what happened to me."

Carmen stepped into the fray. "I'm a friend of Mrs. Downey's. I'll make sure she gets home safely." She stepped in, replacing Stan, and wrapped her arm protectively around Barbara. "We can have the head nurse take a look at her, make sure nothing's broken."

"I'm okay," Barb said in a shaky voice. "Just a few bruises. He knocked me down."

"Did you get a good look at the man who did this to you?" a female police officer asked.

Barb shook her head. "He was wearing a black ski mask. I could feel the wool against my neck as he—"

"Did you see which way he went?"

"I did!" Carmen pointed to the park on the other side of the building. "He ran through that little park over there, heading south towards the lake. He nearly ran me down coming around the side of the building."

"Did you get a look at him?"

"Not much of one. He was still wearing the mask."

"Height and build?" the officer asked.

"Five-ten maybe. Heavy-set, wearing black. That's all I noticed," Carmen said apologetically and wondered why she felt like such a failure. She couldn't blame herself for not catching a man who was nearly a foot taller than she and likely outweighed her by a hundred pounds, yet she did. "He ran into me, knocked my head back against the brick. I chased him, but I lost him in the park."

Two more officers were dispatched to check out the park.

"You sure you don't want to go to hospital?" Carmen asked. "I'll come with you."

"I just want to go home," Barb said tiredly. She looked up at the circle of faces around her and blushed with embarrassment. Carmen could understand how she felt. It must be a strange feeling of violation, all those people peering at her pain, her fear.

Carmen spotted Wayne Goodman talking to one of the uniformed officers. Some nodding and note taking later, they left with Stan and disappeared through the back door into Royal Hospital.

"Inside," Wayne said, dismissing the ambulance. "If you won't go to the General, I intend to make sure you're all right." Looking every bit the boss and in control of the situation, he marched up to the switchboard. "Page Charles. Have him meet us in the first floor examining room." He turned to Barbara. "Let Charles take a look at you, then you can call your daughter. I'll drive you home."

"I've got my car here," Barb said, sounding more like herself. "I can drive myself home."

Goodman shot her a look that said he doubted she was in any condition. Carmen came to her rescue. "I'll drive."

The president nodded. "Wait here for Charles. I'm going to check if they got anything on the security camera."

"It won't show anything at all," Barb said as the door swung shut behind Goodman. "Except a big guy in black clothes and a ski mask."

"Better than nothing." Carmen tried to suppress the pang of guilt that taunted, *If you hadn't lost the tape, this might never have happened.*

"I don't suppose you got a look at his hand?" she asked as gently as she could.

Barb shook her head. "He was wearing black leather gloves, and—" Her upper lip trembled. Ever the lady, she tried to smooth her disheveled hair.

"Hush," Carmen said. "I shouldn't have asked you."

"No, it's okay. I need to remember everything I can so I can tell the police. I think he was looking for something. At first I thought he wanted money. But he wasn't interested in my purse, he just knocked it to the ground. Then he started to rip off my lab coat. I thought—" She dragged in a shaky breath, then continued, "I thought he was going to rape me. But then he started going through my pockets." Barb felt the pockets of her lab jacket, finding them empty. "My God, Carmen. I think he was looking for the disk!"

"How could he possibly have known?"

"I don't know. I'm sorry I lost the disk after you gave it to me to keep safe."

"Don't worry about the disk." Carmen tried to keep her friend calm. "As long as you're all right."

Barb changed the subject. "I tried to get a look at Andersen's hand in our meeting this afternoon. But he kept his hands lodged in the pockets of his lab coat while he ordered me around."

"Sounds typical," Carmen agreed. Ordering was Andersen's usual method of conversation.

"The guy who jumped me—" The conversation turned again as Barb tried to order her chaotic thoughts. "His voice was muffled by the mask. I couldn't tell if it was Andersen's voice or not."

"The...guy..." Carmen couldn't bring herself to say attacker, not in front of Barb. "He spoke to you?"

Barbara nodded. "He said I'd complicated things. Why couldn't I just mind my own business, and that was the main problem with the damned place, people just couldn't mind their own business. Then he said something about Max and budget cuts and how it would all have been fine if people would learn to just let others do their jobs."

"What about his speech patterns? Anything familiar?"

"Vaguely familiar, but I just can't place it."

"He has to be someone who works at the hospital. Who else would know what's going on here?"

"That could be almost anyone. It just gives me the creeps to think that I could have run into this guy twenty times a day and not know."

"It's spooky," Carmen agreed, remembering the look of utter hatred in his eyes as they'd collided outside the hospital. "He knows who we are, but we don't know who he is. Are you sure you didn't recognize anything about him?"

Barb shuddered. She wrapped her arms around herself, for warmth or protection, Carmen couldn't tell. "He wasn't anyone I speak to regularly. I'd have recognized someone like Goodman, or Charles White."

Carmen glanced around at the pale green walls of the treatment room, as if even there invisible eyes and ears could be following their every move. Someone knew when Barbara would be leaving. Someone knew she carried a disk with incriminating evidence on it.

"And now he's got the disk." Barb repeated. "I'm sorry Carmen."

"Don't worry." Carmen pulled her copy from the pocket of her blazer. The way things have been disappearing, I figured I'd better make another copy."

"You shouldn't go carrying it around, Carmen. We don't need anyone coming after you."

Carmen tucked it in the inside pocket of her purse. "As soon as we're finished here, I'm going to mail it to myself express mail. It ought to arrive at my apartment by Monday. Whoever's behind this won't be able to get his hands on it over the weekend."

The door to the treatment room flew open. Both women jumped as Wayne Goodman and the D.O.N. entered the cubicle.

"Sorry, I didn't mean to scare you." The look on his face said he'd really like to scare someone else.

"Did the security camera pick up anything?" Carmen was almost afraid to ask after the incident with the disappearing tape.

"No." Wayne ran a hand through his tousled blond hair. His expression turned from disturbed to murderous. "Someone turned the camera off."

He let that thought sink in.

"Are you sure Stan didn't just forget to turn it on tonight?"

"Positive. Time code on the tape stops about ten minutes before—" He shot a quick glance at Barb.

"It's okay, Wayne," Barb said. "I'm not going to faint if you say the word attack."

"The point is, the tape ran for about four hours after Stan came on duty. When he left to do his evening rounds, someone unlocked the security office and turned off the tape."

"Someone who had keys to both security and my office," Carmen said. "That narrows it down just a little."

"Not much," Wayne said grimly. "There's still all of maintenance, housekeeping, switchboard, and all the people in weekend administration."

"Is anyone missing from their post?"

"Stan's checking. So far everyone's accounted for."

"He wouldn't be stupid enough to assault someone on his shift, would he?" Barb craned her neck to see around Charles who was trying in vain to examine a patient who refused to stay still.

Wayne sighed. "He might."

"Who knows what goes on in the mind of a maniac," Carmen said.

"Could you two take this discussion outside. You're distracting my patient." Charles hustled them from the room.

"I'm trying to help with the investigation," Barb insisted.

"We have policemen for that, Mrs. Downey." He shone a flashlight in Barb's eyes. "If you must discuss this, do it after a hot bath and a good night's sleep. I'm also going to give you the number of a hot line that specializes in helping victims of assault. Is there someone who can stay with you tonight?"

"My daughter's at home," Carmen heard Barb say through the door. "Carmen's going to give me a ride home."

Thrust out in the hallway, Wayne and Carmen stared at each other awkwardly.

"I'm sorry I gave you such a hard time when your office was broken into," Goodman said at last. "I didn't realize what we were up against."

"Easier to believe that I'd be careless?"

"You're never careless, Carmen. I should have known that."

"It's been a hard week."

Goodman pinched the bridge of his nose, as if trying to ward off a headache. "For all of us."

"There's more, Wayne."

"There always is." He covered his face with his hands. Then ran a hand through his hair and looked at her. "Okay, shoot."

"Barb said the attacker said something about downsizing and how it would have all been fine if we'd just let people do their jobs." A sudden thought occurred to her. "Could it be someone who's already been given notice?"

"The only people who've been notified are from those services we're planning to contract out. Housekeeping, maintenance, the lab. Everyone else is waiting."

"Yes, but everyone else suspects they might be let go next. It could even be someone in management."

"I doubt that," Wayne snapped.

"How many people are in the two departments that have been notified?"

"Thirty or so."

"And how many of them are male?"

"I'd have to check, say half."

"Do any of them have a wicked scar on their hand? Across the palm?"

"None I can think of. Why?"

"Just a hunch." She debated telling Wayne about her suspicions, then decided against it. He'd forbid her to investigate the matter further. He'd hand the evidence over to the police who would decide the blurry frame proved nothing. No, she wouldn't get Wayne's hopes up again until she knew for sure.

Wayne gave her a skeptical look, but just then Barb emerged from the treatment room, Charles in tow.

"Just bruises, no permanent damage done."

"That's good," Wayne said, obviously relieved. "When you feel up to it, the police would like to talk to you some more."

Barbara was attempting to stay cheerful, Carmen realized. The false bravado didn't fool her best friend, or the D.O.N.

"Not tonight," he said, standing between Wayne and Barb as if Wayne might drag her off for a police interview this moment. "My patient's going home to bed."

"I'll drive you home." Carmen led Barbara down the hall toward the switchboard and the exit to Royal Hospital. "Let's just get you out of this place."

The attacker shrank back into the shadows as they passed. Damn that Carmen Day woman and her meddling friends! If she thought she had him, she was wrong. Those idiots in security thought they knew everything. Sure, he'd have to be extra careful right now, but all the doors in the hospital were open to him. He hadn't heard all of their conversation that afternoon, just happened to pass by on his way to nursing in time to hear them discuss the incriminating file on the computer in Carmen's office.

He'd been careless that first time, but the problem was nearly solved. He had the security tape, the back-up disk the infection control officer thought she had hidden in the pocket of her lab coat. Now all he had to do was take care of that computer up in medical photography and he'd be home free.

He watched as the Medical Photographer drove the car right up to the front doors of the hospital, frowned as Goodman himself held the door open for the Downey woman to get in. What did it take to get on Goodman's good side? he wondered. To become immune from layoffs and downsizing.

That Carmen Day woman would have to be dealt with first. Then he'd think of a fitting punishment for the Big Boss and the fool who caused all the trouble, Max the Axe.

Carmen held off the tears long enough to drive Barbara home. She managed a brave face while she made sure that both Barb and her daughter were safely locked in their own house for the night. She main-

tained her composure through the long cab ride back
downtown with the chatty cab driver who had a desperate desire to impress her with his witty insights
about everything from restaurant food to baseball.
She even had a polite smile for Mrs. Landreth who
peered at her with beady eyes and glowered as
Carmen unlocked her door.

Without incident she made it up the steep staircase
into her apartment. It was the sight of the living room
still in disarray from last night, the pizza box on the
floor, the cushions on the couch still askew from their
lovemaking that finally undid her.

Big, fat tears welled up in her eyes, then splashed
over, soaking her cheeks and the front of her blazer,
surprising her with how much pain inside was bursting to get out. Noisy, wrenching sobs followed.
Carmen hugged one of the cushions and let them
come, helpless to contain them any longer.

Listen to that, Mrs. Landreth, and maybe you'll be
nicer next time you see me.

Traitorous thoughts reminded her of the soft crush
of his chest hair against her breasts, the way he'd run
his hands all over her body, as if he were mapping the
feel of her so he would remember it always. His musky
scent, mingled with undertones of his cologne perme-
ated the cushions. Even in memory the passion that
ignited between them brought a hot rush of wetness to
her loins.

There was nowhere else to go. She could have
stayed at Barb's, but Barbara seemed to want some
time alone with her daughter to sort her thoughts out.
Despite her love of gossip and intrigue, Barb was a
private person. Carmen was likely the only person
who really knew that. But as her best friend, she knew
when to leave her alone. She'd visit tomorrow after

Barb had had some sleep and a chance to put her thoughts in order.

No, she had nowhere else to go, except the tiny apartment, every inch of which had been touched by Max Deveraux. Carmen glanced into the bedroom, wiping at the tears that flowed anew at the sight of the disheveled bed. Would she have to move to get rid of his memory?

The cramped apartment virtually walked with ghosts tonight. Her mother's furniture, her mother's china, not to mention the ghost of Max the Axe. The idea of moving gripped her, refusing to be shaken loose. Why not? She'd spent the last of her teen years working to help her terminally ill mother. Most of her twenties she'd devoted to making the Department of Medical Photography a viable—and she thought indispensable—part of Royal Hospital. Never in the past decade had she spared the time to think about what Carmen wanted. Except for Max Deveraux, and he'd turned out to be one of the biggest mistakes she'd ever made. She'd made her mark on Royal Hospital, but not on the world. And if the job at Royal Hospital vanished along with Max Deveraux, what did she have left?

"Nothing!" Carmen sobbed, throwing herself fully dressed into the center of the rumpled bed. She lay there for several long moments, staring at the cracks that snaked across the old ceiling in the path of her tears.

Why did it never occur to me there might be more to life than living in a rundown old house in a crimeridden neighborhood and working for a floundering institution?

"Because the only questions I've ever asked were what other people wanted from me," she answered aloud.

Her stomach growled, angry at being deprived of food for yet another day. Carmen leapt from the bed. Stripping off the sheets, she tossed them into the laundry basket. Tomorrow, she'd wake up early, take everything Max had touched to the laundromat. She could hang the couch cushions on the clothesline outside to air out.

There was nothing in her cupboards but an ancient box of oatmeal. She made some anyway. After she visited Barb tomorrow, she'd hit the library, do enough research to write a killer report. After that, she'd go to the supermarket, buy a month's worth of groceries.

If the report didn't save her job, at least she'd have the satisfaction of knowing she did her best.

"From now on Carmen Day is going to take care of Carmen Day," she told the silent bedroom.

□ □ □

Max Deveraux sat on the dock outside Andersen's chalet. It was still early in the season for stargazing, but the whiskey in his stomach warmed him.

The cold had driven Andersen back to the fire burning in the chalet's main room. He desperately wanted to go there, too. To stretch out in front of the mesmerizing flames and let their warmth work the weariness from his bones. But Andersen had done nothing but talk about his department and his plans for Royal Hospital since they left. Four hours of this and he was willing to brave the cold just to get himself some peace.

Carmen was right, a little thought nattered at the back of his mind. He silenced it with another sip of whiskey. Doomed to spend another two days listening to Andersen rant, his mood couldn't be darker. He should have seen through the ploy. Andersen had been furious at not being able to shake his reaction to his report from him, then suddenly he offered Max a fishing trip at the chalet.

How could I have been so blind? Why didn't I bring my own car?

And then there were the thoughts even the cold, the stark beauty of the country sky and the whiskey couldn't keep at bay.

Thoughts of their passionate lovemaking eased the cold at least. Wish I'd brought the cell phone. Then I could call Carmen, tell her she was right.

If she was still speaking to him, which he doubted.

He didn't want her to be angry with him. He wanted to hold her close, to warm himself against her body. To do all those things they'd done last night together. And more.

And what are you going to do if it turns out you have to fire her? You'll be every bit as bad as she already suspects you are.

The stars offered him no easy answers.

□ □ □

"Really, Carmen, I'm okay." Barb dumped the load of laundry she was doing into the washer and slammed the lid. "People get mugged all the time. Life goes on. And I have a million things I want to do around the house this weekend. Summer's coming and I haven't washed down the patio furniture. I want to paint the deck, and—"

"Slow down." Carmen tried to take the box of laundry detergent from her friend's hands and earned herself a slap on the wrist instead. "I'm sure Brenda

would do the laundry if you asked. And it isn't summer yet. The deck and the patio furniture can wait."

"Brenda's studying for exams. She needs to get her
marks up so she can get into university."

Barb's daughter Brenda stopped in the laundry
room door. The knowing look she offered Carmen said
she'd already had a similar conversation with her
mother. "It's okay, Carmen. She wouldn't listen to me,
either."

"Don't you have trigonometry to study?" Barb
asked sharply.

With a shrug, Brenda retreated upstairs.

"I can look after the laundry. I'll even wipe down
the patio furniture if it makes you feel better."

"And what am I supposed to do? Sit in a chair with
an afghan over my knees like an invalid while I pon-
der in great detail everything that happened to me
last night? You're missing the point, Carmen. I don't
want to think about it. I want to be busy. At least I'll
get some of this stuff done around the house."

"As long as you're sure that makes you feel better."
Carmen could see the logic behind it. But leaving Barb
to her own devices made her feel helpless. And that
made her feel scared. That stupid desire to save the
world again. Her subconscious refused to let her pin a
more gentle label to it. But it doesn't prevent you from
feeling frightened, does it?

Before she could deal with her own dark thoughts,
Barb steered her out in the hallway. "I know you have
a report to write. So go do it, Carmen. I promise I'll
call if I need a shoulder to cry on."

Barbara opened the front door. Carmen found herself standing on the front step. "Promise you'll call if
you need me."

"I promise," Barb said, shutting the door. "Go look after yourself for once, Carmen." The door clicked shut.

◻ ◻ ◻

Show them! Carmen looked up from the microfilm article she was skimming. Statistics leaned in her favor, proving that the right kind of feedback and optimism could greatly enhance a patient's progress. Other studies offered percentages of how images improved information retention.

But pages of statistics alone wouldn't move Max Deveraux or the Board of Governors to loosen the purse strings to Royal Hospital's shrinking budget. For that, she needed a more emotional presentation. Pictures, videos, slides. Show them the path of a patient's progress. Someone like Tyler, a young life interrupted by tragedy. Royal Hospital offered him the optimism of a future not confined to a hospital bed.

The materials she needed were in her office at Royal Hospital. She'd start with the statistics, make them into a colorful graph. She'd transfer snippets of video, slides, photos to computer and arrange them all in a riveting presentation. Then she'd write the most heartwrenching speech she could think of.

No boring paper report would ever move the bean counters, so she wouldn't give them a piece of paper to pour over at their leisure, picking holes in her arguments. She'd transfer her file to Wayne's laptop and present it on the big screen in the boardroom. She'd make them sit through her speech, hit them with the real-life faces of Royal Hospital. And then she'd leave them to their decision.

At least she'd go out with a bang.

Carmen made a copy of the article, meticulously citing the source as a footnote. Her argument had to be airtight. The stats didn't lie, neither did the photos. Packing up her materials, she paid the librarian and hopped the bus back to Royal Hospital.

Fear prickled down her spine as she walked up the curving path to the front doors. In the spring sunlight with the first flowers overflowing the many beds, the Hospital looked welcoming. Relatives pushed patients in wheelchairs, enjoying the warm weather. But a glance at the back door where both Barb and Judy had been attacked and she'd nearly been run down as the attacker made his escape, brought a chill in spite of the warm sun.

She waved at Stan in his post at the security desk. The security guard looked doubly serious. Last night's events had obviously ruined his weekend as well.

"Working overtime?" he asked as Carmen passed.

"I've got a report due. Unfortunately I need my computer to do it, or I would have worked at home."

"Too nice a day to be inside," Stan observed. "Did you happen to talk to Mrs. Downey this morning?"

"She's fine, Stan. Not to worry. I dropped by her house and she was talking about painting the deck."

"That's good to hear," Stan said with relief. "She was pretty shaken up last night."

"Any news from the police?"

"Nothing. At least nothing anybody told me."

"It's not your fault," Carmen said, as much to Stan as to herself. "This case has everyone stumped."

Stan smiled, an expression so rare it surprised her with the way it illuminated his face. "Thanks, Carmen. Be careful upstairs, it's pretty quiet up there on the weekend."

"I'll yell if I need you," Carmen promised and hit the elevator button.

Doors opened to the eleventh floor. The quiet tread of her sneakers against the carpet sounded loud in the silence. Mandy's desk sat empty in its glass enclosure.

Carmen stopped her hand on the doorknob to her office. A quick search of her purse confirmed her suspicions. She'd left the keys to her office at home. She groaned in frustration. Now she'd have to go all the way back downstairs and take Stan away from his station so he could open the door for her.

But the knob turned easily beneath her fingers. The door swung open, admitting her to the dark and silent office.

Don't go in there. Go downstairs and get Stan first. Even as her subconscious blared its warning, Carmen crept into her office.

The outer office looked as she'd left it on Friday afternoon. She glanced into the equipment cubicle. Nothing obviously missing. Flattening herself against the tiled wall, she peered around the corner into her production room.

And gasped aloud.

Whoever had been there didn't know much about computers. The attacker's file could easily have been deleted from the hard drive. Anyone with a little computer know-how could have initialized the hard disk. But the intruder had taken a more direct approach— he'd used a baseball bat on her computer.

□ □ □

Stan paled as he surveyed the damage done in Carmen's office. "Whoever did this knew what they were looking for. They obviously meant business."

Carmen sat in her swivel chair just inside the doorway to her computer room. She hesitated to venture further in and risk disrupting anything that might be important to the police. "But why would they do so much damage? All they had to do was steal my back-up disks and initialize the hard drive."

Instead of electronic computer vandalism, the intruder had smashed the screen of her monitor. Shards of glass lay all over her computer table and the floor. Not satisfied, he'd continued on, smashing the outer case of the computer. Dents marred the metal casing. Carmen could see where the screws had given way, exposing the electronics inside. Thorough in his destruction, the vandal had reached inside and torn out the bowels of the computer. Green circuit boards lay scattered across the floor. What he couldn't rip out, he'd simply smashed. When he'd finished with the main computer, he'd set upon her file box of back-up disks with the same single-minded destruction. Blue, gray, and black plastic casings littered the floor. Scattered among the crumpled casings were the tiny magnetic circles, also crumpled and torn.

"Obviously, he meant to send you a message," Stan remarked. "What do you think he was looking for in here?"

"I don't know."

But she did know, all too well, what the intruder hoped to find in her office. The same thing he'd been willing to assault Barbara on hospital property to get his hands on. The disk containing the only evidence that might link him to the crimes. A blurry frame from the original videotape of Judy's attack showing a masculine hand with a thick scar running across the palm.

Carmen glanced around the office. But how had he known? The only time they'd discussed the matter had been in the privacy of her office. Did he have the room bugged? Paranoia offered James Bond-type images of a man sitting in an unmarked van across the street, listening to every word uttered in her office. She glanced out the window. The street was vacant except for an ancient, rusting car that had accumulated a handful of yellow parking tickets. If the room wasn't bugged, then someone must have been listening at her door while she so conveniently outlined the evidence against him and Barb volunteered to keep a copy of the disk safe in the pocket of her lab coat.

"I'd better get back downstairs. The police ought to be here any moment. Mr. Goodman's on his way in as well. I should make sure nothing else is breaking loose around here."

Poor Stan. The vandalism, the attacks wouldn't enhance his work record, either.

Work record. Just when she thought she couldn't possibly feel worse, Carmen realized the loss of the computer also meant the loss of the presentation she meant to put together for Monday.

Whoever was behind the vicious attacks and acts of vandalism had effectively signed her termination.

She wondered if he meant to. Did he want not only to regain the evidence that could lead to his conviction, but to put her out of work as well? Judy's description ran hauntingly through her memory. He said people like that don't deserve the jobs they have.

Did someone hate her because she was still working, no matter how temporarily? Or was it Andersen plotting to make her look so incompetent that Max would be obligated to reallocate her budget? When that didn't work, did he plan to scare her off? Was he lurking in the halls, waiting to exact a personal revenge on her?

"I'll come with you," she said quickly, joining Stan just as he reached the elevator. "I don't want to stay up here by myself."

"Probably not a good idea." Stan's acquiescence didn't make her feel any better.

◻ ◻ ◻

Carmen could see the strain of the past few days etched in Wayne Goodman's face. The young president seemed to be aging by the hour. Dark circles ringed his eyes. She couldn't recall the last time she'd seen him without a tan. Being athletic, Wayne spent most of his weekends outdoors, biking, skiing, sailboarding, playing tennis. Not even noon, and already the president looked like he needed a good night's sleep and maybe a few weeks' holiday in the sun.

Police officers crawled through the debris in her office. Neither the doorknob or the equipment yielded any fingerprints.

"Obviously he didn't get what he was looking for last time," the detective remarked. Today, he was wearing a brown tweed jacket instead of the trench coat reminiscent of a television cop show.

"Any idea what they might have been looking for?" Wayne asked. Carmen looked up to find all the police officers and the two detectives waiting for her answer. She was going to have to tell them, she realized. The situation was simply getting too dangerous.

Carmen pulled up the swivel chair and sank into it. Bad idea, she realized. Looking up at the circle of faces made her feel even more guilty. "I think he may have been looking for a file on my computer."

"What kind of file?" Wayne demanded.

"A frame from the tape that was stolen."

Wayne's fist collided with the top of the computer table. "You had a piece of evidence and you didn't tell us!"

"I didn't know it was a piece of evidence." Carmen's voice rose to match his. "The tape was stolen while I was running the dub. All that got copied were some shots of the parking lot and a hand coming into the frame. I wanted to enhance it, see if I could find anything that might link it to the attacker."

"Why didn't you tell us?" Goodman's voice sank to a menacing whisper.

"I didn't want to get your hopes up. Not after the theft in my office." Perilously close to tears, Carmen stopped talking before she embarrassed herself further. And still there was more they had to hear. "I copied the file to disk and gave it to Barbara Downey to keep safe. I think that's what the attacker was looking for last night."

Tears betrayed her.

"Any other copies?" the detective in the brown tweed asked quietly.

Carmen wiped away the tears streaking down her face. Never had she cried on the job. Not since grade school had she cried in public. "Just one."

"Let's see it," Wayne said.

"You can't. I sent it to myself by express mail for safe keeping."

Wayne cursed under his breath. The detective turned away in disgust.

"I want that disk as soon as it arrives in the mail." There was a quiet anger in Goodman's tone Carmen had never heard before.

"We better have a look at the surveillance tape," Stan said, breaking the tension. As the team filed out of the office. Carmen mouthed a thank you to Stan and followed them.

Empty hallways in the administrative sections of the hospital zipped by on fast forward. Stan slowed the tape as the eleventh floor came into view. But the cameras showed only black and white images of empty hallways. The tape leapt ahead to the next sweep. More empty hallways and quiet elevators. The time code showed early Saturday morning. The door to Carmen's office was closed, showing no signs of what had or was about to happen in there.

"There's nothing more?" the detective asked.

"That's the whole tape," Stan said. The weekend security supervisor was starting to look as stressed out as the rest of them. This won't improve his next performance evaluation, Carmen thought with a sympathetic twinge of anxiety.

Another, more disturbing thought occurred to her. "Could this have happened last night, before we knew the security camera was turned off?"

A sea of faces turned toward her, Wayne Goodman, the police officers, Stan, the detective in the tweed jacket.

"I guess it's possible," Stan said. "We were all out front with Barbara waiting for the police."

"If that's true the guy had one hell of a busy night," the detective remarked.

"But if he knew Barbara had the disk, then he must have been listening in on our conversation. If he was, then he would have heard me tell Barb that I had another copy on my hard drive." She shuddered as her mind worked through the rest of that chilling thought. "And if that's true, then he might also have heard me tell Barb that I'd mailed a copy to myself."

"Get some more men on security," Wayne ordered. "And call a locksmith. Get a new lock on the door to Medical Photography."

Stan left to make the call.

"We'll post an officer here for the rest of the weekend." The detective turned to Carmen. "Do you have somewhere to stay for the next couple of days, Ms. Day? Just in case this guy decides to pay you a visit?"

"Perhaps I can stay with Barb."

Wayne Goodman stared over her shoulder at the group of patients and family members enjoying the garden. "We need to protect ourselves, but I want to keep this as quiet as possible. The last thing we need is to start a panic."

Suddenly his expression changed. Carmen followed the line of his gaze just in time to see one of LKVW TV's mobile satellite vans turn into the parking lot.

Chapter Ten

*M*ax Deveraux stared into his coffee cup, wishing he could disappear into its dark depths. They'd barely finished their bacon and eggs before Andersen launched another assault. Fate was on Andersen's side. Before he could find some excuse to stay at the chalet while Andersen went fishing, it started to rain.

The thought of being cooped up in the chalet for the entire weekend, while Andersen extolled his virtues and the virtues of his plans for Royal Hospital, made him want to scream.

"I've already told you, Jim," Max snapped. "I'll consider your report once the others are in. It's only fair," he added lamely, trying to take some of the bite out of his tone.

"And Goodman," Andersen continued, undaunted, "how do you think he's leaning?"

"Whatever's on Goodman's mind, he's keeping it to himself. And so he should, it's only professional conduct."

"Come on," Andersen taunted. "You can tell me."

"I'm not going to tell you," Max said, rising from the table. "If that's the only reason you invited me up here, it was a wasted tactic, Jim."

"Take it easy." Andersen's eyes followed Max as he snatched his jacket from the hook by the door. "You can't blame me for trying. Everyone's curious."

"And everyone's going to have to wait until all the input has been considered. Like I said, the decision hasn't been made yet, and it won't be until I've considered all the information." Max hauled open the door and reached for the screen.

"It's her, isn't it?"

He turned towards Andersen, clamping down on his temper. "What's that supposed to mean?"

"It's that Carmen Day woman. I hear she's been doing lots of off-hours soliciting of your good will."

Max felt his face darkening, his anger threatening to break free of his will. "My personal life is none of your business." He uttered the words in a whisper that was threatening in its understatement.

If he stayed another moment he'd lose it completely. Max pulled open the screen door and stepped into the biting, damp air.

"It's raining out," Andersen uselessly observed.

"Yes, it is," Max said, choosing the rain over Andersen's company.

Unlike Andersen, Max didn't mind the rain. Andersen no doubt considered rainy days bad weather, something to be avoided, along with budget cuts and other unpleasantries. Max's Mohawk ancestors would simply have called it rain. Rain made the crops grow, ensured a good harvest. Sure, it was wet and if he stayed out long enough he'd be cold as well. But one had to be wet and cold in order to appreciate being warm and dry. It was all a matter of balance, just like the finances of Royal Hospital.

Jim Andersen wanted only to govern in times of plenty. Which was as impossible as a lifetime of sunny days. Andersen gave no thought to what would happen when the money ran out. Carmen, having experienced poverty, understood a lot more about balance than Jim Andersen.

The best thing about the rain was it drove Andersen inside and left Max in peace. At least he would have been at peace in the silken whisper of the rain, had his thoughts not kept straying back to Carmen Day.

She was right, he thought, tramping through wet brush that soaked his jeans within minutes. Powdery rain beaded on his hair and settled like a damp cloak over his coat.

Why hadn't he canceled on Andersen and stayed in the city? He could have spent the entire weekend with Carmen. Thoughts of waking up to her sun-filled bedroom after making love all night warmed him in spite of the rain. They could have bought buttered croissants from the bakery...except that now she was furious with him. The longer he delayed, the more he risked losing her trust completely.

To beg Andersen to drive him into town so he could rent a car and head home would ruin his credibility. That was the way it worked between men. Showing your weaknesses was an invitation to be taken advantage of.

He couldn't blame Andersen—not really. If his department were in danger, he'd be trying to sniff out the results as well. It irked him that Andersen's words held a grain of truth. He put himself at risk of a serious conflict of interest in befriending anyone at Royal Hospital. And he'd strayed irretrievably across the line of fair play when he'd shown Andersen's damning report against her to Carmen.

So many times he'd sworn off mixing business with pleasure. The last time had nearly discredited him permanently. Taking a position outside Ottawa was his salvation. Accepting the Royal Hospital contract improved the situation by keeping him away longer. But the health care field operated like gossip in a small town. Word spread like wild fire.

Problem was, knowing all that, he still couldn't stay away from Carmen Day. Sweet and lovely, with equal parts determination and intelligence, she charmed him. Consequences be damned, he wanted her. He wanted to spend his life with her.

Now where did that thought come from? Max took a seat on the wet pier, knowing that when he stood up, he'd have a wet smear on the back of his jeans. For most of an hour he sat in the rain, staring out across the slate gray lake practically indistinguishable from the horizon and the clouds. His mind ran in circles around his predicament, coming to the same conclusion time after time.

He had to go back to Carmen, even if it meant the termination of his contract at Royal Hospital.

The decision made, the pieces of the rest of the plan fell into place. He'd convince Andersen to drive him to town or drive him home.

Andersen was in the spacious den watching the Lakeview station on satellite television. No roughing it for Jim Andersen, Max thought darkly. Even the cavernous main room of the chalet sported a kitchen with dishwasher, microwave and all the conveniences of home.

"Jim, I've been thinking—"

"Shh!" Andersen held up his hand for silence. Reaching for the remote, he turned up the volume so he could hear over Max's interruption.

Max turned his attention to the news item that had Andersen so enraptured. His heart jumped when he recognized the exterior of Royal Hospital.

"...a number of women have been attacked on hospital property. Several cases of vandalism have also been reported. Police are warning women in the area not to walk alone after dark..."

"We have to go back," Max said. "This changes everything."

☐ ☐ ☐

Carmen sat at the desk in Barb's basement den.
Barbara and her daughter had gone out of their way
to make her comfortable. Still, she always felt out of
place staying in other people's homes. Allowing someone to rig up an impromptu video editing suite in their
basement had been asking a bit much, but Barb worried about Carmen's safety, insisting she come stay for
the weekend.

"This isn't necessary," Carmen had insisted as
Wayne helped her pack up the video editing equipment that hadn't been damaged in the break-in.

"The last thing I need is another of my staff members getting attacked," Wayne had said. "If you must
work this weekend, do it somewhere else."

Carmen pulled a stack of videotapes off the shelf.
Tyler's archives. The material she'd hoped to use had
been stored on her computer's hard drive. Lost now.
Forever.

Fortunately, her tape library housed almost as
many moving stories of patients' recoveries. She'd edit
them together, juxtaposing the disheartening injuries
with miraculous cures. The statistics she'd have to
give in a written report. It wouldn't have the impact of
the multimedia presentation she'd intended, but it
was the best she could do under the circumstances.

"I don't see why this can't wait until next week."
Wayne grunted as he lifted the heavy editing equipment onto a cart. "I'm sure Max Deveraux would be
willing to give you a couple of days' grace."

Carmen tried not to wince at the sound of Max's
name. "A few days isn't going to make any difference,
is it Wayne? We both know that with all the cutbacks

I'm not going to get budget to replace the equipment that's been damaged, am I?"

Goodman ran a hand over his face. "Probably not," he admitted.

"This whole thing sets the department back five years in technology. Even the equipment I have is going to need budget to repair."

Wayne set the heavy box down on the cart and leaned against it. "It's the same story across the whole hospital. There just isn't the money to do what we'd like to do anymore."

"Are you telling me that even if I write the best report ever set to paper, I don't have a hope of getting funding? Should I give up now?"

He gripped her lightly by the shoulders and looked down into her eyes. And for a moment, the old Wayne was back, the one she knew before the budget cuts, before downsizing, before Max Deveraux arrived at Royal Hospital. "No, Carmen, don't give up." The ghost of a smile drifted across his face. "You wouldn't anyway, would you? Even if I ordered you to."

Carmen laughed for the first time in days. "Of course not, Wayne."

He shook his head. "Just as I thought. So go to Barbara's for the weekend. Put your presentation together. We'll see you Monday."

Monday, Carmen thought, looking around at the paneled walls of Barb's den, was only a day and half away.

□ □ □

Max Deveraux jumped out of the Andersen's BMW before it stopped moving. He raced across the parking lot, conscious of Andersen following close behind him.

He found Wayne Goodman in his office preparing
another statement for the media. Martha Jones, the
head of PR, sat in the chair opposite his desk, looking
every bit as harried as the president.

"We've got to tell them something." Dressed in
jeans and t-shirt, Martha looked nothing like her
usual career woman persona. "The report's been on
the news all afternoon. I've got calls from all over the
province. We have to put together some kind of statement that makes it clear we're taking every precau-
tion to keep our patients and staff safe."

"Invite the media back." Wayne thought for a
moment. "Line the halls with every security guard we
can scrape together. Make the place look like a garri-
son. Then at least if the perpetrator is watching, perhaps he'll think twice about his next move."

"What are we going to say about the allegations
that it's an inside job?"

"Don't say anything about it being an inside job."

"Too late," Martha said. "They've already talked to
the police."

"Then tell them the police are conducting an under-
cover investigation. That'll scare whoever's behind
this."

"Have a shave and put on a suit jacket. I'm sure the
cameras will be back." Martha grabbed her notes,
ready to do battle with the media.

"Hello Max," Goodman said wearily, taking note of
Max standing in the doorway. "I thought you were out
of town for the weekend."

"I saw the news report. Figured you could use
another hand."

"Things are under control for the moment. This bad
publicity can't help our case with the Ministry."

"Depends on how it turns out," Max said noncommittally. He didn't want to talk about the Ministry or

the hospital's adverse publicity. The only thing he wanted to know was whether Carmen was all right. "Was it the Medical Photography office that was broken into again?"

Wayne opened the doors to the closet in his office and rooted around for a clean shirt. "Carmen discovered the damage when she came in to do some work this morning."

"Carmen? She's here?"

Wayne's eyes narrowed shrewdly. "She's staying with Barbara Downey for the weekend."

"I can't see how that could be safe since Barbara Downey was attacked last night."

"The police thought it was a good solution," Wayne snapped, annoyance plain in his tone.

"We haven't done enough to protect her," Max continued undaunted. "Her office was broken into before. There should be a guard on that door."

"We couldn't be sure it was a break-in." Wayne turned to him, his quest for a shirt forgotten. "And we didn't have the budget to hire another security guard just to sit on the door."

"But you can afford a whole slew of them for your publicity shot, can't you?" Max felt the temper he'd held in check all weekend start to unravel.

"I can't see how this is any of your concern." Goodman gave him a measuring look. "So, it's true, isn't it?"

"What's true?"

"The rumors about you and Carmen. You're seeing each other, aren't you? That's why you're so concerned."

Behind him, Max heard Andersen grunt, then mutter, "Figures."

"Leave my personal life out of this."

"You obviously haven't," Wayne Goodman said. "I would have expected you to be a bit more discreet. I can't see how you expect to make an objective decision when you're involved with one of the department heads you might have to fire."

Andersen stepped from the hall into Wayne's office. "My point exactly."

Goodman stepped in front of him, blocking his path. "In case neither of you noticed, I have a press conference to prepare for. Go home, both of you. We'll discuss the rest of this on Monday."

Chapter Eleven

*M*ax Deveraux cursed the time lost going home and getting his own car. Barbara Downey lived way out in one of the numerous suburbs, the names of which he still couldn't keep straight in his mind. He had to see Carmen, convince her it wasn't safe to keep living in a bad neighborhood, even if it was close to the hospital.

He gripped the steering wheel, anger flooding through him. The thought of Carmen in danger released a whirlwind of conflicting emotions. He wanted to hold her close, keep her safe. He wanted to shake her for putting herself in danger. He wanted to get them both far away from Royal Hospital where their relationship was simply something between them and not entertaining gossip for every busybody in the place. He wanted...

Her.

The realization hit like a tidal wave. He simply wanted Carmen. The contract at Royal Hospital be damned.

Once the decision was made it didn't seem so much like the conflict of interest Wayne Goodman accused him of. He could always resign, turn the project over to one of his colleagues. It wouldn't help his reputation, but there were other places besides Lakeview and Ottawa to work.

Max cursed as he realized he'd taken yet another wrong turn. More time wasted. He couldn't turn up on Barbara Downey's doorstep in the middle of the night. The clock on the dashboard read 9:30 p.m. Not too late for a Saturday night. Not yet.

◻ ◻ ◻

In the basement the sound of the doorbell was muffled, even more so by the sound from the videotape she was editing. Carmen ran the tape again, cueing up the edit. Deciding it adequate, she hit edit. The tape shuttled back and forth, cueing itself to the right place.

Doorbell. What if it wasn't Brenda's date for the evening? What if the maniac had found out where Barbara lived. Abandoning the tape, she raced up the basement stairs.

And collided with Max Deveraux in the living room.

"Max!"

"I told him you didn't want to speak to him." Barbara crossed her arms and glared in Max's direction. Brenda disappeared from the living room, barely concealing a smirk.

He sported a day's growth of beard. A thick flannel shirt was tucked into those well-worn jeans that did nothing to conceal his physique. The flannel looked so soft, she longed to put her head against his shoulder and rub its fleece against her skin. Carmen wrenched her gaze away.

Max looked around at the tiny living room in Barb's bungalow. "Is there somewhere we could talk privately?"

Torrid thoughts of what had happened the last time they talked privately gave Carmen pause. Their passionate lovemaking only minutes over, he'd told her he was spending the weekend with the enemy. Max Deveraux couldn't be trusted, not in private.

"Anything you've got to say, you can say in front of Barb." Carmen crossed her arms, mirroring Barb's defiant stance.

Max glanced nervously at Barbara, then back at Carmen. "It will only take a moment."

"Say what you have to say or leave," Barb interjected.

"Fine." Max drew in a deep breath. "I want you to move in with me."

"I think we should discuss this in private."

Carmen grabbed Max by the shirt and propelled him in the direction of the den, conscious of Barb's eyes following their every move.

"Have you lost your mind?" She closed the door and leaned against it as if her body could muffle their words against the curious ears of Barbara and Brenda waiting outside.

"It only makes sense. You're in danger." Max presented his case forcefully enough, but beneath it all was a wounded quality, as if he'd thought long and hard on the topic and her outright dismissal hurt him.

"I'm perfectly fine. Really," Carmen added more gently.

"You're not. Your office has been broken into twice, two of your friends have been attacked. You live in one of the most crime-ridden neighborhoods in the city."

"You live there, too."

"Exactly. You'd be safer with me," he continued, blocking off her protests. "There's lots of room in my house and you've been living in that tiny apartment."

"And what am I supposed to do when you've moved on in a couple of months and I've given up my tiny apartment. Find another one that I'll pay twice as much for in an equally rotten neighborhood?"

Obviously Max hadn't worked out all of the bugs from his plan. "We'd have to talk about that."

"Oh, right. You'd go ahead and rearrange my life and then we'll have to talk about the future?"

Max's eyes shifted to the door, doubtlessly imagining Barb and Brenda with their ears pressed to it. "Carmen, calm down."

"I don't want to calm down, Max. First you decimate my department, then you seduce me, and after you've—" She lowered her voice and continued in a furious whisper. "After you've slept with me, you betray me to the one person who'd like to see me removed from the budget of Royal Hospital. I am in danger, Max—from you!"

"I still don't understand why you're so mad about the fishing trip. Nothing Jim Andersen says has anything to do with my decision or my feelings about you."

"Jim" again—that familiarity with which doctors addressed their peers, yet never expected to be called by anyone else. It rankled that Andersen wouldn't hesitate to play dirty by inviting Max away for the weekend while she followed proper channels. "Are you telling me Andersen didn't mention his budget once while you were away?"

The abashedly guilty look on his face gave her the answer. "That's what I came to tell you. Andersen did nothing but talk about his budget. All the way up north in the car, even over breakfast the next morning."

"So you admit it."

He took a hesitant step toward her. "I'll do more than admit it, Carmen," Max said softly. "I'll even admit you were right."

"Did he convince you to fire me?" She didn't want to know the answer, but she asked anyway.

"I have half a mind to cut his budget to make up for my pain and suffering."

"Serves you right."

"Carmen, you're an impossible person to apologize to." He enfolded her into the circle of his embrace.

Carmen burrowed further into the soft flannel of his shirt, filling her senses with the scent of pine trees and fresh air.

"All I know," Max said, "is, when I saw that newscast, all I cared about was making sure you were safe."

Max rested his head atop hers. One hand stroked her back, easing out tensions that had been there for over a week. Her thoughts filled with memories of his hands on other parts of her body, hot sweaty memories of their bodies entwined. Before she realized it, she was melting into him, comfort dissolving her reluctance, leading her in a direction she still hadn't committed to.

"Come live with me, Carmen. We'll work the rest of it out later."

"And what if you have to fire me, Max? How will we work that one out?"

"I don't know," he said. "I wish I did."

"What you're saying is that you have nothing to lose, while I have everything."

He held her back from him. That wounded expression shadowed his face again. "That's unfair, Carmen. I have lots of money saved, I could support us both for as long as it takes for you to find something else."

"Something else where, Max? At your next posting? You'd take me away from my job, my home and all my friends, while I followed you around the country like a sick puppy."

His arms fell to his sides and he paced away from her. "If you have something constructive to say I'd like to hear it because I'm really trying here."

Carmen opened her mouth for another sharp retort, but the image of another argument sprang to mind. Andersen's face, contorted with anger seared into memory. "Max, what time did Andersen pick you up?"

He turned toward her, confused at this new line of questioning. "What's that got to do with anything?"

"Just bear with me for a moment."

"If this is some weird way of getting out of this discussion, I'm not impressed."

"I really need to know."

"Why?" He set his hands on his hips and regarded her with annoyance.

She wasn't going to get the answer out of him without an explanation. "I think he might have been the one who attacked Barbara and trashed my office."

"That's insane!" He frowned, and stared back at her from under dark brows. "Have you been drinking?"

"Just answer the question, Max. What time was it?"

"It was about nine. Jim said he had an emergency to see to. Whatever it was, he was in a hell of a dark mood."

"About nine," she repeated. Now it was Carmen's turn to pace. "And he didn't say anything about Barb being attacked. It happened around seven-thirty. No one at Royal Hospital could have missed the hubbub. The parking lot was full of police cars. Even the residents were looking out the windows."

"No, he didn't say anything about the hospital, except for the necessity of increasing his budget."

"By laying me off."

"Something like that."

"Think about it, Max. Andersen has keys to my office, and also to the security office. That would explain how the surveillance camera got turned off. It would also explain how my office was robbed without tampering with the lock."

Max sat on Barb's couch and rested his elbows on his knees. "I just can't see him doing such a thing. I mean, why would he have to? He planned to have my ear all weekend."

"A fail-safe maybe. Think of it. Maybe he didn't hold much stock in convincing you. After all, there are tons of rumors about us. Maybe you were his alibi."

"That's too crazy."

"Is it? You were with him all weekend. Talk about an air-tight alibi. He tells you he has an emergency. He turns off the surveillance camera just as Stan's starting his night rounds. Knowing Stan's in the basement at that time, he lets himself into my office. But he can't find what he's looking for, and he takes his frustration out on my computer. If I don't have the computer, then I can't write that report, can I? He's pretty happy with the results until he remembers overhearing me tell Barbara to keep a disk safe for me. By this time, he's getting desperate and he attacks Barb."

"Wouldn't Barb have recognized him?"

"He was wearing a mask, but she said his voice sounded familiar."

"She'd know Andersen's voice, wouldn't she?"

"Maybe not if she was frightened."

Max considered this new line of thinking with a frown. "So, how do you explain Judy?"

Stumped, Carmen sat beside him on the couch. "I don't know how you explain Judy's attack. Frustration maybe."

"Andersen wouldn't be that stupid."

"Maybe Judy did something to him that we don't know about."

"Perhaps, Carmen, but it still doesn't add up."

"It adds up fine to me," she snapped. "He's always disliked me, he wants to be rid of me. Maybe he got sick of waiting for someone else to make the decision. He knows Wayne and I are good friends. Once he

heard you were involved with me, maybe he just went
nuts."

"Maybe." Max wrapped his arm around her and
pulled her close. "I don't know about your theory, but
I don't like what's been going on. If you won't move in
with me, then at least stay with me for a couple of
days. Just until this all blows over."

Her heart longed to do what he wanted. To stay in
his old, but charming rundown house. To sleep in his
large bed, warmed by his body and his love. But before
she could do that, there was another mystery she
needed an answer to. "I can't, Max," Carmen said,
pulling away from him. "Not until you tell me about
the assistant administrator from Kanata."

Max stared back at her, dumbfounded. The four-
hour drive from Andersen's chalet had been excruciat-
ing. LKVW TV's sensationalist coverage of the event
had only fueled his overactive imagination. Carmen
trapped in the midst of a number of gruesome scenarios taunted him all the way home. When he'd seen her
standing in Barbara's living room unharmed, he
almost threw his arms around her.

And now, after all the worry, after swallowing his
pride and admitting he was wrong, after inviting her
to move in with him, she chose to quiz him about an
ex-girlfriend.

"I don't believe this." Indignation swept those cozy
thoughts from his mind. "I drive four hours just to
make sure you're all right and that's all you have to
say to me."

"I have to know where I stand." She walked to the
window, putting her back to him. From her rigid posture and the uninviting set of her jaw the window's
reflection allowed him, he could tell the conversation
wouldn't be over any time soon.

"You should know that already. I came back because I was worried about you. I asked you to move in with me because I care about you. What more do you want, Carmen?"

"I want to know what's behind the rumors I keep hearing."

"Rumors!" His hold on his temper slid rapidly through his fingers. Walk out, his temper urged. Forget her she doesn't care. But he did care, that was the worst of it. His feet wanted to walk away, his heart wouldn't let him. "What about the rumors I have to put up with? Andersen practically accused me of giving you funding because you're my lover. Even Goodman's been on my case about it. How'd they know a thing like that?" He jabbed a finger in the direction of her rejection. "It sure wasn't me who blabbed it all over the hospital."

She whirled to face him. Green eyes that her short hair cut made larger, blazed at him. "I haven't said a word, except to Barb." Realizing what she'd said, she rallied for another attack. "Perhaps your reputation has already convicted you."

"What reputation?" Angry now, he glared at her, marveling that a woman who stood little more than five-feet tall could put him on the defensive so quickly.

"What reputation?" Carmen mimicked, edging his anger up another notch. "I don't suppose you remember being involved with the assistant administrator at the General in Kanata."

Her broadsided attack took him by surprise. Max opened his mouth to defend himself, but fury, mixed with a sudden stab of pain, silenced him.

Carmen continued without even drawing a breath. "And I've heard a lot more than I wanted to about your lovers in Kingston, Sudbury, London, and Hamilton."

"Hamilton!" Max gripped her arms, turning her towards him. He wanted to yell at her, to shake some sense into her, but the moment he touched her, she felt so tiny in his arms he only wanted to hold her closer, to protect her. The smell of floral shampoo mixed with her own scent and he had to restrain himself from nuzzling closer, from kissing those full lips that were parted to argue with him. "Carmen, I've never had a contract in Hamilton."

"But Tamara Brown said—" She sputtered, then fell silent.

"Who the hell is Tamara Brown?"

"A college buddy of the assistant administrator from Kanata."

"I see. And how well do you know this Tamara person?" The urge to shake her returned. Max let her go, taking up her spot by the window.

"I don't, she's a friend of Barb's."

"Oh right, Barbara whom you confided in and now it's all over the hospital."

"I'm sure Barb didn't say anything too personal."

"Except to Tamara, who's a good friend of the assistant administrator from Kanata. Someone was bending Wayne Goodman's ear about it, and Jim Andersen sure had an earful for me."

"Barb wouldn't be gossiping with Dr. Andersen. He doesn't even bother to say good morning to anyone who doesn't have an M.D."

"Someone obviously said something to someone. The problem is, Carmen, now that the secret's out, anything we do is going to be subject to scrutiny. If I fund your department, everyone's going to say it's because you're my lover. If it turns out that isn't possible, you'll end up another name on that Tamara woman's list."

"You're just saying that to throw me off topic so you won't have to tell me the truth."

"We're talking rumors here, Carmen. Not truth."

He wasn't going to dissuade her, he could see that. She wouldn't give up until she wrestled the truth out of him. And the truth was going to hurt.

"So you weren't in Hamilton. That leaves Sudbury, Kingston, and London." She glared up at him, her bottom lip jutting out in defiance. He longed to nibble on that lip, even though he was furious with her.

Max leaned against the windowsill. Weariness crept into muscles cramped by the long car drive. He just wanted to go home, have a long hot shower, preferably with Carmen, if she didn't drive him completely to distraction first. "If I told you I was not romantically involved with anyone during my contracts in Sudbury, Kingston or London, would you believe me?"

"Is that the truth?"

"That's the truth."

She eyed him warily. "You didn't mention the assistant administrator from Kanata."

Carmen Day had missed her calling, Max decided. She should have been a police interrogator. "The assistant administrator's name is Marnie. And yes, we did have a relationship that...ended badly."

"Ended badly? What did you do?"

"For God's sake, Carmen! Why are you so certain it was me?"

"Was it?"

He sighed wearily, resigned to having to deal with the pain after all. "I made some mistakes, so did she. Neither of us got out of it unscathed. If it makes her feel better to blame me, then so be it. I certainly blamed her for a time. I just didn't have anyone to talk to about it."

"Guys don't do that kind of thing?" she asked.

"What kind of thing?"

"You know, commiserate about women over beers."

Her innocent question cut through his anger. "Sure, we complain, but moving around makes it hard to keep in touch with people."

"I guess it does." She looked at him, much like someone would examine a specimen, full of interest and skepticism. "Are you going to tell me what went wrong?"

Just when he was softening towards her, getting over his anger at being betrayed to her best friend, she renewed her attack. "No, I'm not going to spill my guts here in your friend's house. I came here because I worried about you all day, and all you've done is cross-examine me like a suspect in a murder case. I'm thirty-one years old, Carmen. Of course I've had other relationships. Why don't you tell me about some of yours."

"My romantic history wouldn't fill five minutes," she snapped.

A great deal of pain hid behind that admission. He wished he could take the question back. Anything to wipe that sorrowful look from her face.

"Listen," he said, tracing the path of a tear that spilled down her cheek. "This isn't the way I wanted this to turn out. I was worried about you. I'm still worried about you. I don't care what Wayne Goodman or Jim Andersen or Tamara Brown have to say, I just want to make sure you're safe."

She leaned against him, buried her face in the front of his shirt. Through the flannel he felt the dampness of her tears. "Come home with me, Carmen. Just until this thing blows over and that lunatic is behind bars. You'll be safe and we'll have a chance to talk privately."

"I can't." His shirt muffled her words. "How can I possibly prepare a confidential report, with you watching over my shoulder?"

Would he never convince her? "I rent a fourbedroom house, with a separate living room and dining room. I'm sure you can find a private place to work. You can even have your own bedroom, if you insist."

She sighed and he watched the strength go out of her. "It's not just that, Max."

"For God's sake, what now?"

Lips pursed as if there were a million things bubbling up inside, she blurted, "It's your whole life!"

"Well, thanks a lot." What more would it take? He'd driven all day to be with her, embarrassed himself in front of her, only to have her throw it back in his face. He turned to leave.

Carmen caught his sleeve. "Wait, let me explain."

Max stopped, making no move to turn back into the room. She had two seconds to redeem herself he decided. If her next words showed no promise of reconciliation, he was out of there.

"You move around so much, a few months here a few months there."

Not going so good, Max thought. Two more seconds. "It's my job, Carmen."

"I know it's your job. And you're good at it. And I'd never ask someone to rearrange their life just for me, but I grew up in an unstable environment and then my Mom died and...well, security means a lot to me."

That explained a great deal: why she'd had only one job in all her adult life, why she hung on to it against all odds. She stood a couple feet away from him, her chin jutting out, daring him to ridicule her for that heartfelt admission. He gripped her shoulders, ran his hands up and down her arms, massaging

out some of the tension. "Why wouldn't you ask someone to rearrange their life for you?"

Green eyes widened in shock at his question.
"There was never anyone there for me," she said finally.

"And if there was? Don't you think it would be
worth fighting for what you needed?"

"I don't know, Max. It's never come up. I guess I
just always assumed no one would think I was worth
it."

"Why?"

She shook her head. I grew up in an unstable environment. Her words haunted him. And she had yet to
mention her father. It didn't seem like a good time for
him to ask. "I'm not the villain here. I'm willing to
make some compromises for our relationship. Just like
you will. But I refuse to be judged by Barbara Downey
and the rest of the rumor mill. So, here's the deal.
Come home with me. At least I'll know some crazed
lunatic hasn't broken into your apartment and kid-
napped you, and we can talk the rest of this out." He
gave her a long measuring stare. "Or say no now, so
we can both get on with our lives."

Silence stretched out over several seconds. Max
gathered his courage for the coming rejection.

"Okay," Carmen said just as he had given up. "Let's
go home. Let's talk. But I'm going to have to work all
day tomorrow."

"So am I," he said tiredly.

◻◻◻

"I can't believe you're going home with him," Barbara
hissed, while Max waited on the porch for Carmen.

Not after he went fishing with that...that maniac Andersen."

"We have a few things to work out." Carmen tried to keep her voice to a whisper. Above all she didn't want to make the situation with Max any worse. Not until she decided whether that situation was on or off. "And if Andersen is involved in this whole mess, I'm pretty certain Max didn't know about it."

"What makes you so sure?" Barb cast an accusing glance at Max's shadow. "What if it's him?"

The accusation sent a cold bolt of fear down her spine.

"Max is not the attacker."

"How do you know? Were you with him on either of the nights of the attacks?"

Carmen thought back through her memory. No. The word lodged in her throat. Memories of gentle hands caressing the most intimate of places swept through her mind. Max's gentle lovemaking wouldn't convince Barbara of his innocence. "I just know, Barb. Okay?"

"No, it's not okay. I don't want you going with him."

"I have to, Barb. We've got to work this out."

"So, work it out over lunch on Monday. In a public place where you'll be safe."

"A public place is nowhere to discuss a relationship." Max coughed discretely outside. "Look I've got to go. Tell you what, I'll call you tomorrow."

"Promise." Barb didn't look at all convinced.

"I promise."

An hour later, her makeshift editing system was set up on the bulky wooden desk in one of Max's three extra bedrooms. The room was stuffy from lack of use. But once the windows had been opened for a few minutes, clean sheets and the comforter from Max's own bed completing the furnishings, Carmen felt quite comfortable.

She lay back, sinking into the creaky old bed. Tension eased slowly from her body. Max had been the perfect gentleman during the ride home, not forcing a conversation, helping her unload, then set up her equipment. He hadn't pressed her to join him in his bedroom, merely said that they were both tired and bad-tempered, and they would talk again in the morning.

Still, even as she drowsed off, Barb's words followed her into sleep. What if it's him?

Carmen came awake with a start. Shadows played across an unfamiliar ceiling. The moon cast silver fingers of light through tattered drapes. Dark shapes of furniture rose up around her, each shadow hiding potential danger.

Fear paralyzed her. For a moment she couldn't hear above the thumping of her heart. Until she remembered the strange ceiling belonged to Max's spare bedroom. Odd shapes took on the recognizable form of bulky furniture. The shadows in the ceiling became the intricate plaster work she remembered. Carmen burrowed back under the covers, determined to get one decent night's sleep out of the week.

But the old house seemed to have taken on a life of its own. As the late May night cooled from pleasant to chilly, an ancient furnace wheezed to life in a series of bumps and bangs. Antiquated duct work creaked in response.

Within that eerie chorus she heard again the sound that had awakened her. From outside came a scrape of metal on metal. Someone putting a ladder to the side of the house.

Her hand closed on the bedside lamp. The old plug came away from the wall easily enough, trailing its cord like a tentacle across the floor. The base was made of marble. Carmen tested its weight in her hand. Pressing herself against the wall, she inched toward the window.

A can blew down the street, impossibly loud in the silence. Sudden gusts of wind sent an unearthly moan through the trees.

She clutched the edge of the lace. Her hand tightened on the lamp. She jerked back the curtain.

Behind her, the wooden floor creaked. She spun around.

In the doorway she made out the broad silhouette of a man holding a large club.

Her scream drowned out the pounding of her heart.

Instead of lunging for Carmen, her attacker let out a hoarse cry of his own. Screams ricocheted off the walls. Then silence.

"Carmen?"

She shrank back against the wall. A shape detached itself from the shadows, moved into a puddle of moonlight.

Broad shoulders materialized into more recognizable form. He was bare-chested, wearing only a pair of thin pajama bottoms that clung to every muscle. Light caught the thing in his hand, illuminating pink cherubs on an over-decorated lamp. The shade was still attached, so was the electrical cord that trailed behind him.

"Max?"

He let go a harsh rush of breath. "You scared me half to death."

"I heard something outside." Already she felt foolish. For jumping at shadows, for disturbing his sleep, and most of all for allowing Barb to convince her Max was the attacker. He looked every bit as startled as she was.

From outside came another crash. Max strode to
the window and jerked back the curtain. In the shadows between the houses Carmen could make out the
hunched form of a well-fed raccoon making off with a
crust of bread. Trash spilled from the mouth of the
trash can, littering the narrow alley.

Max groaned. "That raccoon has it in for me."

For a moment they stared at each other,
disheveled, half-dressed and each brandishing their
own lamp. Terror dissolved into hilarity. They clung to
each other, shaking with laughter and relief.

"I'm sorry I woke you up." Carmen leaned against
Max, content in the warmth of his arms around her.

"You have a piercing scream. I was sure some
lunatic had you by the throat."

"And you were going to bludgeon him with a china
lamp with cherubs on it?"

Shudders of laughter rippled through his chest.
"Something like that."

"I heard a noise. After all that's happened..." She
looked up into eyes that gleamed like pools of darkness against the moonlight. "I was really scared."

"Don't be frightened, Carmen," he said, pulling her
closer. "You're safe. I'm here."

"Ready to defend me with your handy-dandy
cherub lamp."

He choked back a laugh and said seriously, "I'd
have picked up the house and hit him with it if I
thought it would save you."

Carmen nuzzled into the soft hairs on his chest.
"Thanks, Max."

"Don't know what that raccoon has against me.
Why is it always my garbage?"

"You have the best food," she murmured, lips moving against his chest.

"You haven't tried my eggs Benedict."

"Is that an offer of breakfast?"

"Promise," Max said. Taking the lamp from her hand, he set it carefully back on the bedside table. Then he draped the comforter around them. "Come to bed with me, Carmen. Before we destroy my rented furniture."

His warmth made up for the cold sheets. Together they burrowed into the warm pocket made by their bodies. Max pulled the comforter up around their necks.

"It's cold tonight," he murmured.

He ran his hands over her arms and grasped her cold feet between his own. Tangled, they lay silently for a few moments. Cold noses met. He kissed her long and languidly, stoking hesitant fires inside. Hands drifted from her shoulders, molding the contours of her body, pressing her against him as if they were both made of clay.

Each velvet touch chased away a little more of her uncertainty as he made sure she wouldn't be cold or frightened for the rest of the night.

◻ ◻ ◻

Of course she'd go to him. Didn't take a rocket scientist to figure that out. Once he'd deduced that much, it wasn't hard to find out the rest. Especially for a man with the keys to the kingdom. His pass key even opened the doors to personnel with its neatly organized list of addresses and phone numbers.

The intruder glanced up at the bedroom window above him. He might have had the rest of it, if it hadn't been for that stupid raccoon waking up half the neighborhood.

Soft sighs drifted down to him, borne by the wind. The opportunity had passed, it was obvious they wouldn't be going back to sleep for some time.

Tomorrow, he vowed. He'd see to it all tomorrow. Being a patient man, he could wait that long.

□ □ □

The next morning the tension between them seemed to have dissipated. As they worked in their separate rooms, it was easy for them to be together. Away from the concerns of Royal Hospital, they fell into a simple routine. Max's eggs Benedict proved to be as wonderful as the rest of his cooking. Carmen promised to outdo him at dinner.

The afternoon vanished as she assembled the pieces of videotape into her report. Sitting back in her chair, mind numb and eyes tired from watching the same pieces of video over and over again, she viewed the final cut.

Not bad, she decided. If she'd made the video for anyone else, she would have been delighted with the result. But this video had a special purpose. The salvation of her job. It didn't have the slick presentation graphics she had planned for the multimedia presentation. She'd lost them when the computer had been destroyed. Still, it showed the power of medical photography to tap into the suffering and the hope of the patients of Royal Hospital.

But would it be good enough? This time there was no dry run, no screening session, no approvals to sign off on. This tape would have only one showing.

And what if it wasn't good enough?

Would she feel the same about Max Deveraux after he signed her termination notice?

□ □ □

"In the video I'm about to present—" Carmen groaned in frustration. She'd rehearsed about ten different introductions, none of them sounded any good. "I sound like James Andersen giving one of his deadly boring in-services. I'm even putting myself to sleep."

She paced some more, wearing a deeper impression in the carpet beside her desk, and debated doing one of those sensationalist intros that tabloid television shows used. "Imagine you're eighteen. Your whole life stretches before you in endless possibilities. Until, one day disaster strikes! You end up doomed to a life in a specialized care setting, at the mercy of miserable opportunists like Dr. James Andersen." Carmen laughed at her own sarcastic finish. "I don't think I could say any of that with a straight face. But it's the ugly truth. I am at Andersen's mercy. And Max's."

They still hadn't talked. Sunday vanished as they worked separately on their own projects. The issue of Max's nomadic lifestyle and Carmen's impending unemployment remained undiscussed. Tip of the iceberg. Events at Royal Hospital absorbed so much of their thoughts there'd been no time to discuss the normal issues, like commitment.

□ □ □

As she sat in her office the next morning, the phone rang, cutting into her dark thoughts.

"Just called to wish you good luck," Max said as soon as she answered.

"I'm going to need it." Carmen doodled more sensationalist introductions on her note pad.

"It'll be over before you know it."

"That's what I'm afraid of." She couldn't help wondering if he phrased it that way on purpose.

"What I meant was that the presentation will go by quickly once you get started."

"I can't even think of an intro," she wailed, and hated herself for whining.

"Sure you can." Max sounded certain of her victory. Or was he bolstering her confidence to make the inevitable fall easier to bear? "You just need a little of that fire you had when you barged into my office that first day."

Carmen smiled in spite of her performance anxiety. "Won't work. Wayne's heard me rant before."

"Worked on me." In the background his intercom buzzed. "Listen, I've got to go. I've got a ten o'clock with Andersen. Don't want to add any more grist to the rumor mill."

"Wish me luck again."

"Knock 'em dead, tiger. See you at eleven-thirty."

One hour to come up with a riveting preamble. One hour to save her job.

She was lucky even to get on the agenda. Perhaps Wayne had taken pity on her after everything that happened last week and shuffled the schedule. Andersen was giving his report first. She wasn't invited to that part of the program. But as a department head and member of the senior staff, Andersen would sit in on hers. Goodman, the chairman of the board and Max would make up the rest of her audience. The video was ten minutes long. She'd give a five minute introduction. They'd probably ask her five minutes of questions. Ten to twelve it would be all over, just as Max had said.

The senior management staff would have little half-sandwiches and coffee in a silver urn delivered to the boardroom. Carmen would go back to her office and try to force a stale muffin into her churning stomach.

The phone rang again, cutting into her valuable preparation time. Carmen answered it anyway, vowing to have Mandy pick up her calls for the rest of the morning.

"Carmen? It's Joan from O.T. I think you'd better come down here."

"I can't, I've got a meeting in"

"Bring your video camera," Joan blurted before Carmen had a chance to reply.

□ □ □

HI, MY NAME IS TYLER. I LIKE PLAYING DEEP SPACE SHOOT OUT, AND LISTENING TO THE GROUP GUNS A BLAZING. WHEN I GET BETTER I'M GOING TO BUY A PAIR OF IN-LINE SKATES.

Even seen through the tiny black and white viewfinder, a miracle was in progress. Carmen zoomed in over Tyler's shoulder, showing the perfectly formed words moving across the computer screen.

"That's great," Joan said in the background. "A really big improvement, Tyler."

Carmen caught the smile he beamed her way in profile as he turned toward the camera. "I've been practicing," he said proudly.

"You sure have." She set up the camera for another shot.

"He's been working hard at all his exercises." Joan sounded every bit as proud as Tyler. "Not just the ones on the computer."

"I really want to get better," Tyler added.

"Now we can see that you are. This is going to look great on your tape. We'll edit them all together and then you'll really be able to see how far you've come." His happiness lifted her dark mood. Moments like this kept her working at Royal Hospital, through the budget cuts—

It occurred suddenly to Carmen that Tyler's recovery was the proof her presentation needed that medical photography really did have an impact on learning, on a patient's state of mind.

"Can you do a bit more typing, Tyler. I just need to get a few more close-ups." Carmen glanced at her watch. Half an hour. She'd edit it right on the end. If she hurried, she'd just have time. The introduction she'd have to wing, it wouldn't matter so much. Tyler's story would speak for itself.

Excitement took its toll. A dramatic improvement, but Tyler was still a long way from a complete recovery. "My arms are getting tired," he said apologetically.

"Maybe we should call it a day," Joan offered.

The camera ground suddenly to a halt. Carmen heard its motor die into silence, watched helplessly as the red recording light flickered, then went out. She popped the video compartment open. It sprang free with a sickening crunch, a ribbon of tape spilling out.

"Oh no!"

"Did you get any of it at all?" Joan asked, her enthusiasm evaporating. Tyler looked crestfallen.

"I'd better take it upstairs and have a look." Carmen gave Tyler a reassuring smile. "You rest your arms, Tyler. I'm sure we got most of it. But you're so much better, we can always reshoot it another day."

Her office door closed behind her, Carmen almost burst into tears, would have if it weren't for the presentation she had to make in twenty minutes.

It took her five minutes just to wrestle the damaged videotape from the camera and another couple to
manually wind the tape back into its case. Playback
showed what she'd been dreading. The best shots were
crunched beyond salvation, rendering practically
everything she'd taped unusable except for a few seconds of typing and Tyler's beaming smile at the end.

Carmen rested her head against the monitor's cool
glass and resisted the urge to dump the camera down
the back stairs. "Think!" she muttered. There had to
be a way to use what remained.

The clock in her outer office ticked loudly. Fifteen
minutes.

Carmen lunged for the tape lying on her desk.
Fingers shaking, she fed it into the editing system.
She scanned the neat rows of the tape on the shelf, her
gaze zeroing in on the raw material of Tyler's tape. A
short reprise was the answer. She'd cut those few sal-
vageable seconds around some old footage, contrasting
Tyler's previous condition with his dramatic recovery.

No time for fancy graphics, no titles to make the
transition cleaner. It worked like magic regardless.
Tyler's broken body edited against the beaming youth
in the last shot was a story warm enough to melt the
coldest of hearts.

She glanced at the clock, noticing with despair it
was already eleven-thirty. No time to check the tape to
see if all the edits were clean. No time to prepare that
slick introduction. Carmen ejected the video from the
editing system and dashed for the elevator.

Chapter Twelve

They gathered like vultures around the boardroom table: Andersen looking as he did when he was about to deliver bad news to a patient's family, Max looking as if he'd rather be somewhere—anywhere—else, and Goodman barely recognizable as the fun-loving executive she used to know. The chairman of the board offered the only support. The impeccably dressed older woman smiled at Carmen as she entered, giving every indication she was anxious to hear what her younger colleague had to say.

"We're waiting for you, Ms. Day," Andersen snapped as soon as she set foot into the hushed room. The grim face was merely a facade, she realized, catching a glimpse of the hunger in his eyes. Perhaps his presentation hadn't gone well. All the more reason for him to hope for her failure.

"Sorry, the elevator was crowded." The apology sprang from her lips, force of habit. Carmen ground her teeth together, refusing to defer further. Explanations, apologies, only weakened her position. She smoothed the wrinkles in her power suit and walked to the front of the room.

A videotape machine stood in the corner of the boardroom. Dusty with disuse. She should have taken the time to check it this morning. If it didn't work, she'd only look more the fool.

She walked confidently toward it anyway. It powered up easily. Carmen wiped dust off her hands and inserted the tape, listening intently for any indication the machinery might be chewing up her only copy. But the tape cued smoothly. She forced a breath of air into her lungs and faced her audience.

"I've come to offer a rebuttal to the premise that medical photography doesn't have an impact on patient care."

She leveled a long slow stare in Max's direction.

He wore a suit she hadn't yet seen, looking every bit the executive he was and not the sweatshirt-and-jeans Max she'd come to know. His three-button suit with its narrow lapels seemed too avant-garde for conservative Royal Hospital. Though the high collar of his white shirt was freshly starched and his face was clean-shaven, wisps of dark hair tumbled over his collar. Wildness, itching to escape. It was hard to think of him as Max the Axe now. Not after she'd seen him without his executive armor. Not after their lovemaking last night. Now he was her lover, putting her in an uncomfortable situation.

Max appeared to be having similar thoughts. Though his expression remained somber, he offered her a conspiratorial wink. Andersen intensified his deathbed glower. Wayne just looked tired. The chairman's eyes darted from Max to Carmen. A ghost of a smile crossed her face, then she resumed her look of polite interest.

Carmen rattled through the statistics, how many slides she'd made that year, the number of videos she'd produced, how much it would cost to buy those services from the local university. Once again she wished for the fancy charts and graphs the computer could have provided. Stats were impressive by themselves, she realized as she explained how visual aids shortened teaching time and increased information retention.

They looked as bored as she predicted. This was what they'd been expecting. Carmen had a surprise up her sleeve.

"But those are merely statistics," she said, holding each of their gazes in turn. "Medicine is never about statistics. It's about people. Let me show you the real face of medical photography at Royal Hospital."

Please let the machine work, she prayed. And hit play.

Tyler blossomed before their eyes. The wounded young man curled up in his wheelchair repeating the same lyrics over and over was difficult to watch. She noted the change in their faces as the video revealed his improvement, ending with the glowing teenager who faced the camera and said, "Can I see the rest of the videos, Carmen?"

Even Wayne Goodman was smiling as she froze the video on Tyler's triumphant expression and turned back to face the committee. Plainly, she'd won the chairman's heart. Max shot her a smile of congratulations for a presentation well done. The look hinted at another type of celebration altogether, but he smothered it when the chairman glanced in his direction.

"Now that we've had our 'feel good' moment of the day, can we get down to business?" Andersen cut in.

The scientist in him would abhor her use of an emotional ploy to win them over. No doubt his own presentation had consisted of charts, graphics and scientific study.

A shudder swept through her as Carmen stared into the heat of his fury, imagining the hands he clenched on the table tearing at Barb's lab coat, around Judy's neck, wielding the baseball bat that had destroyed her computer.

A man who could pack that much undisguised hatred into a single glance could be responsible for those horrible acts. In the company of senior management she was safe enough. But what about later? Carmen vowed to call a cab for the ride home.

The computer disk! Her report had absorbed her thoughts for most of Sunday. Max had monopolized the rest. She'd forgotten that the disk was on its way to her through the mail. What if the attacker knew that? Carmen sneaked a glance at her watch. Nearly noon. The mail didn't come until late afternoon. Too early to run home and check.

Wayne caught her stolen glance. "Are there questions for Ms. Day before we break for lunch?"

The chairman cleared her throat. "While you've given us a provocative insight into the power of medical documentation, the question comes down to whether we can afford to allocate money to your budget to begin with. Can you think of any ways the department might be able to generate its own revenue?"

"Well, we could implement a charge-back system," Carmen stammered sounding every bit the fool she felt. That she might have to prepare a rebuttal hadn't occurred to her.

"And make the rest of us pay for your services," Andersen growled. "I don't think so, Ms. Day."

"Internal billing hasn't been successful for other hospitals," Wayne said. "Most of the photography departments ended up closing down."

"We could sell the materials we produce," she blurted, anxious to have some kind of answer. 'I don't know' simply wouldn't suffice, whether it was an honest response or not.

"That would require additional staff and budget for marketing." Andersen's expression turned murderous. "With no guarantees of success."

"We simply can't afford it," the chairman agreed.

"We simply can't afford medical photography," Andersen added.

Carmen held Andersen's gaze, matching the anger she saw there with her own. "How can we not afford it?" She motioned to Tyler's face frozen on the VCR behind her. "How are you going to tell that young boy his future isn't worth it? Hope was as much a part of his recovery as medical procedure. Would you take that away from him, Dr. Andersen?"

The question hung in the air. Neither Goodman nor the chairman offered a rebuttal. Max wisely kept silent, but she caught the proud gleam in his eye.

"You have no proof of your claim," Andersen chortled.

Carmen rested her hands on the table and leaned forward. Let him strangle me here and now, at least I'll go down fighting. "Neither do you," she said.

Andersen rose from his chair and took a step toward her. "That's untrue." He directed his next comments to the chairman. "Ms. Day talks the talk as they say. However, her department's record isn't quite as impressive on paper. On five occasions this year, I've had equipment break down during important presentations. Recently an irreplaceable piece of videotape was ruined because equipment wasn't maintained. In addition, she was responsible for losing—"

"That's enough, Jim." Goodman's voice broke the tension in the boardroom. "It's noon. Let's break for lunch."

"I think we should," the chairman said, visibly relieved. "Thank you for a thought-provoking presentation, Ms. Day."

Caught in an act of open aggression, Andersen had no choice but to take his seat. Wayne Goodman opened the door and motioned for the dietary assistant to wheel in the coffee and sandwiches. Carmen collected her videotape and fled.

"You prepped her, didn't you?" she heard Andersen accuse Max as she passed. She didn't wait long enough to hear his reply.

A thought-provoking presentation, Carmen mimicked to the empty elevator. Yeah, I bet. A few banal pleasantries, the obligatory 'thank you' and they'd hustled her out the door so they could debate her future without her.

"Hope you choke on your crustless egg sandwiches," she growled, letting herself into her office.

Since last week, she'd developed the habit of checking the back room every time she came into her office. She even found herself holding her breath as she unlocked the door, checking to make sure it was locked and not standing open the way she'd found it before. Nothing out of place. She sat on her desk, her feet resting on her swivel chair and wrapped her arms about herself for comfort.

Why hadn't she prepared a rebuttal? Why hadn't Max at least told her what to expect?

The adrenaline surge that had been sustaining her since morning abruptly ran out, leaving her feeling completely drained. She should take the afternoon off. Certainly she deserved it. She'd worked all weekend. Wayne had ordered Barbara to take a couple of days off work. Her staff could handle an outbreak of flu, he'd argued. They were trained professionals. Carmen sorely missed her company. At any other time they might have stolen half an hour sitting in Barb's office with the door locked, eating chocolate chip cookies and complaining about the world's cruelty. Barbara had already experienced enough of the world's cruelty firsthand, her conscience reminded her. The only remedy for today's bad mood was hard work.

Carmen eyed the growing pile of requisitions, suddenly remembering poor Mr. Harding. She'd promised

him an enlargement of his late wife's picture to hang
in his living room. He'd probably look at that photo
every day. At least someone appreciates my hard
work.

Once she was fired, there'd be no one to question
about the photography allocation, who that one
enlargement had gone to. Carmen picked up the pile
of requisitions and headed for the darkroom. She'd
make Mr. Harding a 16 X 20.

But the darkroom door didn't lock. The velvet
blackness she usually found a refuge from work made
her uneasy. Squinting into the darkness, she imagined she saw shadows moving in the depths of the
room. Footsteps crossed the outer office. Opening the
door would ruin the print she was working on.

Relax, it's probably Mandy coming to dump some
more requisitions in your in-basket. Mandy knew better than to open the darkroom door when the red light
was on.

The feeling of being watched intensified. There's no
one in here but me, she told herself. Maybe darkroom
work wasn't the best remedy for her bad mood. She'd
finish Mr. Harding's photo, then file negatives for the
rest of the afternoon.

She turned her attention back to the outline of the
photograph developing in the red shadows of the safety light. Mrs. Harding in the last weeks of her life,
smiling at the sight of the birthday cake bearing a
multitude of candles. And behind her—

Carmen gasped. The wet photograph slid from her
grip, back into the developing tray. Carmen seized it
with the tongs, hands shaking. She tilted it again into
the light, straining to see the detail in the crimson
shadows. If what she thought she saw was accurate...then the attacker's identity lay beneath her very
fingertips.

Carmen held the sopping photograph closer. Her gaze slid past smiling Mrs. Harding, scanning the row of staff members behind her. Nurses, health care aides, Joan from O.T.

Standing right behind Mrs. Harding, his hand reaching out in a posture that had come to be terrifyingly familiar to her, was John Forbes. It had just been announced that the services of maintenance and housekeeping would soon be contracted out and the staff laid off. That would give him a motive.

Question was: Did John Forbes have a nasty scar across the palm of his hand.

Her eyes zeroed in on the blurry photograph. Forbes reached out his hand to take an offered piece of birthday cake. But it was his stance that reminded her vividly of another—the frame of videotape she'd captured from the surveillance camera.

Nearly identical, the pose, the angle of the hand. Reaching out for birthday cake, or reaching out to strangle an innocent woman. Her heart skipped a beat, then resumed double-time. She wouldn't know until she enlarged that section of the photograph.

In the outer office, the phone rang. Carmen dumped the photograph into the wash.

"Screening your calls?" Max asked.

"Just trying to get some darkroom work done." The words came out hollow, distracted.

"I had a heck of time getting by that receptionist of yours. You'd think she was working for the CIA." When Carmen didn't respond to his half-hearted attempt at a joke, he continued. "I wanted to congratulate you on an amazing presentation, but Goodman had me tied up in that meeting for hours. I'd say you've got the Chairman on board, but Andersen spent most of the time trying to convince Wayne you have absconded with my brain and I'm now incapable of

making a decision by myself." Carmen heard his
words with half her attention, her mind racing ahead.
Silence stretched between them. The phone line crack-
led. "Carmen, are you all right?"

"No," she said too quickly, then, "Listen, Max. I
have a hunch that might be useful in solving the identity of Barb and Judy's attacker. But I need you to do
something for me."

Another hesitation, broken only by static on the
line. Voices seeped into her office from outside in the
hallway. Shift change. "Are you sure it's safe for you to
get involved in this? Look what happened to Barb and
Judy."

"I'm already involved in it, Max. As long as I sit
here passively I'm a victim. I'm not going to be safe
until that guy's in custody. I think I might be on to
something that will speed up the process."

"Okay, you're right. I'm convinced. What do you
want me to do?"

"I mailed myself a copy of the disk. The one Barb
was carrying in the pocket of her lab coat when she
was attacked. I think that's what he was after. He
kept saying people ought to mind their own business
and stuff like that. Don't you see, Max. He knew I was
on to him. He knew Barb had the disk."

"So you put the last copy in the mail, putting it
beyond anyone's reach, even yours," Max finished.

"It might be sitting in my mailbox this minute. My
mail usually comes at three o'clock, sharp. I can't risk
leaving it there." Carmen drummed her fingers on the
desk impatiently.

"And you want me to rob your mailbox?"

"It's not stealing, Max. It's my mail and I asked you
to go get it."

"What if the neighbors see me? What if the mail-
man catches me?"

"Now you're being paranoid. Just stroll up to my house. There's only one mailbox. All the tenants use it. If there's anything at all for me, bring it back here."

"Tampering with the mail is federal offense, Carmen."

"I'll testify on your behalf if you get caught," she snapped, growing impatient. I'd do it myself, but there's one more clue I need to nail down so I can be sure."

"Can't you do it somewhere else? I don't like you being up there alone after what happened Saturday and that lunatic letting himself into your office."

"I need the darkroom. The negative's sitting in the enlarger. It'll only be a few more minutes." Carmen craned her neck to see into the darkroom. Everything lay as she had left it, the enlarger waiting for another exposure, the red light spilling out into the lengthening shadows of afternoon, the incriminating print drifting in the wash tray.

Max let go his breath in a rush. "Okay, I'll check your mail, but I'm coming up there as soon as I get back and both of us are going home to my place. No overtime tonight, Carmen. I don't like the sounds of any of this."

"Thanks, Max."

"Be careful until I get back. Promise?"

"I promise." A sudden thought occurred to her. "Watch out for Mrs. Landreth downstairs. Don't let her catch you rifling the mail. She's a really busybody."

"Great," Max said without much enthusiasm.

"Hey, I said I'd testify. Just tell her you're my brother."

"After all the noise we made on Thursday, I doubt she'd believe that."

"Probably not," Carmen agreed. Hanging up the phone, she shut the door to the darkroom and went back to work.

Squinting into the enlarger lens, Carmen sectioned off a piece of the picture. If she blew it up too far she'd lose definition and end up with a blurry, flesh-colored smear. An eight-by-ten would be too big. Even a five-by-seven would be risky. Maybe a four-by-six. She decided to make them all, just in case.

Halfway through the first exposure, she realized she'd forgotten to check the outer office.

□ □ □

I have a hunch... Her words echoed in the silence of the room. He knew she was dangerous, even before he'd eavesdropped on her conversation. She had him pegged.

It was his own fault. He'd been remiss. Instead of jumping the Downey woman he should have dealt with that Carmen Day character first. Fate made the choice for him. He had to act. Now, before she discovered anything else.

The key slid into the lock. Getting a new key had been no trouble at all. He hired all the tradesmen.

Glancing behind him, he made sure the hallway was clear. A dietary aide wheeled a cart down the back hall, not even glancing in his direction. The surveillance camera pointed in his direction was no threat. A metal slug strategically placed in the coaxial cable looked after that problem. In a few minutes Stan might realize the feed from the eleventh floor was blank, but by then he'd be long gone.

He flexed gloved fingers, testing the length of wire in his hands. Hopefully, he wouldn't need it. If he could destroy the evidence, there'd be nothing to link him to the crimes. If not, well, it was all her fault anyway. If she'd been smart enough to mind her own business, neither of them would be in this situation.

Silence greeted him in the outer office. He yanked the black ski mask down over his face. He checked the back room where she kept equipment. An empty counter still bearing the telltale square of dust where the computer used to sit stared back at him. He drifted back into the outer office, his gaze settling on the phone on the desk. Reaching down, he ripped the jack from the wall. Wouldn't do to have any unscheduled interruptions just now.

So where was she?

A flashing red light drew his eyes upward. Darkroom in use. How very convenient. Being trapped in the darkroom would make it doubly difficult for her to escape. Insulation would deaden the sound. Best of all, it would offer him the privacy he needed to get the job done.

His fingers closed on the handle to the darkroom door.

□ □ □

Your imagination's running away with you. You were just out there. Surely you'd notice someone lurking in your office.

Vibrations she'd taken for footsteps crossed the floor. Inching closer to the darkroom door.

It's probably just someone walking down the main hallway. The darkroom's outer wall bordered the hallway. Vibrations carried; she'd noticed that effect on a few occasions. To open the darkroom door now would ruin her last few minutes' work, not to mention waste the supplies she'd already taken liberty with in making a free print for Mr. Harding.

She dumped the second exposure into the developing tray and transferred the first to the fix. With a furtive glance in the direction of the outer office, she counted off the minutes before she could open the door.

Outside, she felt another of those shuffling footsteps that could be an intruder in her office, or the dietary cart being wheeled down the adjoining hall. Impulsively, she took the negative from the enlarger. Can't be too careful with the evidence around here. Sliding it back into its wax-paper sleeve, she tucked it in her pocket.

Footsteps stopped in front of the darkroom door. Definitely not in the mail hall. Carmen whirled toward the sound.

The door flew open.

◻ ◻ ◻

Max Deveraux straightened his tie. Wrapping himself in an air of authority, he strode up the path to the front door of Carmen's apartment as if he were its owner.

Like they wouldn't arrest a mail thief in a suit. He paused, looked both ways, and climbed the last few steps. I can't believe I'm doing this. And sometime that day he had to prepare his final recommendations to present to Wayne Goodman tomorrow. He should be at his desk working. Instead, he'd let Carmen talk him into one of her conspiracy theories.

He peered through the glass window into the tiny entrance. The stately old house had been divided up into apartments years ago, but he could see where the original foyer had stood, its grandeur crudely partitioned with drywall to give the tenants privacy. If old Mrs. Landreth—he had no doubt that was the woman who had glared at him as he was leaving last week—was about, she kept behind the partition of her own door and was silent.

Max slid his hand into the mailbox, fingers closing on a thick bundle of mail. He pulled it out into the light. Names he didn't recognize, a couple of letters for a Mrs. B. Landreth. Finally at the bottom, a padded express mail envelope addressed in Carmen's handwriting to C. Day.

"What do you think you're doing?" a voices said, sounding remarkably like an old gate creaking.

Max whirled, finding no one in his line of sight. The door to the house was still shut. No one stood behind the glass window.

"Answer me! What do you think you're doing with my mail?"

His gaze was dragged downward by that grating voice, down to the hedge-obscured path that ran between the houses. Standing at the base of the front porch was the glaring woman he recognized from his early morning escape. With her tiny figure obscured by a voluminous apron and shawl, she didn't seem so imposing when he looked down on her from a height of six feet or so.

Until she rapped the wooden handle of her rake against the porch. "Stay right there while I call the police."

As if she expected him to. He had the frightening suspicion that's exactly what she had in mind. The thought brought a smile to his lips. Her frown deepened. And then it struck him who she reminded of.

Carmen. Ms. Carmen Day, who would storm into his office and give a stranger what for. Flash forward sixty years to a wizened old Carmen who just might threaten a man fifty years her junior with a rake.

"No need to call the police, ma'am." Max hastened down the steps. Mrs. Landreth backed up a step, still brandishing the rake. "I'm just picking up a piece of mail for a friend." He held up the package for her to squint at through her bottle-thick glasses.

"Who's your friend?" she demanded, giving away the fact that she couldn't read what was written on the envelope.

"Miss Day." Her scowl intensified, deep lines spreading out from the corners of her mouth as if her face might fold up on itself. Beady dark eyes held him transfixed. "I'm..." His own words shocked him. "I'm her fiancé." He held out his hand in introduction. "Max Deveraux."

She left his hand hanging there in midair, glancing at it as if it might bite. "She never mentioned no fiancé."

"We just got engaged this weekend." She wasn't buying it, he realized. He handed over the package for her to scrutinize close up. "Carmen needs this package for work. But she's tied up, so she asked me to come and get it."

Mrs. Landreth glanced from the package back to him. The expression in those bird's eyes told him she didn't believe the story one bit.

"But I've got a meeting myself in a few minutes, so I'm going to have to leave." He pried the package from her gnarled fingers.

"Fine, sonny. You run along." Mrs. Landreth leaned on her rake. "But rest assured, I intend to discuss this with Miss Day. If she doesn't profess to know you, I will be calling the police."

Max backed away down the path. "Good day, ma'am."

Only his pride stopped him from running back to Royal Hospital.

◻ ◻ ◻

Light. Impossibly bright. A shadow raced toward her.

Blinded, Carmen raised her arm. An ineffectual protection against the impact that sent her flying backward into the counter.

She hit with a jarring blow to the kidneys. Developing trays scattered beneath her, spraying chemicals. Pain arced through her lower back. The acrid smell of developer filled the air.

Wetness seeped through her suit. The door swung shut behind him. Pinned against the counter by his weight, she could only stare up at his shadow above her, illuminated by the ghostly glow of the crimson safety light.

"Where is it?" he hissed, thick gloved fingers groping around behind her.

Carmen freed a hand. Levering it between them, she tried to pry herself loose.

"Stay still, you meddling little fool." He thrust his weight against her, dissuading her from further movement. She could feel every muscle through the rough clothes he wore, smell the scent of an unwashed body, the smell of which had been unsuccessfully covered up with deodorant. The sensation sickened her. His maleness didn't feel at all like...

Like Max. Who ought to be returning any time. Perhaps she could stall him that long.

"Where is what?" she gasped.

"The evidence you were telling your damned friend about. Sleeping with him, are you? See if you think he's so fine when you're standing in the unemployment line."

"What evidence?" Carmen shut her eyes. Max, hurry please!

Iron hands closed around her throat. "You know damned well what I'm talking about. Hand it over, before I have to choke it out of you."

Stale breath laced with old tobacco gusted across her face. His maleness pressed against her as he pinned her to the counter. A desperate urge to be sick washed over her.

She thrashed against the counter, freeing a leg. Getting it between them, putting the force of her will in that one kick to his groin.

Her attacker uttered a grunt of pain. He doubled up in a vain attempt to protect himself.

Carmen sprang free. Through thick, red air, she raced for the door. Her fingers brushed the door knob.

A hand seized the fabric of her jacket, yanking her abruptly backward. Flailing, her grasping fingers closed on one of the overturned trays still dripping chemicals across the counter and onto the floor. In the crimson light it looked like blood.

He turned her toward him, hands already closing again on her neck. Using the tray as a club, she attempted to bash him over the head with it. A thick arm arced out of nowhere, sending her aim wide. The tray collided with the side of his head.

Stumbling, he dragged her with him. Her hands clawed at the side of the counter, sliding through red liquid, leaving wet trails.

Until the two of them crashed to the floor.

Breath burst from her lungs. Carmen gasped, but the weight atop her wouldn't allow her lungs to expand. She hauled in an insubstantial breath of pure fire. Her attacker's mask hovered inches from her face, a black smear against the blood-red light.

Stale sweat filled her nostrils. Her stomach heaved.

"If you want to be nasty about it..." He reached into his pocket, holding her with his weight to the wet floor. Something thin, black sprang loose from his hand. A length of wire.

"Please." Carmen forced the plea from her lips.

□ □ □

Late already for the meeting. Something he'd never been in all of his career. Max tried the door to Carmen's office. Locked.

Had she been called away? Possible, but somehow it didn't seem right. She sounded so desperate on the phone, as if her very life depended upon him retrieving that piece of mail.

"Carmen?" He pounded on the door.

Nothing.

Max pressed his face against the frosted glass. The lights were on inside. He peered inside, noticing the red smear of the darkroom light. She'd said something about working in the darkroom. Had she forgotten about him while he risked his professional reputation running her errands? A pang of anger shot through him.

He knocked again and was greeted only by silence. Putting his ear to the door he listened intently.

A scraping noise followed by a clatter, like something had fallen.

"Carmen?"

The meaty impact of something hitting the floor. A body? He felt the vibration through the soles of his shoes. A scream quickly silenced and muffled by the double doors.

Max threw his weight against the door, but the heavy fire door held securely. He looked wildly around him, but the hallway was empty.

No time to call security. No time to wait while he explained the situation to Stan. No time to wait while the security guard made his way up eleven floors.

Carmen was in there, every instinct shouted at him. And she was in danger.

He turned, raced down the hallway to the emergency phone hanging by the staircase. Dialing the operator, he issued the universal command no one who worked in a hospital would ignore.

"Code Gray, Room 1118!"

Royal Hospital sprang to attention.

Fire doors whooshed into operation, segmenting the hallway in a dance of ghostly closing doors. Alarm bells rang. Emergency personnel ran to their stations. Elevators returned to the basement level.

And the one thing he dearly hoped would happen: power locks sprang open.

Max tore down the carpeted hallway. Slowing down too late, he slammed against the door to Carmen's office. With a click, the lock disengaged and he tumbled into the room.

□ □ □

Carmen thrashed against the attacker's weight. Ramming one of her high heels against his shin brought no results. The wire descended to within inches of her throat.

"Now," her attacker growled. "Are you going to tell me where it is, or do I have to kill you?"

"I'll tell you," she wheezed, stealing in a breath of air laden with his repulsive scent.

He would kill her anyway, she realized. After all, she knew who he was.

Alarm bells sounded overhead. She heard the hiss of locks disengaging.

And then the announcement, to be repeated over and over again until the emergency was declared under control. "Code Gray, Room 1118." All emergency personnel in the hospital were on their way to her office. By the stairs, in directly routed elevators, running down hallways. She just might survive.

Her attacker froze, listening intently. Vibrations betrayed the pounding of heels coming down the hall toward them. Certain he would run now, she renewed her attempts to unseat him.

Instead she felt the bite of wire around her neck. Strangely detached, she wondered how long would it take to die. How long did she have?

Breath choked from her throat. Stars danced in the strange, red light. Her arms flailed, grasping for anything that might save her...

Fingers snatched at the wool fabric of his mask. She yanked it from his face.

The door sprang open, shooting bolts of blinding fluorescent light into the shadows. Bodies poured over the threshold: Max, Stan, Goodman, even Andersen.

Arms seized the attacker, hauling him from her chest. Air rushed into her lungs. She gasped. Acid followed the path of the air. She choked, a terrible wheezing sound that did little to help the situation.

Max's arms around her. His hands, massaging her back, her throat. "It's okay, Carmen, you're safe."

"Try to breathe normally," she heard Andersen say, acting for once like a physician instead of the crusading administrator. She could barely force air past her

bruised throat and lungs. As soon as she could talk
she'd tell him off, but for the moment it took all her
strength just to concentrate on breathing in and out.

"Where the heck are the lights in here?" Wayne
Goodman's voice, disembodied in her red shadows.
The click of a switch.

Light everywhere, her eyes teared after so long in
the darkness. As if gazing through a fish tank, she
watched Wayne walk to the counter, where Stan and
the other security guards had the attacker pinned
between them.

His audible gasp caught the attention of everyone
in the room. "Good God! It's John Forbes."

Forbes glared furiously at Carmen.

"Being maintenance supervisor, he's got keys to the
entire hospital," Stan remarked.

Goodman looked stunned. "But why, John? Why on
earth would you do such a thing?"

"Why?" Forbes whipped his head around to glare at
Goodman. "I'll tell you why. A man works hard all his
life. And what thanks does he get?"

Silence answered his question as Wayne stared
back at him, dumbfounded.

"A damned pink slip. That's the thanks he gets."

The president found his voice. "I knew you were
upset about losing your job, John, but we planned to
keep you on as long as we could to give you a chance
to find another."

"Right, like anyone's going to hire a guy my age,"
Forbes growled, then realizing he was incriminating
himself, fell silent.

"Is that what this is about?" Goodman asked.
Forbes turned his face to the wall.

"I can't see how all this has anything to do with losing a job," said Andersen.

Andersen, the perpetually obtuse, Carmen thought. After a few breaths, her lungs became accustomed to air and she began to breathe deeply. "I do," she croaked.

Andersen and Goodman turned to look at her.

"He got scared and took his frustrations out on the people he considered to be more fortunate than himself. The first of those people just happened to be Judy. But he forgot about the security camera."

Forbes pointedly ignored her, keeping his face to the wall. Goodman nodded for her to continue.

"But he was standing in the security office while you viewed the tape, so he knew it was only a matter of time before you figured out who he was."

"And I gave you the tape to see if you could enhance it," Wayne finished.

"So he staked out my office. When I left, he let himself in and took the tape."

"That would have been the end of it, except that you managed to copy a frame," Max added. He patted his pocket. "Got your mail for you."

"He didn't understand the equipment enough to know a dub was running. And I did manage to salvage a frame of a hand with a scar on it. While Forbes was staking out my office, he heard me tell Barb to keep a copy safe for me." Carmen covered her mouth with her hands. "Oh God, I practically set Barbara up to be attacked."

"Should have kept your damned nose out of it," Forbes said.

"Be quiet," Goodman ordered.

Talking hurt her throat, but Carmen continued anyway. "I saved the file to my hard drive just in case, and made a third copy for myself."

"Not knowing computers, he figured taking a baseball bat to your computer would solve that problem."

Stan tightened his grip on Forbes. "Where on earth are the police?" he muttered. The sound of sirens answered him.

Carmen quickened the pace of her story, knowing she would have to tell it all again to the police. It would hurt her throat more, but she had to get it all off her chest this very minute. "Once the computer was destroyed, I knew I had to guard the only evidence I had, so I mailed the disk to myself. That way no one could get their hands on it."

"Why didn't you tell us this?" Goodman faced her with equal parts anger and concern. "You've put yourself in a great deal of danger."

"I wasn't sure until I saw the photograph."

"What photograph?" came a chorus of voices.

Carmen motioned to the carnage in the dark room. In the light she could plainly see the evidence of their struggle. The overturned trays, supplies scattered across the counter, the halfdeveloped prints lying on the floor. "The photograph I was enlarging for the husband of one of our late residents."

Supported by Max, Carmen got unsteadily to her feet. Picking up the abandoned print, she turned it into the light, revealing a blurry image of a hand, marred by the shadow of scar running through the center of the palm. Hopelessly underexposed and grainy, but if the negative hadn't been damaged, she could still make another copy. "This is what I found in the background."

Goodman looked over her shoulder. "That's what he was after?"

Carmen nodded. "He heard me tell Max to get my mail, so I could compare the two images." She jutted her chin in Forbes' direction. "Have a look at his hand."

"I don't have to show you anything without talking to my lawyer," Forbes snarled.

Outside, sirens screeched to a stop. "Tell that to the police," Wayne said.

But Stan yanked Forbes' right hand into the light. Across his right palm ran a thick, jagged scar.

"It's him all right," Goodman said. He squeezed Carmen's shoulder, and for a moment she saw a glimpse of the old Wayne. "Good work," he said quietly. "Once we clean up this mess with the police, perhaps this place can get back to normal."

Back to normal. For Goodman maybe, but not for her. She'd narrowly escaped death only to find the impending loss of her job still hanging over her.

And the man she loved was the one who'd have to fire her.

Chapter Thirteen

"They're going to fire me anyway, aren't they?"

Keeping one eye fixed on the road, Max turned to stare at her. "That doesn't sound much like the Carmen Day I've come to know."

"I don't feel much like myself." She addressed Max's reflection in the glass. "I feel beaten."

"The Carmen Day I thought I knew would never give up so easily."

"What's left to do once you've done your best and it wasn't good enough?"

"You re-think the situation," Max said softly. "Sometimes all it takes is a change in attitude."

"You sound like Wayne Goodman. If I hear one more word about attitude adjustment, I'm going to—" She stopped, dismayed to hear John Forbes' desperation in her own voice. Deep down, she could understand how knowing no other way to express his pain, Forbes had lashed out at others. Others he thought were more fortunate than himself.

"You're jumping to the wrong conclusions, Carmen. Aside from the services we're going to contract out, nothing's been decided yet. Wayne Goodman clearly values your services. You certainly won the chairman over with your presentation. And you've proved yourself as a forensics expert as well."

"What about you, Max? Did I win you over with my presentation as well?"

He glanced back at the road. "You've won me over in a lot of ways."

"You didn't answer my question." She turned to look at him. Max pointedly directed his attention to his driving.

"I can't answer your question, Carmen. That would land me right in the middle of a huge conflict of interest. Andersen's already on my case about my relationship with you."

"Our relationship is a conflict of interest for both of us," Carmen snapped.

"Yes," Max agreed, "it is."

"Which means you're going to have to make a choice."

He glanced furtively in her direction. "We both will."

The question hovered on the tip of her tongue. If she didn't ask, she might be afforded a few more days of deluding herself that Max cared more about her than his career. Realistically, that was foolish. They'd known each other only a brief time. Was she prepared for his answer?

After the ordeal she'd been through, heartache was the last thing she needed. Today was the turning point, Carmen decided. If Max planned to leave her, she had to know now. "Which way will you decide?"

With a curse, Max pulled the car off the road and on to the shoulder. Head lights swept by them. He undid his seat belt and slid toward her. "I can always get another assignment, Carmen. But as long as I have this one, I have to maintain an unbiased opinion." He placed a finger beneath her chin and turned her face toward him. "That doesn't mean I'd let it destroy my personal life."

"What if Andersen leans on Goodman to fire you because of conflict of interest? Then we'd both be out of jobs."

Soft lips settled against hers, tenderly, so as not to
hurt any of her many bruises. "I'm a consultant," Max
whispered. "I'm always out of work. We can job hunt
together."

It sounded so simple when Max said it. The
nomadic life suited him. Carmen pulled out of his
embrace. Somehow she had to make him understand.
"It's not so simple for me, Max. My entire life has
revolved around Royal Hospital since my mom became
ill. I have no one I can turn to, no family..." Her words
trailed off into silence.

"No family at all?"

"Just an aunt on my father's side. But I haven't
seen her for years."

Now why had she told him that? He was going to
ask the question, the one she couldn't answer without
tears.

Streetlights glittered in Max's dark eyes. "What
happened to your father, Carmen?"

Her mouth moved. Tears choked her voice. She'd
sobbed even when she'd told Barbara about it.

"Is he dead?" Max asked softly.

His father died in a horrible accident. One he'd wit-
nessed. Loss of a parent was something Max would
understand.

Carmen shook her head, squeezed the words past
her bruised throat, choked now on tears. "He left when
I was very young."

"I'm sorry."

She waved him to silence, struggling to get the
words out intact. "He remarried, had a son, forgot
about us. But I guess all my life I harbored the dream
that he'd come back, say he was sorry, that it had all
been a big mistake."

"All children wish these things," Max said. "It's
only natural. I used to imagine my dad's accident was

a mistake, too. Mom spent her days in school and her nights working, trying to support us. I had far too much time on my own. Too much time to think. I made up little scenarios in my mind that Dad hadn't been killed, that he was suffering from amnesia in a hospital somewhere and any day he'd regain his memory and come home."

He paused. His shoulders heaved with his indrawn breath. "Even though I saw him climb into that car myself. Even though I went to his funeral. It's not a crime to wish things were different. But it is a shame to waste your life longing for things that can never be."

He understood, really understood, the way no one else had. Carmen had gone through the same cycle of denial, then painful acceptance. "The whole time Mom was dying, I kept thinking he would come. Day after day, I watched her slip away. Each day I waited for him to come. He never did. That's when I had to face up to the fact that he never would."

Max reached for her, pulled her closer. She rested her head against the warmth of his wool suit jacket, realizing she wasn't going to cry this time after all. His next words surprised her. "Is that what you're afraid of? That I'm going to leave too?"

She raised her head. "I guess I am. It's hard to believe in the power of love when the first man in your life thought you were so worthless."

Warm hands circled her neck, tenderly massaging her nape, tipping her head back so he could look deeply into her eyes. "It's also a crime to let your fears prevent you from living your life."

□ □ □

He just couldn't do it.

Max leaned against the door frame. Carmen sprawled in the middle of his large bed. Sleep relaxed her features, making her seem much younger. Her complete abandonment offered him a rare insight into the Carmen he'd seen only once; the first night they'd made love. What kind of person would she be, he wondered, if she'd grown up loved and cherished? If fate hadn't stolen both parents at a young age? Would she still have the steely determination, the fire he so admired?

Or would she be more like the confident sleeper, sure in her talent, her beauty, her place in the world? Which would he like better?

Of one thing he was sure. He couldn't be the arm of another cruel fate. He couldn't steal her job and leave her to flounder alone again.

Goodman and Andersen were right. If he didn't know her, none of it would matter. But he did know her. Just like he'd known another department head whose inner fire had once captivated him.

In those early days, none of it had mattered. Drunk on money and power, he'd reveled in the reorganization of hospitals like a well-matched chess game.

It didn't seem like so much fun, once he'd had a glimpse into the human cost of downsizing. He dismissed the many rumors about him as so much gossip, but Carmen's accusations stung. As much as he hated to admit it, perhaps some truth lay at the heart of the matter. Though his personal philosophy involved bringing order to chaos, adding balance and harmony, he did put people out of work for a living.

Budget just wasn't there for everyone who needed it anymore. Work followed him home, leaked into his thoughts. He found himself worrying about the fate of all the people he was going to have to fire. Not all of them would find new jobs. Some would lose their homes, maybe even their spouses as marriages cracked under the pressure.

Like John Forbes, the strain would unravel their lives completely.

He could take only one of them into his life. Carmen would be safe, he'd make sure of that. He made good money. He could afford to support her. But what about the others?

Carmen turned over in her sleep, stealing both pillows and most of the blankets. He'd have a battle even getting a foot of space to sleep on when he came to bed.

She filled his life the same way, rearranging things, changing his perspective forever.

"Max, my boy, I think it might be time for a career change," he muttered in the same inflection as his late father, then smiled. Perhaps it was. He had his MBA, other careers besides downsizing hospitals existed.

His gaze lingered wistfully on Carmen for another moment. Then Max went downstairs toward the make-shift office he'd set up in the dining room.

To find a way to keep Carmen's job.

□ □ □

Numbers danced before his eyes. Columns of numbers swaying, totals rippling as if under water. Max rested his forehead against his hands. He'd already trimmed to the bone. Further trimming netted him only a pathetic ten thousand dollars more. A gruesome budget at that. He needed another thirty just to pay her salary. She'd scream when she saw the ten thousand dollar budget.

With good reason. Equipment rotted in the dark room, growing decrepit from disrepair. Repair shops had trouble even finding parts for some of her photog-

raphy equipment. The computer lay in pieces in the
evidence cupboard at police headquarters. Video documentation depended on an unruly camera that
screamed for the services of a qualified repair technician.

Axing the department was the only logical conclusion. Out-source the services. Let the local university
worry about maintaining and buying new equipment.
Crusaders like Andersen would have to find the cash
for medical photography within their own budgets.

But the medical photography department at the
local university wouldn't have Carmen's intuitive
touch. No one would take the time to listen to a disabled teenager who desperately wanted to be well
again. The university wouldn't be buying "Deep Space
Shoot Out" out of their own pockets. For reasons that
had nothing to do with hard cash and bottom line,
Carmen would be terribly missed by Royal Hospital.

He rubbed tired eyes and picked up his red pencil.
Ten thousand was a start, better than his previous
forecast. Carmen had gained serious support by solving the mystery of the vicious attacks, by her participation in Tyler's recovery. If he could find the means
to keep her department, administration just might
buy it. Goodman wanted to keep her. His admiration
was obvious. If both Goodman and the chairman voted
in her favor, Andersen would just have to live with it.

Andersen. Max tapped his pencil against the table.
Time to have another look at Andersen's budget.

Dr. James Andersen was used to a more generous
budget than the staff that he supervised. Certainly he
could trim a couple of thousand dollars more, Max
thought. Penny change. Not the thirty thousand he
needed. He was tired. He should go to bed. But he
couldn't give up on Carmen. Not after his gallant
speech in the car. Too much depended on his word. If

he proved untrustworthy, she'd never trust another man again.

He rubbed his eyes again forcing his blurry vision into focus. Columns of numbers shimmered, settled.

And then he saw it.

A curious pattern running throughout Andersen's budget. Duplicated entries, cleverly disguised as other expenses. A healthy expense account labeled medical supplies. If he hadn't looked at the print-out, he never would have noticed that several thousand dollars of "medical supplies" had been purchased from L'Ambiance restaurant.

Several columns ingeniously labeled, duplicated other columns. Miscellaneous expenses and purchased services all contained the same sort of entries. Max whistled, his lethargy suddenly vanishing. None of the columns added up to expenses that were out of line. Wily Dr. James Andersen wasn't that stupid. At first glance, nothing at all seemed out of order. Andersen had made a point of commenting that each year he'd brought his expenses in just under budget.

No wonder, Max thought. He billed everything, including his personal dry cleaning, to Royal Hospital.

Max dug into the filing box sitting on the floor of the dining room and brought out the last two years' budgets.

Purchased services contained several billings from the medical photography at the university. Max scratched his head. Carmen's services were more than adequate. Superior to what he'd seen at other institutions. So why, if he already overloaded Carmen's production schedule, did he depend so heavily upon "purchased services" from the university?

Exorbitant long distance bills, made on one of the only phones in the hospital that had long distance clearance. Max shook his head. Who on earth was

Andersen calling? A curmudgeon like Andersen could-
n't have that many friends. He pulled out the supplies
budget for nursing. The two should be comparable.
But Andersen's named a sum several times that of
nursing services, and all neatly labeled, disguised in
plain view of administration as "other expenses."

Long distance phone bills, supplies, entertainment,
the list was starting to sound remarkably like Max's
own accounts as a private consultant.

The pencil fell from his hand, rolling across the
table before falling silently to the carpet. Max leapt
from his chair. Where had he put the phone books the
technician had given him when he installed the
phone?

Half an hour of slugging through boxes later, Max
found the directory, lying on the faded carpet buried
beneath a mountain of file crates. He flipped open the
personal section, easily finding Andersen's personal
number, ANDERSEN, DR. JAMES H. followed by a
slew of initials signifying an impressive list of medical
degrees.

Max turned to the business section. Nothing under
Andersen. He grabbed the Yellow Pages. Nothing in
the alphabetical listing. Max cursed under his breath.
He was on to something, he could feel it.

His eyes settled upon a two-by-two-inch square
advertisement in a thick black border: "J.H.A. Medical
Consulting."

He flipped back to the residential listing. Same
exchange. Probably because it was housed in
Andersen's residence. The old chime clock in the dining room signaled twelve. Too late to call.

But he had to know. Assuming Andersen didn't
have call identification, he could always hang up. Or
he could claim a desperate need to clarify something

in Andersen's budget, say he missed Andersen's listing in the white pages.

Hell, Andersen probably turned the ringer off his
business phone at that hour, just like he did.
Throwing caution to the wind, Max dialed the number.

"You've reached J.H.A. Medical Consulting, an
answering machine informed him.

Andersen's voice. Max hung up the phone. "You
worm," he whispered.

"Who is?" asked a sleepy voice from the doorway.

He looked up to find Carmen standing on the
threshold, wearing his sweatshirt and nothing else.
Her short hair was disheveled, her green eyes still
heavy with sleep. Fleece hung to mid-thigh, covering
her modestly enough, but he couldn't keep his mind
from conjuring up images of what he knew lay
beneath. His conscience slammed the brakes on such
thoughts, reminding him of what she'd been through
in the past few hours.

"Who's a worm?" she repeated.

"Andersen." He ground the name out like a curse.

Carmen smiled. "The whole world knows that,
Max."

She was right about that. Andersen had few sup-
porters, except himself. Hospital management
deferred to him out of respect for his position as chief
of staff, but he'd never heard anyone mention his
name fondly. "No, really." He held out a hand, and she
came toward him. He caught the gentle sway of her
breasts beneath the fleece, the smell of his own soap
and shampoo that she'd borrowed. "Tell me what you
make of this."

"What am I looking at?" She leaned over the table,
hiking the sweatshirt's hem even higher.

Max forced his mind back to the spreadsheet.
"Andersen's accounts."

Red-gold eyebrows raised in surprise. The last vestiges of sleep vanished from her face. "Should you be showing me this?"

"No, actually. It's highly confidential. But if what I think is here, then Andersen's committed enough improprieties to last himself a lifetime. Maybe even earn himself a jail sentence."

Taking a yellow highlighter, he marked the suspicious entries, tracing them from the account summary back to the breakdown on the more detailed printouts.

"My God," Carmen breathed, following the line of his evidence. "What do you think he's doing with all those supplies."

"Here's where it gets really interesting." Max ripped the advertisement from the Yellow Pages and handed it to her.

"J.H.A. Medical Consulting?" Green eyes narrowed into slits. "He's running his own company and subsidizing it through Royal Hospital. The worm!"

"My sentiments exactly."

"That would explain why he needed so much work from me, why no matter what I did, it was never enough." She stopped, pondering a new train of thought. "Do you think he was selling my work?"

"Probably."

"But why would he want me fired?"

"So he could have all of your budget, I'd imagine."

Carmen picked up another spreadsheet, stared at it for a moment, then tossed it down in disgust. "How long did he think he could get away with this?"

"Forever, I guess. Those entries are buried deep. Likely figured he'd hide it all in plain sight."

"No wonder he wanted to make you his friend. No wonder he turned nasty when he figured out you weren't."

"He certainly didn't want me looking too closely. Since he found out about us, he's been trying to undermine me with Goodman."

"No one at Royal Hospital would dare question him. He's been there too long, he's a powerful part of the administration."

"It's about time someone shook the place up," Max said, then added, "I mean, if there's stuff like this going on."

"Royal Hospital's been around for over 150 years. While I don't agree with you, the way we used to do our budgets was to take last year's figure and add fifteen percent. Administration okayed it. Just like that. Under that old system, I guess you could get away with something like this for quite awhile."

"Re-thinking a system that doesn't work isn't a crime, Carmen. There are times when it's the only decent thing to do."

She scowled her disagreement at him. But then her eyes caught something in the spreadsheet. Her finger moved along the column. "Max, look at this."

He followed the line of the yellow as she marked off a series of billings from a pharmaceutical company. All were marked as supplies, syringes, gloves, gauze. But the prices quoted were way out of line. "It can't be," he muttered in disbelief. But the figures didn't lie.

Carmen spoke aloud the dark revelation dawning on him. "Andersen's selling drugs!"

They looked at each other in the dim light of the dining room.

"What are you going to do?" she asked finally. "He's not going to take this lying down."

Max felt his shoulders tightening already with the threat of the upcoming confrontation. Proof was needed. If he went barreling in there without solid documentation, he'd lose his credibility forever. "First, I'm going to go back over these figures, back up my allegations. Then I'm taking this to Goodman and the chairman of the board."

"Let me come with you."

He pulled her close, pressed a kiss to her forehead. She was still warm from sleeping, and more than anything he wanted to take off that sweatshirt and crawl back into bed with her. "You can't, little tigress. As much as I'd appreciate your support, you've got to stay out of this. Royal Hospital has some serious decisions to make in the next few days. The ruling regarding your department should be made on your own merits. Don't get yourself involved in this. It's going to be ugly enough as it is."

"Why is it always the decent hardworking people that get hurt?"

"Devils like Andersen only get away with their tricks for so long, Carmen. Don't let one scheming jerk ruin your outlook."

"I had a less flattering word in mind for Andersen."

In spite of his exhaustion, Max laughed. He pulled her close again for one last hug, then turned her in the direction of the staircase. "Go to bed. I think I'm going to be at this for awhile yet. One of us should get some sleep."

◻ ◻ ◻

Max looked in the mirror and groaned. Dark circles ringed his eyes. Even a cold shower couldn't make up for the sleep he'd lost last night. Carmen, under orders from Wayne Goodman, agreed to take the day off. She made eggs for breakfast, forcing him to fortify his body with something other than adrenaline. The strong black coffee helped, but only a little.

Taking in recommendations for the reorganization of an institution always turned out to be difficult. No one wanted to hear the bad news. No one wanted to hear about downsizing and lost jobs. But this time he was walking in with news of embezzlement and black market drug sales. News he might even have to deliver to Andersen's face if he couldn't snag Goodman beforehand.

He drove the couple of blocks, too tired even to walk. A message from Wayne Goodman greeted him as he entered his office. The meeting had been moved up two hours from eleven to nine. Ugly didn't begin to describe what awaited him. Max straightened his tie, grabbed the incriminating paperwork and walked into the boardroom.

They were waiting for him, three grim faces set around the boardroom table just like they anticipated a bad prognosis for a dying patient. The patient would be fine, Max knew. His recommendations allowed Royal Hospital to continue its good work. Without the participation of Dr. James Andersen.

"Let's hear it, Max," Goodman said before he'd even had a chance to sit down.

Andersen's vicious expression made him do a double take. He knows I know, Max thought then dismissed the idea. How could he? Unless he did have a telephone number identification system on his phone.

"Can I have a word with you in private, Wayne? Before we get started."

Goodman shot him a scrutinizing stare. "Any comments you want to make can be said in front of our present company."

Blue eyes held his a moment longer. At nine in the morning Goodman's hair was already disheveled as if he'd been running his hands through it. He did that when he was stressed, Max noted. His heart sank. Andersen's already been at him. So much for the element of surprise. Perhaps he should have called Wayne Goodman at midnight after all.

"Fine," he said tightly. "If you'll turn your attention to my summary on page three."

A rustling of pages, three sets of eyes fastened on his opening remarks. Andersen, he noticed, was busily flipping forward to his revised budget allocation.

"Son of a—"

The chairman jumped at Andersen's outburst.

"Jim?" Goodman asked, equally surprised.

"He's cut my allocation by more than fifty percent! This is totally unacceptable." In emphasis he tossed the report back at Max.

"Perhaps we should let Mr. Deveraux finish his remarks before we begin arguing the fine points," the chairman counseled. A steeliness settled in her gray eyes that Max had not seen before.

But Andersen had snatched back his report. Flipping pages, his face darkened to a shade just above crimson. The report crunched in his fist.

"That's what this is about. He cut my budget so he can fund the woman he's sleeping with!" Shoving the offending page under Goodman's nose, he stabbed at the entry with one thick finger.

"Sit down, Jim," Goodman warned. He glanced down at the budget summary for medical photography.

"If he'd been thinking with his brain instead of his di—"

"Dr. Andersen!" the Chairman protested.

"—he'd realize what a stupid move this is. I won't allow it. This man calls himself an expert, but it's plain to me he doesn't know the simplest things about the running of a medical institution. He's cut medical services so he could fund a non-essential service."

"I disagree. Ms. Day proved in her presentation that medical photography is an essential service," the Chairman remarked.

Time to drop the bomb!

"The budget submitted by Dr. Andersen is far in excess of the funds needed for the running of such a service—"

"How the hell would you know that?" Andersen's complexion darkened yet another shade.

"I've compared it to the budgets of similar institutions and found it to exceed those figures by more than half."

Andersen's fist collided with the table. His lips drew back into a snarl. "I refuse to listen to this uninformed nonsense."

"Enough, Jim," Goodman said sharply. "If you can't control yourself, we'll have to continue this discussion without you."

"After careful examination of these accounts, I've found the reason for these inflated entries to be due to duplication of accounts."

"He's lying!" Andersen rose to a half crouch.

"If you'll turn to the next page, my analysis proves I am not lying."

Goodman ran a hand through his blond hair, tousling it further.

The chairman pulled a pair of half-lens glasses out of her purse for closer look. "This is outrageous," she commented. "These figures are far out of line with the amount of medical intervention we're doing. I can't understand why we require so much." She put down her glasses and stared accusingly at Andersen.

"The truth is, we don't." Max took a deep breath. Here goes. "I've traced all these duplicated entries back to a company called J.H.A. Medical Consulting."

"J-H-A," Goodman said, slowly rolling the letters off his tongue.

"When I called the number listed in the Yellow Pages, it was answered by a message recorded by Dr. Andersen."

"That's a bloody lie!" Andersen lunged across the table, clenched hands aimed for Max's throat.

□ □ □

She never should have let him go in there alone. Carmen paced back and forth in front of the window in Max's living room, debating her course of action.

Max had only met Andersen in the polite confines of the old boy's club of senior management. Fishing trips, after work drinks. He'd never seen Andersen lose it. A glimpse of Dr. James Andersen, senior executive, his face purpled with rage lanced through her memory.

He wouldn't be prepared for Andersen's explosive temper. But she couldn't rush in Royal Hospital wearing only Max's faded sweatshirt and the tailored pants she'd had on yesterday. Surely it would be safe to go back to her apartment now, Carmen thought. Forbes was in custody. Andersen, unfortunately, was still a respected member of Royal Hospital's senior staff.

Until Max dethroned him.

Grabbing her purse, she headed back to her own apartment to change.

A meeting was already in progress when she arrived at Goodman's office. Relieved, she noticed Judy back at her post.

"Welcome back, Jude—" she started to say. A heavy thud, followed by the sounds of a scuffle cut off the rest of her sentence.

□ □ □

Max stepped back abruptly out of range of the hands aimed for his throat, but not fast enough to avoid a spray of spittle. The chairman shot to her feet. Her chair teetered on two legs, then fell to the floor with a clatter.

Having missed Max the first time, Andersen rounded the table intent on his target. Goodman stepped between them.

Thwarted by Goodman, Andersen stabbed a finger at Max. "That is a very dangerous allegation, mister. You're going to hear from my lawyer."

"It's not slander if it's true," Goodman said. "Is it true, Jim?"

Andersen's color had faded from crimson to gray-white. "Who are you going to believe? Your colleague of over ten years, or a man who's clearly in a conflict of interest? Are you really going to let him axe my department so he can give the money to his lover?"

"Rest assured, Royal Hospital will be looking into both of these allegations before making any decisions." The chairman crossed her arms. "I certainly hope for your sake, Dr. Andersen, that Mr. Deveraux is wrong."

"I can't believe you're not going to do anything about him!" Andersen took another step towards Max, sandwiching Wayne Goodman between them.

Seeing the situation deteriorating quickly toward violence, the chairman opened the door and stepped into Goodman's outer office.

"Judy, call security to the Boardroom immediately." She glanced back into the boardroom, then added quickly, "Call the police as well."

Judy was already staring in the direction of the boardroom, alerted no doubt by sounds of a scuffle on the far side of the wall. Carmen took a step a step toward them, but just then Andersen burst from Goodman's hold, half-falling into the reception area.

"It's all her fault!" he growled, eyes fastening on Carmen. "He's sleeping with her!"

Judy's mouth fell open in shock. But before she could say anything, Andersen whirled on Max. Goodman restrained Andersen with a firm hand against his chest. Foiled, Andersen clawed at Max as if his arms could stretch the distance between them.

Hurried footsteps sounded outside in the corridor.

"He's the real criminal," Andersen shouted. "He's the one with the conflict of interest."

"You're right," Max said. "But unlike you, Jim, I'm willing to admit it." He glanced at Carmen, then looked directly at Goodman.

"The only way to rectify this situation is to resign," Max finished. "My resignation will be on your desk tomorrow morning, along with a list of consultants you can contact to finish the job."

"Max, no!" The words burst from her lips before Carmen realized she'd spoken. "You can't," she finished.

Impossibility stretched before her. Long days without Max. Lonely nights at home. Frozen dinners eaten on the couch watching television. The strands of her life unraveled. She reached with tortured words to hold it together.

Working together last night in Max's dining room, she'd almost believed in the dream of their life together. How could he throw that dream away with one curt sentence? If Max left Royal Hospital, he'd be on to his next assignment sooner than either of them expected. Gone were even the brief weeks she thought they'd have.

She'd have to leave Lakeview if she wanted to be with him.

Gone was the dream, the brief interlude, and soon the only home she'd ever known. Uncertainty clouded every avenue.

Max offered her a lifetime of playing catch-up, always in the town behind him as he moved on to new and more exciting assignments. If things didn't work out between them she'd be truly alone, far from everything and everyone she loved.

Keeping a cautious eyes on Andersen, Max cast her a pleading glance. "Carmen, I have to. Aside from Andersen's embezzlement, I shouldn't be making budget decisions about a department headed by the woman I love."

Love, he'd said. In front of everyone. Andersen uttered a growl of disgust.

Before Carmen had a chance to digest this new development, the door flew open as Stan and a trio of uniformed police officers and a pair of detectives wearing tweed jackets burst into the room.

Are those regulation jackets? Do they give them out at the station? Carmen wondered.

Overturned chairs, the boardroom table knocked askew, Andersen still bodily pinned against the wall by Wayne Goodman, mapped out the recent drama. Stan's expression hardened as he accepted yet another emergency with resignation.

"Busy place," commented the detective in the brown tweed jacket as Wayne explained the situation. His partner wore a jacket almost identical, but in blue.

Carmen recognized him from the "incident" with Forbes in her office yesterday.

Was it only yesterday? Seems like a year.

At the sight of the handcuffs, Andersen renewed his efforts to escape Goodman's grasp. Freeing a hand, he threw a punch in Max's direction. It took all three police officers to wrench his arms behind him long enough to snap on the cuffs. Even then, he tossed himself from side to side, trying to break their grasp.

He didn't look like a distinguished physician with his lab coat creased, his tie hanging crookedly and his face crumpled with hatred.

"I demand to speak with my lawyer!" he snarled as the officers hustled him from the room. "I'm innocent!" He shrugged a shoulder in Max's direction. "He's the real criminal."

"Tell that to the nice people downtown," one of the officers muttered. He thrust Andersen past the threshold and into the hall.

Max slumped against the wall. "I wish you'd let me tell you all that in private."

Goodman grunted in agreement. He ran a hand through his hair and grimly surveyed the office, looking as if he'd like nothing better than to slump into a chair, close the door and forget about his growing list of troubles.

"We're going to need to have a look at your records." The detective in the blue tweed helped himself to Judy's phone. "I'll call someone from our corporate crime unit to give us a hand."

"Better get someone from narcotics down here as well." His partner glanced into the boardroom and shook his head.

"Judy, pull the records for Andersen's accounts for the past five years," Goodman said. "Order us some coffee and sandwiches." He offered the chairman an apologetic half-smile. "And you'd better call our auditor. We've got our work cut out for us this afternoon."

"My report should be simple enough to follow," Max said. "And since I no longer work for Royal Hospital, I might as well go home."

"Stay close to the phone," Goodman cautioned. "Just in case we have questions."

"What about me?"

Wayne jumped as if he'd forgotten Carmen was still in the room. "Do I still work for Royal Hospital?"

"I'm going to have to go over the figures myself. If what Max charges is true, there shouldn't be a problem funding your department. But I'll let you know in a couple of days for sure, once I've got this problem with Andersen out of the way."

"You mean I'm going to be able to keep my job?" After so much worry, it didn't even seem like a possibility.

"That's what I mean," Wayne said. "Now go home, Carmen. Take the rest of the week off. Leave us to solve the rest of our problems here at Royal Hospital."

"I get to keep my job," she repeated, following Max out of Wayne's office. In a matter of minutes the tables had turned.

Keeping her job, meant losing the man she loved.

Chapter Fourteen

"So what now?" Carmen asked.

She and Max were sitting among the spreadsheets still scattered over his dining room table, brooding over their coffee, barely making eye contact.

"I have a few job leads to follow up." Max took another long gulp of coffee and contemplated the faded painting on the far wall.

"Job leads? Where?"

For a moment she was afraid he wouldn't answer. Keeping his gaze squarely focused on the painting, he said, "Ottawa."

"What good is a job in Ottawa if I'm working here?" she blurted. Better to get it all out in the open. Over the past week her life had changed irrevocably. Best to let it unravel altogether. Easier to start over that way.

"I have to work somewhere, Carmen."

"There's got to be somewhere in Lakeview you could work."

Max drummed his thumb against the table. "I doubt it. I've downsized most of the institutions in the city."

She uttered a bark laughter at the bitter-sweet irony. "What about us?"

The question lingered between them as his gaze drifted from the painting reluctantly back to her. "You could come with me."

"And lose what I fought so hard for? What I almost got myself killed for?"

A deep sigh escaped his lips. His shoulders fell. "Then stay in Lakeview. It would be difficult to maintain a long distance relationship, but it has been done."

"When you're finished in Ottawa, what then? A few months in Vancouver, a year in Calgary. Where does it end, Max?"

"It doesn't." He stared into the black depths of his coffee. "That's the way my life is."

In that second she could almost see inside him, see the fear that kept him moving all those years. "You're afraid."

His head jerked up. "What?"

"You're afraid if you settle down long enough, life will steal what you've gained. Like it took your father?"

"That's ridiculous," he snapped. "It's just the way I make my living."

"Is it?" she whispered. "Or do you make your living taking things away from other people to make up for that one cruel thing life took from you?"

"You don't understand." Even as he found himself protesting, the truth in her accusation rankled. Certainly he tried to bring order to an outdated medical system sorely lacking for funds, while overlooking the lack of balance in his own life. He lived a nomadic existence, moved from job to job, relationship to relationship. Max reined in his thoughts. Just because he admitted it to himself, didn't mean he wanted to argue the point with Carmen.

"I think I understand far too well."

Her words chafed the wound further. "Enough, Carmen." Max set his coffee cup down on the table with enough force to send dark liquid sloshing over the side. The tablecloth caught against his wool pants as he stood up. "I'm going upstairs to make some of those calls."

The dining room door slammed closed behind him.

Carmen watched a tear roll down the bridge of her nose. It hovered for a second on the tip before splashing into her cup. "Damn." Her fist connected with the table. Spreadsheets fluttered, then settled. "Why are all the important decisions so painful?"

Upstairs she could hear the dull murmur of Max's voice, talking in that business tone he only used with his peers. Getting up took more strength than she had. She laid her head against the embroidered tablecloth and closed her eyes.

Above her the floor creaked. A door opened. Footsteps sounded on the stairs. Max stood in the doorway behind her.

"So?"

"I have an interview in Ottawa. Day after tomorrow."

He pulled up a chair and sat next to her. His hand was warm against the back of her neck. Slowly, he began to rub her back in calming circles. "Don't take it so hard, Carmen. Let's wait and see what happens. It will all work out."

She raised her head. "I don't see how it can."

"A week ago you told me what you wanted most in the world was to keep your job." Annoyance crept into his tone. "And I found a way to make that possible. What else do you want from me?"

What indeed? He'd said he loved her. But in order to accept his love she'd have to give up everything else. This wasn't supposed to happen. Somehow she found the strength to lever herself from the chair.

"Where are you going?" Max demanded.

"Home," she said. "Where else do I have to go?"

"Carmen—"

She fled down the sidewalk, back toward the calm certainty of her own life.

❑ ❑ ❑

"Did you get your mail?"

The scratchy voice came from somewhere behind her. Carmen jumped. Leaving the keys to her apartment dangling in the lock, she turned, finding Mrs. Landreth leaning on her rake on the pathway below.

"Your mail," she reminded her. "Your fiancé picked it up yesterday. Said you needed it at work."

"My—" And then she remembered. She'd sent Max home to retrieve the computer disk. The one John Forbes had almost killed her for.

"Nice looking man, that fiancé of yours."

Max had called himself her fiancé. The word tugged at her heart. But if she cried in front of shrewd Mrs. Landreth, she'd never be free of the old lady's questions. "I think so, too," she choked out.

Mrs. Landreth's eyes narrowed. "I suppose you'll be moving soon, when you get married and all."

"Moving?" Carmen caught herself opening her mouth to deny it. What on earth had Max said to her?

Thanks a lot, Max. She's probably already rented out my apartment.

"Oh, we haven't set a date yet." She forced herself to sound lighthearted. With a twist of her hand, the door to her unit sprang open. She stuck her head out, waved to Mrs. Landreth. "But I'll let you know," she said.

Coming home was a mistake. Ghosts still occupied every corner of her apartment. Her mother's ghost, a constant reminder in the delicate furniture, the bone china and the lacy doilies that covered every surface.

And the ghost of Max Deveraux who loomed in memory, in the bed where they'd slept together, on the couch where they'd made love for the first time. Now that she had her job back, she'd lost Max. In the past week everything had changed.

She might still be employed by Royal Hospital. Her driver's license still had the same address, but the Carmen Day who'd lived in this apartment was irrevocably changed.

Dust danced in the afternoon light streaming through the window. Carmen crossed the floor and threw open the windows. It helped to relieve the stuffiness in the air after the apartment had been closed up for several days. But still the cramped quarters suffocated her.

Carmen grabbed last week's newspapers from the recycling bin. On the covered porch sat a stack of boxes she kept to wrap Christmas presents in. She took them in, sat them in the middle of the floor and went to work.

Two hours later, she'd stripped the couch of its throw, the bed of its lace coverlet and the furniture of all their doilies. China and figurines nested in newspaper crammed the rest of the boxes.

Carmen turned slowly, surveying her handiwork. The threadbare couch would have to go. Once she got the confirmation from Wayne Goodman that her job was definitely hers to keep, she'd spend what little money she had saved on the cream leather couch she'd admired in a store downtown.

She'd cultivated that tiny savings account for years, terrified out of old habit to spend a cent of it. During her mother's illness, what little money they'd had was badly needed. But the worst emergency in recent memory had passed. Time to start living, she decided. Instead of carrying around the baggage of old ways of thinking and other people's lives.

There was room to move now in the living room with the porch stuffed full of dainty end tables and boxes. Carmen swung her feet up on the coffee table and leaned back.

Moping around the apartment was the last thing she needed. Tomorrow, she'd go back to work.

◻ ◻ ◻

"How's the hospital detective?"

Carmen gripped her desk and vowed for the millionth time not to jump at every little noise.

"Barb!" She rose, hugged her friend tightly. Still pale and drawn looking, Carmen noted, but Barbara, determined to put on a brave face, was smiling. "C'mon in."

"I'm gone a couple of days and the rumor mill is buzzing like no tomorrow. Can't a hard working woman take a break?" She planted her hands on her hips and gave Carmen a measuring look. "Pretty smooth, the two of you getting the goods on Andersen like that. Not to mention John Forbes." Barb shook her head, her expression sobering. "I never would have thought it was him, Carmen. I used to talk to him all the time. He was always so polite."

"Fear can make monsters of us all," Carmen said. The proclamation had a ring of truth to it. After all, fear had kept her hiding in her tiny apartment, living a shadow of a life.

Barb stuffed her hands into the pockets of her lab coat, searching for the phantom disk. "Hard to feel sorry for him, though. After all the people he hurt."

Carmen gave Barb another hug. Non-demonstrative Barbara suffered her affection good-naturedly. "Don't worry. We're safe now. Forbes is safely locked away where he can get some help."

Barbara claimed her usual post, leaning against Carmen's desk. "What about Andersen? I can't believe I've been working along side him all these years. Looking up to him, respecting him..." She broke off, searching for words. "It's like everything has suddenly changed."

"Everything has changed," Carmen said. "But I'm still here, and I intend to stay."

Barbara focused hawk-like eyes on her. "So rumor has it." She sounded oddly hurt, as if it had some nerve to continue manufacturing gossip in her absence. "So?"

"So? What?"

"What about you and Max the Axe?"

Oh no, here it comes. First I spend a week denying we're involved, and now I can spend the rest of my life explaining what happened. The adage against getting involved with people at work made good sense, Carmen decided. Just the facts, Ma'am. "Max is job hunting in Ottawa." She pursed her lips together, refusing to say more.

"And?" Barb prompted. Shaken up maybe, but still undoubtedly Barb, there was no way Carmen would get away with just the bare facts.

"And we haven't decided what to do about it."

"About Max—" Barbara began. But instead of pressing the issue, she surprised her by saying, "I'm sorry, Carmen. I was wrong about him."

"The whole place was wrong about Max. People really want to believe he's a monster, instead of a hard-working guy with an unpleasant job. I guess it makes it easier that way." Already she'd said more than she intended to. "But we aren't going to talk about him, Barb." Carmen waved a hand at the requisitions overflowing her in-basket. Wayne had released some funds to send the film processing out. She couldn't bear to go back into the darkroom just yet. But that didn't take care of the myriad other requests. "And I've got a ton of work to do. Unfortunately, the hospital doesn't pay me to be a detective."

"That's too bad," Barb said. Not sympathy for her workload, Carmen realized. "I was hoping it might work out for the two of you. I was thinking just the other day, I've never been a bridesmaid." She sighed heavily. "Always a bride and never a bridesmaid. And I'm not even married anymore."

"I guess you'll just have to wait a bit longer for your bridesmaidhood. What about Linda in patient records? Wasn't she seeing that guy from accounting?"

Barb seized that new piece of information. "I don't know, I'll check it out next coffee break."

Relieved the conversation had turned to safer territory, Carmen reached for another requisition. "You on for lunch?"

"What did you have in mind?"

"L'Ambiance," Carmen said. "We deserve it."

□ □ □

They were offering him a small fortune.

Max tossed his suit jacket on the couch. A small cloud of dust rose on the impact. He sneezed. Warm air wafted in as he opened the window in the sunroom.

Having baked in the sun for the couple of weeks he'd been away, the den was far too stuffy to work in. He wandered into the bedroom to open more windows.

Nothing in the refrigerator, except for a stale, half-eaten carton of ice cream. The only thing remotely edible in the cupboards was a jar of freeze-dried instant coffee. He boiled water, mixed up the unappealing brew and dumped a spoonful of stale ice cream in it.

The coffee proved to be as repulsive as he imagined. Tonight he had to go shopping.

The apartment didn't feel much like home with the things he'd planned to move to Lakeview still in boxes and the furniture covered like some long vacant mausoleum. But it was good to be back in Ottawa. He'd spent the latter part of his teens there once his mom became a tenured professor at the university. Ottawa was still the closest place he'd had to a permanent home. It felt good to drive the familiar streets, eat in familiar restaurants. Visit old friends on the weekend.

The interview had gone much better than he could have imagined. His reputation preceded him, resulting in better and better offers and downsizing became a process most institutions went through instead of an emergency tactic.

Another couple of contracts like that and he'd be able to trade up on the condo, buy a house. Something closer to the land, with a yard instead of a two-by-four-foot concrete slab his real estate agent had had the nerve to call a terrace.

With a grimace, Max set the coffee down on the end table and flung himself onto his leather couch. The contract was simply too good to pass up.

But would Carmen come to Ottawa? If he owned a house, would that offer her the security she so desperately craved?

The scenario crumbled before his mind's eye. He pictured Carmen pacing about a living room in his absence, stripped of her job, her place in life. He saw her working out in the gym in the recreation room downstairs, the pool, each slap against the water hating him for his prolonged absences, the loss of her job.

No matter how many angles he examined it from, it just wouldn't work.

He sighed, realizing exactly what he was going to have do. The calmness with which he contemplated that new venture surprised him.

Max reached for the phone. First he had to call his prospective employer, and after that his landlord.

Then he had to have a serious talk with Carmen.

❑ ❑ ❑

"Carmen!"

The voice followed her down the back hall. "Never fails," she muttered. "The one day I have a lunch reservation, someone ambushes me at the back door." Though the hospital was still uncharacteristically quiet after the drama in the past few days, routine had returned to its usual ordered chaos.

Reluctantly, she turned, finding Joan from occupational therapy hurrying down the corridor to catch her.

"Don't go, Carmen. We're having a party, and it just wouldn't be complete without you."

"A party? What's the occasion."

Joan grinned, grabbing Carmen by the sleeve of her jacket. She started to pull her in the opposite direction.

"Wait, I had a lunch date with Barbara."

"Bring Barb along," Joan said, still intent on kidnapping Carmen. "We're having a goodbye party. Tyler's going home."

His condition much improved, Tyler had little trouble making two massive pieces of chocolate cake vanish. Barbara and Carmen had planned on a more nutritious meal than cake and coffee for lunch. But even though she ended up working, shooting off an

entire roll of film on teary goodbyes, Carmen wouldn't
have missed it.

"Mom and Dad moved my bedroom to the den so I
won't have to use the stairs," Tyler announced proudly. "They put a ramp on the front for me, too. But the
best thing," he virtually danced with excitement, "they
bought me a computer with a 500mhz processor and a
DVD drive!" He then rattled off a list of specifica-
tions—64 megabytes of RAM, 13.5 gigabyte hard
drive, etc., etc.—that made her dizzy.

Staff disbursed. Tyler's parents made noises about
leaving. "He's going to miss everyone here," Tyler's
mother said.

"C'mon son," Tyler's father gripped his shoulder.
"We'd better get going, leave your mom time to get you
settled before dinner."

Tears welled in Joan's eyes. Carmen found herself
sniffling as Tyler and his parents started down the
hall and out of Royal Hospital forever.

"Tyler, wait!" Joan disappeared into the O.T. office.
She reappeared a second later, a brightly-colored box
in her hand. "You forgot this."

Carmen recognized the garish packaging of "Deep
Space Shootout."

"Cool!" Tyler tucked the box under his arm. "I can
play it this afternoon."

"This afternoon we're going to talk about school,"
his father corrected, sounding for all the world like the
father of a normal teenager.

They turned a corner in the corridor, cutting off the
sounds of a family argument in progress.

Joan looked at Carmen and laughed. "I guess you
really started something."

"It's great to see," Barb interjected. She looked
fondly down the hallway after them. "The family's

back together. Tyler's going back to school. Days like this I love working at Royal Hospital."

"Me too," Carmen admitted. "Even after all that's happened."

□ □ □

Work occupied the afternoon, seeing to the million details that piled up during the drama of the past week. Carmen found herself busier than she'd been for weeks. But despite the workload, her thoughts kept straying back to Max Deveraux. Two days passed, and still they hadn't spoken. Max presumably left for Ottawa. She didn't call to check if he got off okay. He didn't call to say he missed her.

Procrastinating wasn't going to solve their dilemma. At some point they were going to have to talk. Really talk. Assuming Max did call. Assuming Max actually came back from Ottawa, instead of just hiring a company to move his things back. Assuming she decided not to wait like a love-stricken teenager and call him instead.

Carmen stared at the phone on her desk. It was five-thirty. She should go home. Maybe she'd take a cab uptown and window-shop for that new couch.

Perhaps she'd be brave, call Max, leave a message on his answering machine asking how things had gone in Ottawa. She reached for the phone.

As her fingers closed on it, the phone rang.

"I thought I told you take the week off," accused the voice on the other end.

"Wayne?" Was it Wayne? Or had they strayed into Mr. Goodman territory permanently.

But Goodman continued. "And what's got you in the office so late?" Friends again.

"Late? This is early. You should see the disaster on my desk."

"You should see the nightmare on mine."

"How's it going?"

"Well, the charges have been laid and the rest of the mess has been turned over to the auditors and the police." Goodman uttered an explosive sigh. Carmen imagined his hair sticking out at odd angles while he messed it more. "Which leaves me to tackle the original mess."

"The downsizing plan?"

"The same."

And what about my job? she wanted to say, but instead said, "Oh."

"Have you heard anything from Max?"

"He's still in Ottawa," Carmen said noncommittally. The things she didn't say rang loudly in the silence.

"I guess you're wondering about your job?" Wayne said at last.

"It's been on my mind." Every minute I haven't been thinking about Max.

"Well, just so you can go home and have a great evening, I thought I'd let you know that both the chairman and I agree that you're an indispensable part of Royal Hospital."

◻ ◻ ◻

Couldn't have asked for a better end to the day, Carmen thought as she walked the short blocks home. Summer was coming, the sun setting later in the evening. In the light, Lakeview looked welcoming.

Halfway down his street, she realized where she was going. Her heart might want to delay the inevitable, but her feet took her straight toward Max's house. Not too late to turn around. She scanned the street for signs of his car.

That's when she saw the moving van parked in front of Max's house.

Chapter Fifteen

*M*overs swarmed around the brightly-colored van that squatted in the street. Carmen stumbled to a stop. Max was leaving. The undeniable evidence blocked the road.

Uncharitable as it was, all afternoon she'd been wishing he'd call with the news that it hadn't gone well in Ottawa, that they might be granted a few more days together before fate tore them apart.

There are no happy endings, Carmen, her mind hissed. You've known that since you were a little kid.

But she had hoped. The same vain hope that kept her looking for her father long after he'd left. And now Max would leave. Cruel fate waited until happiness was within her grasp before snatching it away.

Tears clouded her eyes. She'd assumed they'd have a couple of days left together. Time to settle what lay between them. Time to say goodbye.

The moving van was almost full, she noticed as she drew closer. Surely Max hadn't planned to leave without even saying goodbye.

Anger dried her tears. Straightening her shoulders, she stormed up the path to his door.

And was nearly run down by a mover carrying a stack of boxes and a lamp shade.

"Excuse me."

She squeezed past him and narrowly missed being trampled by another. Her footsteps echoed through empty rooms. Dust gathered in the corners and in shadowed places where furniture had been. A spider had taken up residence in the valence, hidden until now by heavy drapery.

Another mover wrestled with the large carpet in the dining room, attempting to command it into an orderly roll. Watching him, it occurred to her that all the furniture being loaded into the van belonged to the previous owner of the house.

"What on earth—?" Empty walls shot her voice back at her, sharpened by the echo.

Having subdued the carpet, the mover flung it over his shoulder and trudged off, throwing yet another cloud of dust into the air. Carmen sneezed.

In the kitchen a conversation died into silence. Max stuck his head around the corner.

"Carmen? There you are! I've been trying to get you all day. You weren't at home, and when I tried you at work, they said you'd left—" He wiped grubby hands on the front of his sweatshirt, then reached for her. Dust coated his hair. His faded jeans were scuffed with dirt. She opened her mouth to protest, but before she could croak out a word, his lips fastened upon hers. "Hang on just a minute," he said, darting back into the kitchen. "We're almost finished." Carmen followed him dumbly.

The kitchen had also been stripped of all his furnishings. Stained lace curtains, the chunky oak table that had occupied the center were all gone. Cupboards stood open, their contents emptied. Only a smear of greasy dirt marked where the old wheezing refrigerator had stood.

Paper littered the kitchen counter, the only writing surface left in the house. Max and a gray-haired man bent over the counter signing a sheaf of official-looking papers.

"That about does it." The older man straightened. Dividing the papers into two, he stuffed one half back into his briefcase and pushed the rest toward Max. They shook hands. Nodding to Carmen, he started down the hall toward the front door. Max followed after him.

Through the narrow space left by the open door, Carmen watched them linger on the front lawn. They shook hands again. She heard the moving van's motor start. Max shut the door, blocking off the rest of her view.

Walking toward her, he looked as if he could fall down where he stood and go to sleep. Still, within his exhaustion lay something else. Relief, her mind supplied. Why? Because he was going home?

"How'd it go in Ottawa?" Carmen forced the words past her constricting throat.

"Ottawa?" For a moment he looked confused, then he said, "Oh, fine."

He could have been discussing the weather for all the emotion in his voice, and yet he was looking at her with such tenderness in his expression. Memorizing her face?

"Sounds like they made you a good offer."

"A very lucrative offer," he said, smiling, and closed the distance between them. How could he grin stupidly at her like that? Didn't he know her heart was breaking?

"I guess I should congratulate you then."

"You should."

His lips brushed hers, shattering the dam inside her. To her dismay, Carmen felt the hot tears spill down her cheeks.

With his thumb, Max wiped her tears away. "But I think you're supposed to bring a bottle of champagne when you visit someone who just bought a house."

"You what?" She twisted in his arms, but he held her tight.

"I bought the house, Carmen." He nuzzled close again, but she levered herself away from him.

"You bought this house? Why?"

"So I could stay here with you." His smile blurred through her tears.

"But what about the contract in Ottawa? The lucrative offer?"

"You're crying," he said with surprise. Grubby fingers brushed at the tears streaming down her face. "What's wrong?"

She burrowed against his sweatshirt, her words muffled by the cloth. "When I saw the moving van, I thought...I thought you were leaving."

"Leaving?" He gathered her closer, linked his fingers through her short hair. "No! The previous owner wanted to go through his mother's furniture, to separate out a few keepsakes and give the rest to charity." With strokes of his hands and lips, he soothed away the last of her doubts. "I could never leave you, Carmen."

He turned, so he was leaning against the counter and she leaned against him, borrowing his strength. "They did offer me a lot of money. More than I'd ever been offered before. And, for a moment, I did consider taking it."

"What changed your mind?" she asked into his chest.

"You did."

Her head came up.

"I thought about how much I'd miss you." Dark eyes looked down at her with a calm that hadn't been there before. "And then I thought about how your father had gone away, and how much it would hurt you if I went away too."

He kissed the tip of her nose, the center of her forehead. "If I left, you'd probably never trust another man again. With your goodwill toward all mankind resting on my head, I figured I'd better not let you down."

Carmen looked around at the kitchen standing forlorn and empty. "You did all this for me?"

"You're worth it."

"But where are you going to find work?"

"There's bound to be some institution within commuting distance from Lakeview that could make use of my talents."

"I thought you said you already downsized them all."

"I did, but I'm looking for a new specialty this time around."

"You are?" If there'd been a chair to sit on, she would have sunk down on it.

Max cupped her chin and tilted her face toward him. "I thought hard about what you said about the way I make my living."

"Oh, Max, I'm so sorry. I didn't mean to say those things. I was really out of line."

He accepted her apology with a nod. "But what you said was also very true. I do make my living taking things away from other people. For a time it helped blind me to what was missing in my own life. That's why I can't do it any more."

"But how will you live? How will you pay your mortgage?"

"I don't have a mortgage. I bought the place outright. It's been on the market for ages. The family was anxious to unload it. I got it for a steal."

"But—"

He laid a finger lightly across her lips, cutting off further protests. "I'm sure some poor unsuspecting firm would be happy to have a director of finance or operations who knows how to keep the company in the black."

Max grinned wickedly. "Besides, the woman I'm hoping will be my wife still has a job. Once things are settled with me, we can start renovating." He turned her toward the door to the dining room. "We could extend the kitchen, redo the floors, put in a garden in the back yard."

It was all to much to take in at once. "Wife? Renovate? Garden?"

"Maybe we should add a fountain and a pond."

"Max!"

Clasping her hands between his warm, dirty ones, he glanced down at the dusty floor and grimaced. But he sank down to one knee anyway. From the pocket of his jeans he pulled a silver ring case, tarnished black with age. The contents sparkled as he opened the lid. Inside was an antique engagement ring, the diamond set in platinum, with a scattering of smaller diamonds on either side of the center stone. "Will you marry me, Carmen?"

She gaped, stared down into his pleading eyes. "Yes!" The word sprang from her lips, as much shock as acceptance.

A long sigh ran through his body, and she felt him relax against her. "I was so afraid you'd say no."

"I love you, Max. I would never have said no."

The ring slipped over her finger, cool against her skin. Max rose to his feet and hugged her tightly.

Shock settled into calm certainty. "A house and an engagement ring in just two days. Mr. Deveraux, I am impressed."

"The engagement ring was my grandmother's." A fond smile crossed his face and she could tell he had adored his grandmother. "She was always calling me a terror when I was young. She left me the ring, saying one day I'd meet a woman who was a match for me." Rich laughter rumbled through his chest. "I

never thought I'd meet one who was more than a
match for me."

"Serves you right for being so arrogant."

"So it does." He cast a glance around the empty
house. Devoid of its furniture it looked forlorn and desperately in need of a new coat of paint. "Just let me
lock up, and then let's go."

"Go where?"

"Your place. The house is filthy, my stuff doesn't
get here from Ottawa until tomorrow, and a shower
and a good night's sleep are starting to sound wonderfully appealing."

Night air, like warm silk, caressed them as they
walked the short block back to her apartment. Caught
in the beam of a streetlight, Max tipped back her head
and kissed her thoroughly. Carmen melted against
him, eager to be alone upstairs, yet too impatient to
wait.

A flash of white drew their heads toward the window just in time to catch a glimpse of Mrs. Landreth
yanking her curtains shut.

"Nosy woman," Max muttered. Heedless of Mrs.
Landreth's prying eyes, he settled in for another
leisurely kiss.

"You told her I was your fiancée!"

His lips moved against hers as he smiled. "And so
you are."

Epilogue

"What do you think?" Barb twirled in a rustle of hunter green taffeta and black lace. "Perfect for a fall wedding," she pronounced.

Carmen looked up from the rack of white and ivory silk dresses that lined the wall. Squashed together like that, they all appeared pretty much the same. Equally impractical, unsuitable and expensive.

She hadn't planned on having an elaborate wedding. City Hall would have been just fine with her. But Barb was determined to wear "a proper bridesmaid's dress." The opportunity to be a bridesmaid finally within her grasp, she intended to play the role to its fullest.

Max's mother had taken charge of the traditional Mohawk aspects of the ceremony. Max just wanted a party with family and friends. Most of his friends lived in Ottawa; she hadn't even met them all yet.

Instead of dashing to City Hall in a floral print dress, she found herself contemplating invitation samples, surveying wedding halls and traipsing halfway across town to try on dozens of nearly identical white gowns.

"Peach roses," Barbara continued, "Maybe even some for our hair." She stopped, finding her friend lost in a wilderness of silk. "Carmen?"

Carmen gave up. "I was thinking maybe a white suit."

"A white—" Barb strode across the mirrored dressing room that was almost big enough to pass as a fashion show runway, and gripped Carmen by the arms. "If you wear a white suit, then I'm going to have to wear a suit as well."

"It's a lot more practical." Carmen plucked at the taffeta sleeve. "Max's mom is making me a traditional outfit for the wedding. And Max's cousin is taking care of the music. It would just be extravagant to add satin and lace."

"It's your wedding day!" Barb's protest drew the attention of the saleswoman, whose helpful advice Carmen had desperately been trying to avoid. "This is the one day you're allowed to be extravagant. Why can't you have both? Why can't you have it all?"

She did have it all, Carmen realized with a start. A beautiful home, a job she loved, a fiancé who adored her, and a wealth of tradition to share between them. She couldn't deny Barb this long-awaited chance to be a bridesmaid.

"Do you really want to spend all that money on something like this, that you'll only wear once?"

"Yes!" Barbara spun her around, marched her back to the rack of lacy white silk dresses in long plastic bags. "I waited all my life for this. Always a—"

"Bride, never a bridesmaid," Carmen finished. "The way you go on, you'd think you were the bride."

"I wore a navy blue suit to my wedding, with a pink corsage." The memory stole the smile from Barbara's face. "And all I ended up with was a blurry photograph that someone took on one of those Polaroid cameras." Her bottom lip trembled. "That stupid picture lasted longer than the marriage."

Carmen squeezed Barbara close. Taffeta crinkled between them. "If you like this dress, then you have it, Barb." She looked back at the rack and sighed. "I'm sure I can find one of these frilly things to wear."

"If you're going to do it, you might as well do it right." Barbara flipped through the dresses in their plastic bags, discarding the ones that didn't meet her expectations. "Max has a new job, you're working, the house is paid for."

"Except for the million renovations," Carmen added. "The contractor's weeks behind on the kitchen. The basement is a total disaster, and Max is adamant about putting a garden and a pond in the back yard."

"All the more reason to have a beautiful wedding photo to hang above that new fireplace."

"You're incorrigible!"

She followed Barb's progress along the rack, noting that ever the efficient manager, Barbara had soon put the saleswoman to work as well. Fear put a damper on her blossoming happiness. It was harder than she ever imagined it would be to put her faith in the positive directions her life was taking.

Max was now Vice President of Operations at a large insurance company. Commuting added a couple hours to his day, but he never complained, directing his efforts and his raise in pay into the renovation of their house and elaborate plans for a honeymoon he kept as a surprise even from his bride.

She was the one who refused to believe in their new prosperity. Every spare cent went into her savings account, insurance against the disasters that had always lurked in the corners of her life.

But Max had done his job well. Royal Hospital's budget was balanced, no more layoffs were scheduled. She should be able to relax, but she couldn't.

"This one!" Barb pronounced.

The saleswoman sized Carmen up and nodded approvingly. "Yes, the ivory would go wonderfully with her hair and eyes."

Barbara propelled Carmen toward the dressing room. "Come on, Cinderella, try it on."

Carmen glanced down at the dress of ivory silk and frowned. "It's kind of elaborate." Beaded lace cascaded down the front. Miles of train bunched within the plastic wrap.

It took all three of them to maneuver her into the dress and out through the dressing room door to the mirrored hallway. Carmen took one look at her reflection and gasped.

The cut of the wedding dress complemented the one Barb had chosen. Its high neckline and sculpted waist played up her petite figure. Beaded lace added highlights that reflected in her eyes. She imagined Max in a black tuxedo standing at her side. Yes, she definitely wanted that photograph on their mantle to show their children, their grandchildren. It was going to be all right, she told herself. Finally, she could imagine it.

Barbara and the saleswoman busily sorted through headpieces and veils. Silk shoes, a veil dotted with pearls, a crinoline to fill out the voluminous skirt, all went into the plastic carrying case the saleswoman prepared. Carmen tried not to wince when she paid the bill.

"Tomorrow you're going to start calling photographers," Barbara said as they rushed from the store to the corner where Max said he'd be waiting for them with the car. "I won't hear another word about you doing the photographs yourself."

"It seems silly to hire someone," Carmen protested, her carefully prepared budget blown away by the dress alone. "It's what I do for a living."

"You're not going to work on your wedding day," Barbara said firmly. "And neither am I."

A car horn beeped. She scanned the street, finding Max parked at one of the meters. He put the newspaper he'd been reading aside, and she realized they'd kept him waiting. But he was smiling as he opened the car door for her to lay the bag across the back seat, taking up much of Barb's sitting area.

"Looks fancy." His dark eyes lit up, and Carmen could tell he was picturing her in her wedding finery much as she'd imagined him. "Can I see?"

She swung the bag away from him, and playfully swatted away his hand. "Oh no you don't. Not until the wedding."

As they drove away, Carmen reflected on her good fortune: the love of a wonderful man, a beautiful home, a fulfilling job and supportive best friend. The evidence was overwhelming.

Now she would have to believe in her future.

THE END

INDIGO: Sensuous Love Stories *Order Form*

Mail to:
Genesis Press, Inc.
315 3rd Avenue North
Columbus, MS 39701

Visit our website at

http://www.genesis-press.com

Name————————————————————————

Address————————————————————————

City/State/Zip————————————————————

1999 INDIGO TITLES

Qty	Title	Author	Price	Total
	Somebody's Someone	Sinclair LeBeau	$8.95	
	Interlude	Donna Hill	$8.95	
	The Price of Love	Beverly Clark	$8.95	
	Unconditional Love	Alicia Wiggins	$8.95	
	Mae's Promise	Melody Walcott	$8.95	
	Whispers in the Night	Dorothy Love	$8.95	
	No Regrets (paperback reprint)	Mildred Riley	$8.95	
	Kiss or Keep	D.Y. Phillips	$8.95	
	Naked Soul (paperback reprint)	Gwynne Forster	$8.95	
	Pride and Joi (paperback Reprint)	Gay G. Gunn	$8.95	
	A Love to Cherish (paperback reprint)	Beverly Clark	$8.95	
	Caught in a Trap	Andree Jackson	$8.95	
	Truly Inseparable (paperback reprint)	Wanda Thomas	$8.95	
	A Lighter Shade of Brown	Vicki Andrews	$8.95	
	Cajun Heat	Charlene Berry	$8.95	

Use this order form
or call:

1-888-INDIGO1

(1-888-463-4461)

TOTAL _____

Shipping & Handling _____

($3.00 first book $1.00 each additional book)

TOTAL Amount Enclosed _____

MS Residents add 7% sales tax

INDIGO *Backlist Titles*

QTY	TITLE	AUTHOR	PRICE	TOTAL
	A Love to Cherish	Beverly Clark	$15.95 HC*	
	Again My Love	Kayla Perrin	$10.95	
	Breeze	Robin Hampton	$10.95	
	Careless Whispers	Rochelle Alers	$8.95	
	Dark Embrace	Crystal Wilson Harris	$8.95	
	Dark Storm Rising	Chinelu Moore	$10.95	
	Entwined Destinies	Elsie B. Washington	$4.99	
	Everlastin' Love	Gay G. Gunn	$10.95	
	Gentle Yearning	Rochelle Alers	$10.95	
	Glory of Love	Sinclair LeBeau	$10.95	
	Indiscretions	Donna Hill	$8.95	
	Love Always	Mildred E. Riley	$10.95	
	Love Unveiled	Gloria Green	$10.95	
	Love's Deception	Charlene A. Berry	$10.95	
	Midnight Peril	Vicki Andrews	$10.95	
	Naked Soul	Gwynne Forster	$15.95 HC*	
	No Regrets	Mildred E. Riley	$15.95 HC*	
	Nowhere to Run	Gay G. Gunn	$10.95	
	Passion	T.T. Henderson	$10.95	
	Pride and Joi	Gay G. Gunn	$15.95 HC*	
	Quiet Storm	Donna Hill	$10.95	
	Reckless Surrender	Rochelle Alers	$6.95	
	Rooms of the Heart	Donna Hill	$8.95	
	Shades of Desire	Monica White	$8.95	
	Truly Inseparable	Mildred Y. Thomas	$15.95 HC*	
	Whispers in the Sand	LaFlorya Gauthier	$10.95	
	Yesterday is Gone	Beverly Clark	$10.95	

* indicates Hard Cover

Total for Books _____

Shipping and Handling _____

($3.00 first book $1.00 each additional book)